This deliciously frightening collection of tales from the award-
winning *Whispers* magazine features today's top horror talents:
David Morrell, F. Paul Wilson, Dennis Etchison, Alan Ryan,
Karl Edward Wagner, William F. Nolan, and many others.
Prepare yourself for a grand celebration of things that go
bump in the night—the unparalleled terror of *Whispers* . . .

WHISPERS V

*Books edited by Stuart David Schiff
from Jove*

WHISPERS V

EDITED BY
STUART DAVID SCHIFF

This Jove book contains the complete
text of the original hardcover edition.
It has been completely reset in a typeface
designed for easy reading and was printed
from new film.

WHISPERS V

A Jove Book / published by arrangement with
Doubleday & Company, Inc.

PRINTING HISTORY
Doubleday edition / February 1985
Jove edition / July 1988

ISBN: 0-515-09641-5

Jove Books are published by The Berkley Publishing Group,
200 Madison Avenue, New York, New York 10016.
The name ''JOVE'' and the ''J'' logo
are trademarks belonging to Jove Publications, Inc.

PRINTED IN THE UNITED STATES OF AMERICA

10   9   8   7   6   5   4   3   2   1

ACKNOWLEDGMENTS

CONTENTS

CONTENTS

PREFACE

Both writers and editors handle similar questions when facing their audiences. The dreaded writers' query goes something akin to "Where do you get your ideas?" We editors field the terror-inspiring "What do you look for in choosing a story?" I could go on and on to these people about manuscript preparation, literacy, and the like, but my stock answer is, "I know them when I see them." It truly is not a wisecrack. I genuinely feel a story in my *Whispers* magazine or *Whispers* anthologies does not follow any set guidelines other than horror, terror, or fantasy orientation. Above all, I look for new and special ideas. I attempt to find something a little bit different. I will not insist that I have been to all the places a specific reader has traversed, and I will admit to an occasional soft spot for familiar grounds (why do you think fast-food restaurants do so well?); however, the successful *Whispers* story lacks the sameness I find elsewhere. I solicit, successfully or not, the out-of-the-common story, the beyond-the-pale work, the unusual twist. I know them when I see them.

Stuart David Schiff
Whispers Press
70 Highland Avenue
Binghamton, N.Y. 13905

1983 was an incredible year for Connie Willis. Not only did she win a Hugo Award, but she also won two Nebula Awards. I would like to think that this story was written in the hope of rounding out her trophy shelf with a World Fantasy Award. The tale exemplifies what I mean by my looking for something different. It is a most unusual haunting.

SUBSTITUTION TRICK
Connie Willis

He had been seasick the whole way. He had not wanted the meeting to be like this. He had wanted to stop at the first heart-shocking sight of her, to whisper, "Mutti!" and clasp his own dear mother to him. Instead, he had staggered to the nearest chair and collapsed onto it, shivering with sweat. His mother had brought her shawl and put it around his shoulders, and he had not even been able to smile his thanks up at her for fear the nausea would rise again and choke him.

He felt a grim satisfaction at the seasickness. "We have left all earthly cares behind, all illness, all suffering," the mediums always said in the hoarse, hideous voices they claimed were his mother's. Liars, he thought. Crooks.

She stroked his hair. "Oh, *mein* beloved boy," she said. "So sick he is, *mein* poor boy." Her voice was even sweeter than he remembered. The floor was still rolling, as floors always did for the first few hours after he landed, and the black and red flowers in the carpet made him

1

dizzy. He stared at his mother's black shoes to steady himself. They were sturdy, sharp-toed shoes, the kind she had always worn. They had made her feet hurt. He wondered if her feet still hurt. "We have left behind all suffering, all care," the mediums had said. He hoped that was true, that his mother's feet would not hurt through all eternity. But I'm seasick, he thought. I'm dead, and I'm still seasick.

"You should wear your slippers," he said.

"Slippers?" she said, and her hand jerked and stopped in its gentle stroking.

"I brought you a pair of slippers from Europe, Mutti, but you didn't get them." He remembered that terrible trip. He had not felt seasick that time. He had not felt anything, as if he were the one who had died. Even the reporters on the dock had not been able to make him feel anything.

"Are you going to the funeral?" they had asked, and he should have felt rage, but he had answered, "Yes," in a voice like the mediums used in their trances, dead and devoid of feeling. "Are you planning a tour, Houdini? Any new escapes? What will you do now, Houdini, try to contact your mother in the spirit world?"

"Yes," he had said in that same hollow voice. He had held onto his wife, Bess, with one nerveless hand and clutched his mother's slippers in the other. She had asked for them when he left for Europe. "*Vergiss nicht. Nummer sechs,*" his mother had shouted to him as the ship moved away from the dock. Her last words. Don't forget. Size six. He had not forgotten. When he went to see his mother in her casket, he had laid the slippers beside her. But they had not gotten through.

"Nothing gets through, does it, Mama?" he said. Thinking about that other voyage, when he had not been seasick, had somehow cleared his head a little. "Not even a message could get through," he said. "So how could a pair of slippers?" Her hand was clutching the back of the chair. He patted it. "I didn't want you to think I had forgotten your slippers, Mutti. I remembered."

"Slippers?" she said again, and her voice sounded troubled, guilty, as if she were a child he had caught in some naughtiness.

He had not meant to upset her. "Don't you remember the pair of slippers you asked me to bring you from Europe, Mama?" he said. *"Die Hausschuhe.* I brought them, but you had already . . ." He hesitated, trying to think what word to use. "Crossed over," he said, and then felt angry because that was a word the mediums used.

He had gone to nearly a hundred seances, sitting at round oak tables, holding the mediums' hands, hoping against hope that he would hear a message from his mother. And what had he gotten? Tilting tables and floating trumpets. Oranges had been thrown by unseen spirit hands. Spirit messages had appeared on blank slates. Tricks, all of it, tricks. How had they expected to fool him, the great Houdini, who had done those same tricks on the stage? Crooks, he thought, spook crooks preying on people's grief and longing.

He was glad he and Bess had decided on the code message before he died, so she would not be fooled by some charlatan. They had used the old code from their mind-reading act, key words that stood for letters, and he was to begin the message with the word "Rosabelle," from the song, "Rosabelle, sweet Rosabelle, I love you more than I can tell." Now he saw that a message was impossible, that he could not get through, but at least she would not be fooled by some spook crook who wanted her money. He had seen scientists, educated men fooled by simple tricks he would not stoop to do on stage, but they had not fooled him.

He was beginning to feel sick again. "May I have a glass of water, Mama?" he said.

His mother was still clutching the back of the chair. When she let it go, her knuckles were white, but she smiled sweetly at him. *"Nein, nein,"* she said, shaking her finger at him. "For you is not *das Wasser*. For you I cook the coffee and *der Apfelkuchen*. That is better than *Wasser, ja?"*

Even the naming of food made the nausea rise again, but he did not have the heart to tell her. She bustled over to the sideboard, and the sight of her stout little figure in the black silk dress he had bought for her and the black shoes that made her feet hurt brought tears to his eyes.

The sideboard filled one entire wall of the room. It had a mirror above it, and above the mirror a clock on a shelf. The clock's hands pointed to a quarter past twelve. Midnight. That was the hour his mother had died, struggling to speak a last message to her son, the hour he had lain night after night on the cold grass of her grave, trying somehow to break through the barrier that separated them, the hour the mediums always insisted on holding their seances. So they could do their tricks in darkness, Houdini thought bitterly. I always did my tricks in the light of day.

The room was much smaller than he had expected. "It is so different over here, so much larger and bigger and more beautiful," Lady Doyle had written in the letter she claimed was from his mother, yet the round table and its chairs filled almost the whole room. The table had a black cloth on it whose fringed edges touched the carpet—so the medium can use her feet, he thought—and in the center a red glass bowl full of oranges.

The wall opposite the sideboard was hung with heavy black drapes. They reminded him of the black velvet curtains he and Bess had used in their substitution tricks. He stood up slowly, hanging onto the backs of the chairs as he walked so he would not set the room rocking again, and went over to the curtains.

He took a fold of the heavy cloth in his hand to draw the curtain aside, and then lifted it, rubbing his thumb over the thin, light cloth. He could scarcely feel the weight of it in his hand. It was as fine, as transparent as a veil. What he had mistaken for black velvet was the darkness on the other side.

He heard a sound, like someone calling from an immense distance. One time, on a crossing to Europe, he had stood on the deck in the dark and heard a sound like that, of someone calling to him over the water, so far away and faint he could not make out the words.

He squinted and peered through the veil as he had peered out over the water that night. It had been so dark he could not tell where the sea ended and the sky began, and bitter cold, though the ship behind him was lighted and warm. He had stood at the railing until his hands were numb, looking out over the water, trying to tell where the voice was coming from. After a time, he had thought he could make out a light. It wavered, like a lamp being lit on the deck of a ship, or a star.

"Bess," he said wonderingly, "is that you?"

His mother put her hand on his arm. "Come and sit down, my poor boy. I have ready for you some nice coffee to make your head feel better and a *gut* apple cake." She led him back to the table, her feet shuffling in the red wool slippers.

"Mutti," he said weakly. The strong smell of the coffee was making him dizzy. "Do messages ever get through to the . . . the other side?" He had started to say, "to the living," but he did not want to upset her. She seemed so easily upset.

"Of course, my *böse* boy," she said, putting him into the chair. She poured a cup of coffee from a china pot. "But first you drink your *Kaffee* and eat your cake. You want to send to Bess a message, *ja?*" She held out a china cup of coffee.

"Mama," Houdini said. "You're wearing your slippers."

She peered down at her feet. "*Ja*, of course. I wear them every day since you have to me sent them. The lace-up shoes they make my feet to hurt." She handed him the cup. "You think I not wear them when my boy the magician brings them all the way from Europe?"

He took a sip of the strong coffee. It tasted wonderful. He suddenly felt hungry. "You're the magician, Mama," he said, and laughed.

She looked at him without understanding, her hand poised over the cake, ready to cut it with the silver knife she held.

"Der Zauberer, Mama. *Der Magicker."* He took a huge gulp of the coffee. "I'm hungry, Mama. Cut me a piece of your *Apfel* cake." He finished his coffee and set the cup down on the table. "More coffee, too, please, Mutti."

She was still holding the knife above the cake, her hands clutching the handle as they had clutched the back of the chair, and her look was the look of the furtive, caught child.

"I am not *der Magicker,"* she said. "I am your own dear mother."

He had upset her again without meaning to. He pried her hands from the knife, laid it on the table, and pulled her over to him. "Of course you are my own precious Mutti," he said. "Come. Let me lay my head against your breast as I did when I was a child, and listen to your heart beat."

"Ja," she said, and held him close. He could hear the slow steady beat of her heart. It had always calmed him and helped him to sleep. After she died he could not sleep for months.

"You want to Bess a message send?" she said. "Like the messages I send my boy?"

The coffee had left a bitter taste in his mouth, and his head was beginning to ache. He should never have tried to eat so soon. He looked up at her. "What do you mean, Mutti? What messages? I went to a hundred seances and I never heard . . ."

"That is because you are *der argwahnish, der* suspicious boy. I write you a letter, and you say, 'It is *der Tricker, der Magicker,'* but it is your own dear Mama."

His head was pounding, and the room tilted dangerously. He was afraid the bowl of oranges would slide off the table. He had not believed Lady Doyle had really gotten a message from his mother. He had discredited her and her husband in the papers, and it had not been a trick after all. It had really been a message from his mother. But why had his mother written in fluent English when she spoke only German and a little broken English? Why had she, the wife of a Jewish rabbi, marked each page with a Christian cross?

And why had there been no sign, no proof that it was really a message from his mother? The letter had been full of vague clichés: "I want to talk to my boy, my own beloved boy. I am preparing so sweet a home for him which one day in God's good time, he will come to." Not one word of his brother or of what he should do.

And Lady Doyle could answer none of his questions. How much money had he sent his mother every week? What size slippers had she asked him to bring her from Europe? What had he given her for Mother's Day?

"But, Mama," he said. "Why didn't you tell me whether I should forgive Leopold? That's what you were trying to tell me when you died, wasn't it, to forgive him? I went to your grave and begged you to tell me. Why didn't you? I would have known the letter was from you if you had told me to forgive Leo." He put his hands to his head, trying to stop the aching.

"If I say to you, 'Forgive Leopold,' you only say again it is *der Magicker*," she said. "And you do not believe. That is a bad thing. Not to believe." She sat down in the chair next to him and put the shawl around his shoulders again. "You don't want your Bess to say, *'Der Tricker,'* when you send your message to her, do you?"

"No," he said. He had made a laughingstock of the mediums, duplicating their tricks on stage to show the audience how they worked, and all the time the messages had really been from his mother. "I'm sorry, Mama," he said. "I didn't know the messages were from you. But Bess will know it is me. She and I worked out a special code." He stood up and started for the curtain. "Do you remember that song of ours, 'Rosabelle, Sweet Rosabelle'?"

"No!" his mother said suddenly, sharply.

He turned around, surprised. "Of course you do, Mama. Bess used to sing it all the time."

His mother was standing by the sideboard. She was holding a piece of notepaper and a fountain pen. "That is not the way a message to send. You must to your Bess a letter write.''

''Oh,'' he said, and came back to the table. ''I didn't know.'' He sat down in the chair, and she put the paper and pen in front of him.

He uncapped the pen and held it above the paper. ''How does the message get to Bess, Mutti?'' he said.

''You write on the paper and on the other side the go-between, *die Hexe,* how you call it?''

''Medium,'' he said.

''*Ja,* the medium writes the message down.''

''A medium?'' he said, ''Are you sure, Mama?''

The shawl had fallen to the floor when he went over to the curtain. She bent over to pick it up. ''*Ja,*'' she said. ''They are good, the mediums. Always the messages they send so we can talk to our loved ones on the other side of the veil.''

He could hardly believe what she was saying. The mediums had not been good. They had all been fakes. They tilted tables with their knees and tied strings to their fingers to make oranges float through the air. They had used those tricks to swindle and cheat, to get money. If he sent his message through a medium, the medium would change it, use it to cheat Bess out of money.

That will not work, he thought triumphantly. If they change the message, even one word, Bess will not believe it is from me. He wrote the word ''Rosabelle'' on the paper and looked at it.

What if they will not send the message at all, he thought? They hated me. I exposed their tricks so all the world could see what crooks they were. And now that I am dead, they will try to get their revenge. They will try to keep me from getting through to Bess. Well, I will not let them stop me. I will think of some other way to get the message through to her.

''Mutti,'' he said. ''Isn't there some other way of getting the message through? Without a medium? What about the curtain?''

She was holding the shawl, gripping it so hard her skin

was stretched tight over her knuckles. "No!" she said. "No! You must write your message to Bess. There is no other way!"

"You don't understand, Mutti. I can't send my message through a medium. They're fakes. They trick people." He reached for her hand, but she snatched it away from him. "Mama, they did terrible things. One of them dressed up his assistant to look like you. In a black silk dress just like the one you're wearing. To trick me, Mama. They're crooks."

"You want some more cake maybe," she said. "It makes you feel better, and then you write your message to Bess."

He crossed out the word "Rosabelle" and put the pen down. "No, Mutti," he said firmly. He stood up. "We have to find some other way to send the message."

She picked up the pen. "I will the message write for you."

He could not make her understand how much they hated him for exposing their tricks. They had made all kinds of threats, but he had only laughed at them. What could they do to him, the great Houdini? He could see through all their tricks. He had never once believed they were in contact with the spirit world, that they could . . .

The room pitched suddenly. He gripped the edge of the table to keep his balance. Suppose they did have powers that extended beyond the grave, as they had claimed? And suppose they hated him so much that they could follow him here to the other side to get their revenge?

His head was hurting so much he could not think clearly. He straightened, gritting his teeth against the pain, and looked around the room, even though it made him dizzy. Oranges and black curtains and a round table. A seance room. A medium's room.

"What is this place?" he said, almost to himself. "What are you doing here, Mutti?" he said. "Did someone make you come here?"

She did not look up at him. "We write the message, and

then you have some cake,'' she said doggedly. ''The first word is 'Rosabelle,' *ja*?''

There was no door in the room. He had not noticed that until now. ''Mama,'' he said softly, and put his hand on her shoulder so she would not be frightened. ''Do you know a way out of here?''

The hand holding the pen jerked a little and blotted the paper.

''Don't be afraid, Mutti,'' he whispered. ''They can't keep us here. I'll find a way out. There's never been anything yet that I couldn't get out of.''

''Bess misses you,'' she said, and the pen scratched on the paper. ''We must send her the message. What is the next word?''

He looked down at the paper. She had written the word ''Rosabelle'' in a beautiful, flowing script, not at all like his mother's handwriting.

''We will tell her to come to us, so we can all be together,'' she said.

The room began to roll, the black and red flowers of the carpet tossing like waves. They had nearly tricked him that time with the woman in the black dress. It was amazing what a costume and a gray wig could do. It had been nearly dark in the room, and he had wanted so desperately to believe it was his own dear Mutti that he had almost believed. But she had not been able to answer his questions.

The headache had gone away. He raised his head. ''Mutti,'' he said. ''Should I have forgiven Leo in spite of what he did?''

''*Ja*, of course,'' she said impatiently. ''The next word is what?''

''What was it Leo did that he needed to be forgiven?'' he said. Her hand tightened around the pen. ''How much money did I send you home every week? When did you ask me to bring you the slippers? What did I give you for Mother's Day?'' Her knuckles were white. The pen jerked and left a black mark, like a cross, on the paper.

He stood up, knocking the chair against the wall, and stumbled toward the curtain. ''Bess!'' he shouted, frantically trying to find the opening in the curtains. "Don't listen to them! It's some kind of a trap!"

His mother's hand closed around his arm. "Come sit down, my poor boy," she said gently, but her grip on his arm was as strong as a man's. "My poor boy has still the seasickness. It makes his head hurt, *ja*?" She pushed him down into the chair she had been sitting in. "You must rest your head against your mother's heart as you used to do when you were a baby. Close your eyes and rest. We will send the message to Bess soon and then we will all be together here, you and Bess and your own dear mother, together forever. Soon, soon," she crooned. She put her arms around him and pressed his head against her breast.

Her heart beat strongly, slowly, but his own did not slow, and he did not close his eyes. He looked at the wall behind the sideboard, searching for a mark that meant a hidden door. He had broken out of locked trunks and straitjackets, escaped from handcuffs and jail cells. He freed one hand and slid it along the wall, looking for a hidden panel.

"*Mein Junge,*" his mother said, and her grip tightened. "Tell me the message, and I send it for you."

When David Drake decided to turn his talents to full-time writing and leave his job as Assistant Town Attorney of Chapel Hill, North Carolina, I must admit I had some trepidations. They were wasted, though, as Dave has done extremely well with his professional writing career. He has, thankfully, still found the time to serve as Whispers *magazine's assistant editor, and in between novels, he was kind enough to write this seemingly routine heroic fantasy whose original twists and shakes makes this a true* Whispers *story.*

DREAMS IN AMBER
David Drake

The man in the tavern doorway was the one whom Saturnus saw in the dreams which ended in nightmare. The bead on Saturnus's chest tingled, and the fragmented dream voice whispered in the agent's mind, "Yes . . . Allectus."

Allectus paused to view the interior, smoky with the cheap oil of the tavern lamps. He was a soft-looking man whose curly beard and sideburns were much darker than his flowing ginger moustache. Allectus wore boots, breeches, and a hooded cape buttoned up the front. All his clothing was farm garb, and all of it was unsuited to the position Saturnus knew Allectus held—Finance Minister of Carausius. The Emperor Marcus Aurelius Mausaeus Carausius, as he was styled on this side of the British Ocean, which his fleet controlled. The one-time Admiral of the Saxon Shore

13

now struck coins to show himself as coemperor with his "brothers," Diocletian and Maximian. In the five years since disaster had engulfed Maximian's fleet off Anderida, there had been no attempt from the mainland to gainsay the usurper's claim.

No attempt until now, until Gaius Saturnus was sent to Britain with instructions from an emperor and a mission from his dreams.

Allectus stepped aside as the agent approached him. He took Saturnus for another sailor leaving the tavern on the Thames dockside, the sort of man he had come to hire perhaps . . . but the finance officer was not ready to commit himself quite yet.

Saturnus touched his arm. "I'm the man you want," the agent said in a low voice.

"Pollux! Get away from me!" the finance officer demanded angrily. Allectus twitched loose as he glared at Saturnus, expecting to see either a pimp or a catamite. Saturnus was neither of those things. In Allectus's eyes, the agent was a tall, powerful man whose skin looked weathered enough to fit the shoddy clothes he also wore.

The finance officer stepped back in surprise. He had been tense before he entered the dive. Now, in his confusion, he was repenting the plan that had brought him here.

"I know what you want done," Saturnus said. He did not move closer to Allectus again, but he spoke louder to compensate for the other's retreat. "I'm the man you need." And Saturnus's arm tucked the cloak momentarily closer to his torso so that it molded the hilt of his dagger. The voice in Saturnus's mind whispered ". . . need . . ." to him again.

A customer had just left one of the blanket-screened cribs along the wall. It was a slow night, no lines, and the Moorish prostitute peered out at the men by the door as she settled her smock. Allectus grimaced in frustration. He looked at Saturnus again. With a curse and a prayer in Greek—Allectus was a Massiliot, no more a native Briton than the Batavian Carausius—he said, "Outside, then."

Three sailors blocked the door as they tried to enter in

drunken clumsiness. Normally the finance officer would have given way, even if he had his office to support him. Now he bulled through them. Anger had driven Allectus beyond good judgment; though the sailors, thank fortune, were too loose to take umbrage.

Taut himself as a drawn bow, the imperial agent followed the official. Maximian had sent him to procure the usurper's death. The dreams . . .

The air outside was clammy with a breeze off the river. All the way from the docks to the fort there were taverns similar to the one in which Saturnus had been told to wait: one-story buildings with thatched roofs and plaster in varying states of repair covering the post and wattle walls. The shills were somnolent tonight. Only a single guard ship remained while the Thames squadron joined the rest of the fleet at some alert station on the Channel. Saturnus knew that the mainland emperors planned no immediate assault. He could not tell, however, whether the concentration was merely an exercise, or if it was a response to some garbled news of a threat. The threat, perhaps, that he himself posed.

There was some fog, but the moon in a clear sky gave better light than the tavern lamps in the haze of their own making. Allectus had composed himself by the time he turned to face Saturnus again. In a voice as flat and implacable as the sound of waves slapping the quay, the finance officer demanded, "Now, who are you and what do you think you're playing at?" The metal of an armored vest showed beneath Allectus's cloak as he tossed his head. His right hand was on the hilt of a hidden sword.

Saturnus laughed. The sound made Allectus jump. He was aware suddenly of his helplessness against the bigger, harder man who had accosted him. "My name doesn't matter," the agent said. "We both want a man killed. I need your help to get close to him, and you need . . . " The men looked at one another. "You were looking for a man tonight, weren't you?" Saturnus added. "A tough from the docks for a bit of rough work? Well, you found him."

The finance officer took his hand from his weapon and reached out slowly. His fingers traced the broad dimple on

Saturnus's forehead. It had been left by the rubbing weight
of a bronze helmet over years of service. "You're a
deserter, aren't you?" Allectus said.

"Think what you like," Saturnus replied.

Allectus's hand touched the other man's cape. He raised
the garment up over the agent's shoulder. Saturnus wore
breeches and a tunic as coarse as the cape itself. The
dagger sheathed on his broad leather belt was of uncom-
mon quality, however. It had a silver-chased hilt and a
blade which examination would have shown to be of steel
watermarked by the process of its forging. The knife had been
a calculated risk for the agent; but the meanest of men
could have chanced on a fine weapon in these harsh times.

On the chain around Saturnus's neck was a lump of
amber in a basket of gold wire. The nature of the flaw in
the amber could not be determined in the light available.

Allectus let the garment flop closed. "Why?" he asked
very softly. "*Why* do you want to kill Carausius?"

Saturnus touched the amber bead with his left hand. "I
was at Anderida," he said.

The truth of the statement was misleading. It did not
answer the question as it appeared to do. It was true,
though, that in the agent's mind shimmered both his own
memories and those of another mind. *Transports burned in
scarlet fury on the horizon, driven back toward the mainland by the southwest wind against which they had been
beating. With the sight came the crackle of the flames and,
faintly—scattered by the same breeze that bore it—the
smell of burning flesh. Maximian had clutched the stern
rail of his flagship in his strong, callused hands. His red
cloak and those of his staff officers, Saturnus then among
them, had snapped like so many pools of quivering blood.
The Emperor cursed monotonously. Still closer to their
position in the rear guard a sail was engulfed in a bubble
of white, then scarlet. Maximian had ordered withdrawal.
A trumpet had keened from the flagship's bow, and horns
answered it like dying seabirds.*

*No one in the flagship had seen a sign of the hostile
squadron. In shattered but clear images in Saturnus's*

*mind, however, a trireme painted dark gray-green like the
sea struggled with waves that were a threat to its low
freeboard. The decks of the warship were clear, save for
the steersmen and a great chest lashed to the bow . . . and
beside the chest, the stocky figure of Carausius himself.
The usurper pointed and spoke, and a distant mast shuddered upward in a gout of flame . . .*

The finance officer sagged as if he had been stabbed. "I
was at Mona," he whispered. "Eight years ago. He took a
chest aboard, bullion I thought, as though he was going to
run. But he caught the Scoti pirates and they burned . . .
He's a hero, you know? Ever since that." Allectus gave a
sweep of his arm that could have indicated anything from
the fort to the whole island. "To all of them. But he scares
me, scares me more every day."

Saturnus felt a thrill of ironic amusement not his own.
He shrugged his cape back over him. Aloud he said, "All
right, we can take care of it now. They'll let me into the
fort with you, won't they?"

"Now? But . . ." Allectus objected. He looked around
sharply at the empty street and the river blurred in cottony
advection fog. "He's gone, isn't he? With the squadron?"

Sure with a faceted certainty where even the high official had been misled, Saturnus said, "No, Carausius is
here. He sends the ships out sometimes when he doesn't
want too many people around. I've been told where he is,
but you'll have to get me into the fort."

The finance officer stared at Saturnus for seconds that
were timeless to the agent. "If Carausius knows enough to
send you to trap me," mused Allectus, "then it doesn't
really matter, does it? Let's go, then." He turned with a
sharp military movement and led Saturnus up the metalled
road to the fort.

The Fleet Station at London had been rebuilt by Carausius
from the time he usurped the rule of Britain. There had
always been military docking facilities. Carausius had expanded them and had raised the timber fort which enclosed
also the administrative center from which he ruled the
island. Now only a skeleton detachment manned the gates

and the artillery in the corner towers. The East Gate, opening onto the central street of the fort, was itself defended by a pair of flanking towers with light catapults. The catapults were not cocked. Their arms were upright, and the slings drooped in silhouette against the sky above the tower battlements. The bridge over the ditch had not been raised either, but the massive, ironclad gate leaves were closed and barred against the night.

Someone should have challenged the men as soon as they set foot on the drawbridge. Instead, Allectus had first to shout, then to bang on a gate panel with his knife hilt to arouse the watch. A pair of Frankish mercenaries finally swung open a sally port within the gateway. The Franks were surly and reeked of wine. Saturnus wondered briefly whether the finance officer's help had been necessary to get him within the fort. But the agent was inside safely, now, and a feeling of satisfaction fluttered over his skin.

Allectus looked angrily away from the guards. "All right," he said in a low voice to the agent. "What next?"

Saturnus nodded up the street, past the flanking barracks blocks to the Headquarters Complex in the center of the fort. "In there," he said. He began walking up the street, leading Allectus but led himself by whispers and remembered dreams. "In the Headquarters Building, not the Palace."

The two central buildings were on a scale larger than the size of the fort would normally have implied. Though the fort's troop complement was no more than a thousand men, it enclosed what amounted to an imperial administrative center. The Headquarters Building closing the street ahead of them was two-story and almost three hundred feet to a side. Saturnus knew that beyond it the Palace, which he had never seen with his own eyes, was of similar size.

The fort's interior had the waiting emptiness of a street of tombs: long, silent buildings with no sign of inhabitants. Occasionally the sound of laughter or an argument would drift into the roadway from partying members of the watch detachment. Others of the troops left behind when the squadron sailed were certainly among the few customers on the strip below the fort. Men who chanced near to

Saturnus and the finance officer ducked away again without speaking. Both the men had the gait and presence of officers, and the foggy moonlight hid their rough clothes.

"How do you know this?" Allectus asked suddenly. "How do you know about—about me?"

"It doesn't matter," the agent said. He tramped stolidly along the flagstone street with his left hand clutching the bead against his chest. "Say I dreamed it. Say I have nightmares and I dreamed it all."

"It could be a nightmare," the finance officer muttered. "He must consult sorcerers to bring storms down on his enemies. He must *be* a sorcerer—I've never seen any others of that sort around him."

"He's not a sorcerer," Saturnus remarked grimly. "And he's not alone." "Alone . . ." echoed his mind.

"I can rule without sorcery," Allectus said, aloud but to himself. The agent heard. He did not respond.

The guard at the front door of the Headquarters Building was a legionary, not a barbarian from the Rhine Estuary as those in the gate tower had been. The soldier braced to attention when he heard the pairs of boots approaching. "Who goes there?" he challenged in Latin.

"The Respectable Allectus, Chief of Imperial Accounts," the finance officer replied. "We have business inside."

The guard walked two further steps until he could visually identify the speaker. Allectus threw back his cowl to expose his face. The guard's spear clashed as he swung it to port against his body armor. "Sir!" he acknowledged with a stiff-armed salute. Then he unlatched the tall double doors before returning to attention. Saturnus watched with a sardonic smile. There were few enough units back on the mainland that could be expected to mount so sharp an interior guard. Whatever else the source of Carausius's strength, he had some first-class troops loyal to him.

"Who's the officer of the watch?" Saturnus asked.

The guard looked at him, surprised that Allectus's companion had spoken. The agent did not look to be the sort of man who entered Headquarters at night. That raised the question of the way Allectus himself was dressed, but . . .

"Standard-bearer Minucius, sir," the guard replied. Discipline held. It was not his business to question the authority of one of Carausius's highest officials. "You'll find him in his office."

When the big door closed behind them, it was obvious how much ambient light there had been outside. The clerestory windows were pale bars without enough authority to illuminate the huge hall beneath them. The nave could hold an assemblage larger than the normal complement of the fort. On the south end, the tribunal was a hulking darkness with no hint of the majesty it would assume when lighted and draped with bunting. "We'll need the officer of the watch," Saturnus remarked. He gestured.

Lamplight was showing through the columns from one of the offices across the width of the hall. "We need to get into the strongroom beneath the Shrine of the Standards."

The finance officer looked sharply at his companion. It was absurd to think that all this was a charade dreamed up by a common thief . . . absurd. "There's nothing in the strongroom but the men's private accounts," he said aloud.

Saturnus appeared to ignore the comment.

The gleam from the office was a goal, not an illumination. That did not matter to the agent. He could have walked across the building blindfolded, so often had he dreamed of it bathed in amber light. Now Saturnus strode in a revery of sorts, through the arches of the aisle and finally into the office section beyond the assembly hall. Allectus and present reality had almost disappeared from Saturnus's mind until the standard-bearer, alerted by the sound of boots, stepped from his office behind an upraised lamp. "Who the hell are you?" the soldier demanded, groping behind him for the swordbelt he had hung over the top of the door.

Allectus stepped into the light as Saturnus paused. "Oh, *you*, sir," said the startled duty officer. "I didn't recognize your, ah, bodyguard."

"We need to check the strongroom," Allectus said unceremoniously. He gestured with his head. "Get your keys and accompany us."

The standard-bearer reacted first to the tone of command. He patted the ring of keys he wore on a leather shoulder belt. Then he frowned, still touching the keys. He said, "Sir, none of that's public money, you know."

"Of course we know!" snapped Allectus. "We need to check it anyway." He did not understand the stranger's purpose, but he was not willing to be balked in any request by an underling.

"Sir, I think . . ." the standard-bearer said in a troubled voice. "Look, the squadron should be back tomorrow or the next day at the latest. Why don't you—"

"He delays us," Saturnus dreamed. His right hand swung from beneath his cape to bury the dagger to its crossguards in the pit of the soldier's stomach.

The standard-bearer whooped and staggered backward with a look of surprise. Saturnus released the dagger hilt in time to take the lamp before the soldier collapsed. Minucius was dead before he hit the stone floor.

Saturnus rolled the body over before he withdrew the knife. Blood followed the steel like water from a spring. None of the blood escaped the dead man's tunic and breeches to mark the stones.

"Gods," whispered the finance officer. His hand hovered short of his sword. "You just killed him!"

"We came here to kill, didn't we?" the agent reminded him bleakly. "Help me drag him back behind a pillar where he won't be noticed till morning." As Saturnus spoke, he wiped the dagger on his victim's tunic, then cut the keys loose from the belt that supported them. "Come on, for pity's sake. We haven't much time." "Time . . ." the mind in his mind repeated.

Allectus obeyed with a quickness close to panic. Vague fears and a longing for personal power had brought the finance officer to the point of murder and usurpation. Now the ordinary concerns of failure and execution to which he had steeled himself were giving way to a morass more doubtful than the original causes.

They tugged the murdered man into the empty office

next to his own. Allectus then carried the lamp as he nervously followed the agent's striding figure.

The Shrine of the Standards was a small room in the center of the line of offices. It faced the main entrance across the nave, so that anyone entering the building during daylight would first see the sacred standards of the unit in their stone-screened enclosure. They were gone now, with the squadron. The lamp threw curlicue shadows across the shrine to the equally twisted stonework on the other side. Saturnus fitted one key, then the next on the ring, until he found the one that turned the lock. His dreams were trying to speak to him, but trial and error was a better technique now than viewing the ring of keys through eyes which were knowledgeable but not his own.

Allectus sighed when the iron door swung open. Saturnus released the keys. They jangled against the lockplate. For safety's sake, the agent should have closed the door behind them. That would have disguised the fact that they were inside. He was too nervous to do so, however. The nightmare was closing on him, riding him like a raft through white water. "Come on," Saturnus said to the finance officer. He had to remember that the other man could not hear the clamor in his own mind. Saturnus bent to lift the ring-handled trap door in the center of the shrine's empty floor. "We'll need the light when we're inside."

The hinges of the door down to the strongroom were well oiled and soundless. Saturnus did not let the panel bang open. Rather, he eased it back against the flooring. The room beneath was poorly lighted by the lamp which trembled in Allectus's hand. In any case, the strongroom was no more than a six-foot cube. It was just big enough to hold the large iron-bound chest and to give the standard-bearers room to work in their capacity as bankers for the troops of the unit. The walls of the dugout were anchored by posts and paneled with walers of white oak to keep the soil from collapsing inward.

Saturnus used the ladder on one wall instead of jumping down as Allectus half expected. "Quietly," the agent said with exaggerated lip movements to compensate for the near silence of his command. He took the lamp from Allectus's hands.

As the finance officer climbed down into the cramped space, Saturnus put the lamp on the strongbox and drew his dagger. "Get ready," he said with a grin as sharp and cold as the point of his knife. "You're about to get your chance to be emperor, remember?"

Allectus drew his sword. The hem of his cape snagged on a reinforcing band of the strongbox. The finance officer tore the garment off with a curse. He had seen battle as a line infantryman, but that had been fifteen years before. "Ready," he said.

An ant stared at Saturnus from the wall opposite the strongbox. The creature was poised on what seemed to be a dowel rod set flush with the oak paneling. The agent's right hand held his dagger advanced. Saturnus set his left thumb over the ant and crushed the creature against the dowel that sank beneath the pressure. The whole wall pivoted inward onto a short tunnel.

With his left thumb and forefinger, Saturnus snuffed the lamp.

Allectus opened his mouth to protest. Before the whispered words came out, however, the finance officer realized that he was not in total darkness after all. The door at the tunnel's farther end, twenty feet away, was edged and crossed with magenta light that slipped through the interstices of the paneling. Allectus chewed at one point of his bushy moustache. He could not see his companion until the other man stepped forward in silhouette against the hot pink lines.

For his own part, Saturnus walked in the monochrome tunnel of his mind. Light suffused the myriad facets through which he saw. He was walking toward the climax of his nightmare, the nightmare which had owned his soul ever since his parents had hung the lucky amulet of gold and amber around his neck as an infant. Unlike other well-born children, Gaius Saturnus had not dedicated the amulet with his shorn hair at age twelve when he formally became a man. The blade that would exorcize his childhood was not in the hand of a barber but rather now in Saturnus's own.

"There," whispered the mind beyond Saturnus's mind
as the agent's hand touched the ordinary bronze latch-lever
on the farther door. Saturnus had enough intellectual control over what he was about to do to check his companion's position. Allectus stood to the side and a step back.
The finance officer's face would have been white had it
not been lighted by the rich glow. Allectus was clear of
the door's arc, however. In a single swift motion, Saturnus
turned the latch and pulled the door open.

The door gave onto a room covered in swaths of ceramic-
smooth substance that was itself the source of the magenta
light. Carausius stood in the center of the room. Three
maggots as large as men hung in the air around him with
no evident support. They were vertical, save for tapered
lower portions which curled under them like the tails of
seahorses. To one side of the room was a large wooden
box with its lid raised. The box had been built around a
cocoon of the same glowing material that covered the
walls. A part of the agent's mind recognized the box as the
"treasure chest" that Carausius had strapped to the fore-
decks of the ships in which he sailed at Mona and at
Anderida, where his opponents burned. The cocoon was
open also, hollow and large enough to hold the maggot
which began to drift soundlessly toward it.

Saturnus's amulet tingled and its commands were white
fire in his brain. There were a score, a hundred ants hidden
against the whorls of the magenta room. The cocoon pulsed
in the myriad facets of their eyes. "The weapon," demanded the gestalt mind behind them all. "It must not
turn toward you."

The burly emperor in the center of the room gurgled like
a half-drowned man recovering consciousness. He fumbled
for his sword as Saturnus ignored him and leaped past.

The agent brushed the drifting maggot as it and he both
made for the cocoon. The creature's skin was dry and
yielding. Had Saturnus thought, he could not even have
sworn that he touched a natural integument and not some
sort of artificial one. He did not think. He reacted with a
panicked loathing uncontrollable even by the group intel-

ligence riding him. Saturnus cut at the maggot with the motion of a man chopping away the spider that leaped on his shoulder. There was a momentary resistance to the point. Then the steel was through in a gush and spatter of ochre fluids.

The maggot fell in on itself like a pricked bladder collapsing. It shrank to half its original size before the remainder slopped liquidly to the floor. By that time, the agent had grabbed the side of the cocoon. The object, crate and all, began to twist as if to point one of its ends toward Saturnus.

Neither of the other floating creatures was moving. Next to the area where the cocoon shifted, a great lens blacker than matter started to form in place of the wall behind Carausius.

The emperor had cleared his sword as much by reflex as by conscious volition. Allectus, almost mad with fear and the impossible present, struck Carausius before the latter could parry. The blade rang on Carausius's forehead. The finance officer was no swordsman, but panic made his blow a shocking one even when the edge turned on bone and glanced away. The emperor staggered. His sword clanged as the hilt slipped from his fingers.

Saturnus gripped the cocoon with his left hand. He could not prevent the object from turning. Like a man wrestling a crocodile, however, he kept the end from pointing toward him the way it or what controlled it desired. Then, as the dream voices demanded, Saturnus stabbed into the spongy wall of the cocoon. His steel hissed in a dazzling iridescence. The cocoon's material boiled away from the metal, disappearing at a rate that increased geometrically as the gap expanded toward itself around its circumference.

There was a crashing sound like lightning. The box that camouflaged the cocoon from human eyes burst into flames.

Saturnus rolled back from the destruction he had caused. The blade of his dagger had warped, though its hilt was not even warm in his hand. One of the floating maggots made a sound like that of water on hot iron.

Allectus ignored the maggots as if he could thus deny

their existence. The finance officer stepped between them to thrust with the full weight of his body at the reeling Carausius. His point skidded on the breastplate hidden by the emperor's tunic. Carausius flung himself back, away from the blade. He fell into the lens and merged with the dim shape already forming there.

Carausius's whole body burned. His iron armor blazed like the heart of the sun. In its illumination, the wall began to powder and the maggots shriveled like slugs on a stove. The mind in Saturnus's mind sparkled in triumph.

Saturnus dragged Allectus back down the tunnel toward the strongroom. The agent acted by instinct rather than from any conscious desire to save the other man. The finance officer had been stunned by events and reaction to his own part in them. His skin prickled where it had been bare to coruscance a moment before, and his eyes were watering.

"What was it?" Allectus whispered. He felt his lips crack as he moved them. "What were they?"

Saturnus had been familiar since infancy with the scene he had just lived and with a thousand variations upon that scene. "Things from far away," he said. It was the first time he had spoken to a human being about the nightmare that had ruled him for so long. "They've been helping Carausius for now, getting his support in turn for their own mission, things they need. When they were ready, more of them would come. Many more. They would smooth this world like a ball of ivory and squirm across its surface with no fellow but themselves."

"What?" mumbled Allectus. They had reached the strongroom. With Carausius gone and no one else aware of that fact, the finance minister could seize the throne himself—if he could organize his mind enough to act. The agent's words rolled off Allectus's consciousness, part of the inexplicable madness of moments before. He did not wait for Saturnus to amplify his remarks, did not *want* to hear more about things whose possible reality could be worse than human imaginings.

Saturnus paused as his human companion began to scramble up the ladder. The agent's left hand closed for the last time over the amulet on his chest. The farther door of the tunnel had swung shut on the blazing carnage within. The hinges and latch glowed. As Saturnus watched, the center of the wood charred through and illuminated the tunnel harshly.

Saturnus jerked his hand down and broke the thin gold chain. The amulet was as clear in his mind as if he could see it through his clenched fist. At the heart of the amber bead was the creature trapped in pine resin sixty million years before Man walked the Earth. Trapped and preserved in sap that hardened to transparent stone . . . Trapped and preserved, an ant like so many billions of others in that age and in future ages . . .

Saturnus hurled his amulet back toward the flame-shot door. A last memory remained as the amber bead left his hand. It was not the world of his nightmare, the maggot-drifting globe Saturnus had described to Allectus.

Saturnus's Roman world view had as little concept of duration as did that of the timeless group mind to which he had so long been an appendage. "Thirty million years in the future" would have been no more than nonsense syllables to Saturnus if someone had spoken them. But he could understand the new vision that he saw. The dream Earth crawled with the one life form remaining to it. To salute Saturnus as they left him, all the billions of six-legged units raised their antennae, under the direction of the single gestalt intelligence which had just saved the world for itself.

Then the amber bead and the vision blazed up together.

FOOTPRINTS IN PERDU
Hugh B. Cave

Toward evening, as the forest filled with silence, they
came to a stream. It was swift but shallow. Their sturdy
little Caribbean horses had no trouble fording it.

On the opposite bank stood the peasant *caille* the young
black woman at the hospital had told them about, with
blue shutters and a grass roof.

"There you will meet an aged couple named Lamartière,"
she had said. "They are good people. On being told the
reason for your journey, they will put you up for the night.
Just mention my name and say you wish to find and help
the little girl in Perdu who is said to be a *loupgarou.*"

It was not the first such trip Dr. Mair and Nurse Foster
had made together into the roadless mountains of Haiti.
Both worked at the Hôpital LaRue in the Plaine du Nord.
Both were keenly interested in the country's history and

folklore, and above all in her people. Happily, they had discovered they were interested in each other as well.

Their journeys at first had been simply a means of escaping the routine of hospital work in a part of the country that offered no recreation. Then as they had come to understand each other better—perhaps to love each other—they had found it interesting to combine their nights out together with their love of being doctor and nurse in a primitive Caribbean country where the barefoot people, especially the children, so sorely needed help.

In the house with the blue shutters (no other parts of it were painted at all) they slept in each other's arms and talked a little about being married on their return to the States, whenever that might be. In the morning they were told how to reach their destination.

"You must ride more slowly now," said old Lamartière, who had suffered from yaws at one time and, thanks to the hospital, still had some of his nose left. "It will take the whole day. The trail is rough, so be careful, please. In Perdu, which is what people call that miserable place though it has a different name on the map, the man to ask for is M'sieu Bravache. He is fat and nasty but will put you up for pay and perhaps help you find the child you seek. Everyone else will be afraid of you because you will be strangers, and because so many babies have disappeared from there."

"So many babies have what?" Dr. Mair frowned, not sure he was translating the peasant Creole correctly.

"Disappeared, m'sieu. Four or five of them now, so we have heard. At any rate, that village is truly a lost place."

Twenty-nine-year-old Tom Mair of Boston, Massachusetts, shook the old man's hand and thanked him. Twenty-six-year-old Andrea Foster of Fort Lauderdale, Florida, embraced the old woman.

"I hope," said Andrea, "that when we come back through here we will have the little girl with us. Because whatever is wrong, I feel sure we can help her. She isn't a werewolf, of course. Nobody is."

"How can you know that, m'selle?" Lamartière protested.

"Well, of course, if you *believe* in werewolves . . . Just what *is* a *loup-garou* in your opinion, m'sieu?"

"M'selle, a *loup-garou* is a person who, through his knowledge of *magie noire,* can assume the form of a wolf and has the appetite of one."

"I see. Well, anyway, we must find this child and help her."

As the doctor and nurse began their long ride to Perdu, the old couple looked at each other. "Nobody is a were-wolf?" Lamartière remarked with a shrug. "Then tell me, please, *maman*—who do they think is carrying off those babies?"

"It takes a little while to learn about our country, Emile. Give them time. They are handsome and in love but have not been here long."

"They speak the language."

"That part is easy."

Tom Mair and Andrea Foster put the miles behind them, though this was a wild region. They dismounted often to rest and sometimes were able to find reasonably level spots where they could rest side by side, touching. Not until late afternoon did they come in sight of their destination.

"It doesn't look so lost," Andrea observed. "Perhaps the name has another meaning here."

"Perhaps it has."

The trail became wide enough to be a driving road, had anything on wheels ever been introduced here. On each side stood a long row of wattle-and-daub *cailles* with banana-thatch roofs. Other peasant houses were half hidden by forest trees.

It could correctly be called a village, though, Tom pointed out, because the setting sun sparkled on the necessary flowing water. But it was certainly a poor one, and about as isolated as a village could be.

"That house near the end must be the one we want," he said. "The one with the zinc roof."

"The big shot. 'Fat and nasty.' "

"But important."

"I'll be ever so polite," Andrea promised.

M'sieu Bravache was indeed fat. Two hundred eighty pounds, guessed Tom, who made a game of guessing patients' weights before weighing them at the hospital. Might they pay M'sieu for the privilege of staying overnight in his excellent house? But of course! Could he perhaps arrange food for them also? Certainly! And would he, as a very special favor, help them to accomplish what they had come all this way to do?

"What is that, m'selle?" the fat man asked as the three of them sat stiffly polite on rude but heavily varnished chairs of Haitian mahogany in what he called his parlor.

"There is a little girl here," Andrea explained, "who is reputed to be a werewolf."

Heaving a loud sigh, the fat man shook his head so vigorously that the starched collar of his white shirt seemed likely to saw his neck in two. (Though he wore no tie, the collar was buttoned, and though he wore no socks, his black dress shoes were highly polished. Obviously he was, indeed, the big man in Perdu.) "Ah yes, I know," he said, as though the subject were a burden he longed to be rid of.

"At the hospital, m'sieu, we do not believe in werewolves."

"But of course."

"Meaning you don't believe in them either?" asked Tom in some surprise.

"I? Certainly not. Good heavens, no! But this child you speak of—though she is not a *loup-garou,* of course, I fear you would be wasting your time trying to help her."

"Why?"

"She is insane, M'sieu Docteur. That is why the people here believe she *is* a werewolf—because of her speech and behavior."

"And because of the babies who have disappeared?" Tom suggested.

The fat man was startled; no doubt of it. A shiver ran across the pouches under his eyes. "You know about that?" he said when he recovered.

"We hear many things at the hospital. Tell us about the babies, if you will."

"Well—" It was a long hesitation. "As you say, they have been disappearing."

"How many?"

"Three—no, four—in the past four or five months. A most unnatural thing, of course."

"And the people believe this child, Marie Roche, is responsible?"

"They do."

A frown rearranged Tom's face. "Werewolves eat *babies?*"

"Normally they would not, of course. I mean to say," the fat man quickly amended, "*I* do not believe in werewolves, as I have already told you, but those people who do believe in them will tell you they prey normally on animals. On goats and pigs. But, you see, we have no such animals here in Perdu. My people are truly backward."

"They must raise food of some kind," Andrea protested. "It certainly can't be brought in."

"They grow yams, mostly. They keep a few chickens. And, sadly, they grow the smoking weed."

"Tobacco?" Tom said.

"Not tobacco. It has no name that I know of, nor do I know of any other place in Haiti where it grows. When one is hungry it quiets the ache in the belly. When one is sick it eases the pain. But it takes away all ambition. And everyone here uses it. Not for nothing is this place called Perdu, M'sieu Docteur."

Tom's frown deepened. "Let me be sure I understand you. The people here believe that little nine-year-old Marie Roche is a werewolf because she talks and acts queerly, and because several babies have vanished. Is that correct?"

"That is correct."

"They believe she has seized and eaten the missing babies because her normal food supply—that is, the normal food supply of a werewolf—does not exist here."

"Again correct," said the fat man sadly.

"You personally don't believe this, however, because you are too intelligent to believe in werewolves."

"That, too, is so."

"How do *you* explain the infants' disappearance, then, m'sieu?"

Bravache turned his hands up in a gesture of helplessness. "Among people as backward as these, anything is possible."

"Such as?"

"Let us say an infant dies of neglect. Perhaps simply of hunger. The mother is ashamed, knowing she is to blame. She buries the unfortunate creature and explains its absence by saying it was stolen away in the night by Marie Roche." He shrugged. "It is so convenient to have a resident *loup-garou,* no?"

"If the people are so certain she is a werewolf, why haven't they tried to destroy her?"

The fat man turned his hands again. "They might have, but for me. There was a meeting, and a committee was appointed to go to her home and do it. But I heard about it and removed her to where she is now, and later was able to dissuade them."

"When was this?" Andrea asked.

"About six weeks ago."

"And where is she now, m'sieu?"

"In a poor house back in the bush, looked after by a not very bright old woman who is paid by me for her trouble. But I would not advise—"

"Oh, we must see her," Andrea insisted. "It's why we came here."

"Very well." He sighed. "In the morning I will tell you how to get there. The path is too rough for you to attempt at this late hour."

"Tell me, M'sieu Bravache," Tom said, "has the child no parents?"

"They are afraid of her, m'sieu. One of the babies who disappeared was her own infant sister." The big man struggled to his feet. "Now, if you will excuse me, I must go out to my kitchen. I live alone here, as you see, and do my own cooking. Please make yourselves comfortable in my absence.''

The evening meal was better than they had expected after his talk of shortages. Meat, he explained again while dining with them, was almost never available here. However, at a village not too far distant a cow and a few pigs or goats were butchered once a week, and a cousin of his who lived there had brought him some corned young pork only yesterday.

Cut into slivers, the pork had been cooked with red peas and rice and was served with boiled leeks from, Bravache said with pride, his own garden. For dessert he served avocados from a tree behind his outdoor kitchen. The strong black coffee came from his own bushes. Despite the backwardness of the village, Bravache himself was obviously not a hardship case.

When they rose from the table, the two from the hospital were pleased with themselves and ready for bed. The fat man showed them to their room. After making love, they lay in each other's arms as usual, though with less peace of mind than they had enjoyed the night before.

Perdu was not a nice place, they decided in their whispered conversation before sleep claimed them. M'sieu Bravache was not a man to be entirely trusted. True, he had no reason to wish them harm, and would be well paid for his food and the use of his bed, but . . .

"I'll be glad to get out of here," Andrea murmured. "It's creepy."

"Go to sleep," Tom advised. And she did. But long before daylight she awoke in need of the bathroom.

Their host had shown them the outdoor toilet before bidding them goodnight. It was at the end of the yard, past the kitchen in which he had prepared the supper. The supper, Andrea decided, was probably responsible for how she felt now.

Having no intention of making such a nocturnal journey alone, she shook her bedmate awake. "Hey, I have to go. Come with me, huh?"

"Of course."

Dressed, and with flashlights, they found their way to the front door—the only door their host had introduced them to—and, holding hands, went across the swept-earth yard toward the outhouse. At the kitchen Tom stopped. "I'll wait here, love. Take your time."

He stood in the doorway of the kitchen shack, aiming the light at his feet so she would have a target to return to. Something winked up at him from the black earth. Stooping to see what it was, he picked up an imitation gold heart with an imitation gold chain attached. *Marchandes* sold them in the larger marketplaces for less than a dollar. Children wore them.

Surprised to find one in Perdu, he dropped it into his pocket to hand over to the fat man in the morning. Then Andrea returned from the outhouse and they went back to bed.

After a breakfast of coffee and eggs, the fat man told them how to find the house in which the child they sought was living. They set out on foot.

Villagers they met murmured, *"Bonjour,"* while looking down at the ground as though ashamed to be seen by strangers. Naked children in doorways stared, round-eyed, and seemed ready for instant flight back into the dark interiors of their hovels. It was easily the most depressing village they had ever visited, Tom sadly remarked.

"What do you suppose that smoking weed is?" Andrea said. "A form of marijuana?"

He reminded her of a book they had both looked at, in the library of a school in the capital, that described and pictured more than three hundred poisonous plants to be found in Haiti. "My hunch is, it's something more potent than pot. Something local."

"If we knew what it looks like, we could take some back."

"Well, we can ask. If we find the right person *to* ask."

Then the house.

It stood by itself in the bush, at the end of a little used

footpath. Of wattle and daub with most of its clay fallen out to expose the inside, it no longer had a door—only an opening in which hung a ragged blanket of the type used under mule saddles. The old woman who answered their hello by drawing the blanket aside clung for support to a staff of bamboo.

They were from the hospital in the plain, they told her while she stood there peering at them as though just barely able to make them out. They had come to see the child Marie Roche. They hoped to be able to help her.

Stepping aside, she motioned with a clawlike hand for them to enter. "I am called *Maman* Lucille." Her voice was surprisingly gentle. "Bless you for coming."

The child sat on a chair in the hut's only room, as though in a trance. Nine years old, not unattractive, she was terribly thin, with large brown vacant eyes that gazed unblinkingly into space. Tom and Andrea examined her.

When they had finished, Tom said in English, "What do you think?"

"I think we ought to ask if there are others here like this. I'll bet it's their smoking weed."

"I think so too." He turned to the woman. "*Maman*, does this child use the smoking weed?"

She shook her head.

"Has she ever?"

"Yes. But not since she came here to me."

"Was she like this when she came?"

"Worse. It affects some more than others, of course."

"*Maman*, do you think this child is a *loup-garou?*"

The wrinkled face became taut with fury. "No! She is just a sick little girl! And a good one!"

"Why is she thought to be a werewolf, then?"

"Because M'sieu Bravache says she is!"

Startled, Tom looked first at the child again, then at Andrea. Andrea said in a tone of incredulity, "M'sieu *Bravache* says she is a werewolf, *maman?*"

"Of course! Unceasingly!"

"But he told us—" She faltered, unsure whether to go

on, and Tom picked it up. "I take it you don't like M'sieu Bravache very much, *maman*," he said.

"Does anyone?"

"Well, of course, we don't know. We're strangers here. Why don't you like him?"

"He is a man who must always have more than the rest of us. More of everything, just to prove he is entitled to it. As for this poor child, he has all but destroyed her by saying she is a *loup-garou*. Please, I beg you, take her away and help her!"

"It would seem," Tom said, scowling, "that your M'sieu Bravache has told us some things that are not true. He said, for instance, that he himself did not believe in were-wolves, and he brought Marie here to keep her from being killed."

"He did bring her here. Yes, he did. And it puzzles me, because he is the one who turned the people against her."

Tom, too, was puzzled, but could see no point in pursuing it. The old lady obviously could not provide a solution. "Tell me something. Is it true that babies have been disappearing here?"

"Yes, m'sieu. One disappeared only two nights ago."

"Two nights ago? He didn't tell us that."

"Just two nights ago the month-old boy child of young Nita Borgne was stolen from his bed, and there were footprints in the mud around the house in the morning. No one has seen the infant since."

"What kind of footprints?"

"Well, m'sieu, they looked like those of a large dog. I myself saw them. But we have no dogs in Perdu, as you must have noticed. When you are hungry, it is better to eat dogs than to keep them for pets and have to feed them." Shaking her head, she looked at the child. "You see how hard it is for me to find food even for her. So it goes here all the time now. Please—will you take her with you?"

"Yes," Tom said, "we will. And here's some money to pay you for looking after her." He was generous, but what she would spend the money on in such a place he could not imagine. "I have one more request, *maman*.

Can you find us some of the smoking weed we have talked about?''

"M'sieu, you must not even think of using any!"

"No, no. We want to have it analyzed. If we can find out what it is, we may be able to help you people. It may speed Marie's recovery also."

"Wait," the woman said, and went out.

What she brought back a few minutes later was not of the marijuana family, Tom and Andrea decided. The leaves were oval, brittle, and as shiny as though freshly enameled. Tom wrapped them in his handkerchief and entrusted them to his shirt pocket. "Thank you, *maman*. Let's hope we can learn something. Now say goodbye to Marie, and we'll go.

The woman and child embraced, and there were tears in the old one's eyes.

As Tom and Andrea walked their charge to the fat man's house where their horses were tethered, they discussed what *Maman* Lucille had told them. Three things puzzled them.

One: Why had Bravache insisted he did not believe in werewolves when all the time he was telling his villagers the child was one?

Two: Why had he saved the child's life after turning the people against her?

Three: Why had he not told them a baby had been stolen only two nights ago?

"Well," Tom suggested, "he's a peasant in spite of his status here. And when we said *we* didn't believe in werewolves, he probably thought he'd better go along with us. You know how they are."

"Then why didn't he mention the baby?"

"My hunch is that he really thinks a *loup-garou* took it, and didn't want us asking questions that would force him to admit it."

"*Should* we ask more questions, Tom?"

He thought about it and shook his head. "What's the use? He won't tell us anything he doesn't want to." A smile of satisfaction touched his face as he looked down at the child walking beside him, clutching his hand. "We've got Marie. Let's just get the hell out of here, pal."

They paid M'sieu Bravache for his food and bed. They bade him adieu. When their wiry little horses paced out of his yard, Andrea led the way and Tom brought up the rear with the little girl sitting in front of him. He looped his right arm around her to keep her from sliding off, for she had never sat on a horse before.

The house was some distance behind them when Tom suddenly remembered he had something in his pocket that belonged to the village big shot. Fishing it out, he looked at it and decided he did not care enough for the man to go back with it.

Disturbed by his sudden shift of position on the horse, Marie turned her head to see what he was up to. He smiled at her. "Here, little one. Here is something pretty to hang around your neck." In English he added, "Call it an unwilling reparation from a man who has done you much harm."

Delighted, she put it on. He fastened the clasp for her. By this time they were nearing the end of the village street.

It happened in front of the next to last house, where a sad-faced young woman leaned against a gate in a bamboo fence, watching them as they approached. Andrea rode on by, murmuring a polite *"Bonjour,"* and lifting a hand in greeting. A picture of total dejection, the woman did not respond.

Then she saw the child on Tom's horse, and her gaze went to the little girl's throat. As though jolted by a charge of electricity, she sprang forward with her arms outflung and fingers clawing.

Rushing at the pony, she began screaming in a voice that threatened to lift the scalp from Tom's head.

"You! Marie Roche! *Loup-garou!* Eater of babies! Look at you—even wearing the necklace my baby had on when you stole him two nights ago!" Her rush carried her headlong into the horse's shoulder and caused it to lunge sideways. Only by a miracle did Tom succeed in holding onto the child while fighting to regain his balance.

He dug his heels into the animal and urged it forward, out of the woman's reach, but her voice pursued them even then, screaming the same shrill words. *"Loup-garou!* Eater of babies!" And the same furious accusation: "Wearing my own baby's necklace!"

On reaching the end of the village he turned for a last stunned look, and she was still in the road, screaming. Just ahead, Andrea had stopped and was waiting.

As he came up to her, she stared as though hypnotized at the necklace on the child in front of him. She had heard the screams of the missing baby's mother, of course. And she knew about the necklace, for he had shown it to her in their bedroom after finding it by the fat man's kitchen. Now as she gazed at it her eyes filled with horror.

"Oh my God," she whispered. "Oh God, Tom . . . that meat he served us . . ."

She began to cry.

"Don't do that!" He knew he had to speak sharply to make her respond. "We have to get back fast and report this!"

She nodded. Wiping her eyes with the back of her hand, she urged her horse forward again. But as he followed, Dr. Tom Mair of Boston, Massachusetts, wondered how they were to report the footprints of a large dog around a missing baby's house in a village that had no dogs.

Dr. F. Paul Wilson is best known for his excellent horror novel The Keep *and his Prometheus Award-winning* Wheels Within Wheels. *The Whispers Press has just published his most recent horror novel,* The Tomb. *The following is unlike his horror novels. It is one of those stories that had to be written to exorcise those ghosts of music past and certainly exhibits the touch of uniqueness of a* Whispers *tale.*

The Last ONE MO ONCE GOLDEN OLDIES REVIVAL

F. Paul Wilson

The announcer broke in with the news—right into the middle of a song by the latest new-wave sensation, Polio.

Philip "Flip" Goodloe was gone. The father and seminal stylist of the rock 'n' roll guitar was dead at age forty-eight.

Lenny Winter leaned back and took a long draw on the Royal Jamaican delicately balanced between his pudgy thumb and forefinger. He certainly didn't mind anybody cutting Polio's music short—this new-wave crap was worse than the stuff he had jockeyed twenty-five years ago. And he wasn't all that surprised about Flip.

Dead . . . the Flipper was dead. Lenny had sensed that coming last week. The only disconcerting thing was that it had happened so soon after he had seen him. Fifteen or

twenty years without laying eyes on Flip Goodloe, then
Lenny visits him, then he's dead, all within a few days'
time. Definitely disconcerting.

He listened for details about the death, but there were
none. Only a hushed voice repeating that the major influence on every rocker who had ever picked up an electric
six-string was dead. Even guitarists who had never actually heard a Flip Goodloe record owed him a debt, because, as the voice said, if you weren't directly influenced
by Goodloe, you were influenced by somebody who got
his licks from somebody else who got *his* licks from Flip
Goodloe. "All roads eventually lead to Goodloe," the
voice said. It closed the break-in with: ". . . The exact
cause of death is unknown at this time."

"I can tell you the exact cause of death," Lenny muttered to the empty room. "Smack. Flip Goodloe the hop-
head finally overjuiced himself."

The disc jockey—whoops, sorry, they liked to be called
"radio personalities" now—yanked the Polio record and
put on "Mary-Liz" from 1955, Flip's first hit record. An
instant Flip Goodloe retrospective was under way.

In spite of his personal knowledge of what a jerk Flip
was, Lenny Winter suffered a pang of nostalgia as the
frenetic guitar notes and wailing voice poured out of the
twin Bose 901s in the corners of the room. Nobody could
play like the Flipper in his day. Flip didn't showboat and
he didn't just doodle around the melody—he got behind
his bands and pushed, driving them till they were cooking
at white heat.

Lenny Winter put his cigar down and pulled his considerable bulk out of the recliner. He was pushing fifty-five
and was at least that many pounds overweight. He wad-
dled over to the north wall of his trophy room—one of the
smaller of the eighteen rooms in his house. Where was it,
now? He scanned along rows of gold records. There—the
45 with the Backgammon label. "Mary-Liz" by Flip
Goodloe. A million sales, RIAA certified. And beneath
the title, the composer credit: (P. Goodloe–L. Weinstein).

Lenny smiled. Not too many people knew that Lenny Winter's birth certificate read "Leonard Weinstein."

He wondered how many copies would sell in the inevitable surge of interest after Flip's death. Look how many Lennon records moved after he bought it. Lenny did not like to think of himself as one who made money off the dead, but a buck was a buck, and half of all royalties from sales and airplay of a good number of Flip's early songs belonged to Lenny and it was only fair that he got what was rightfully his. He made a mental note to call BMI in the morning.

The radio segued into Goodloe's second big hit, "Little Rocker," another P. Goodloe–L. Weinstein composition. A gold copy of that, too, was somewhere on the wall.

Those were the days when Lenny could do no wrong. Flip had it all then, too. But he blew it. Lenny had managed to stay at or near the top. Flip had been nowhere for years.

Which was why Lenny had visited him last week—to give the Flipper another chance.

He shook his head. What a mistake that had been!

It hadn't been easy to find Flip. He had moved back to Alexandria, Virginia, his old hometown. He still played an occasional solo gig in some of the M Street clubs in D.C., but sporadically. He was unreliable. Club owners had learned to expect him when they saw him. Everyone knew he was shooting shit again. No one had a phone number, but a bartender knew a girl who had gone home with him after a recent gig. Lenny found her. As expected, she was young and white. She remembered the address.

It was in a garden-apartment complex that gave new meaning to the word run-down. Waist-high weeds sprouted through cracks in the parking-lot blacktop, where a couple of stripped and rotting wrecks slumped amid the more functioning cars; children's toys lay scattered over the dirt patch that had once been a lawn; on the buildings themselves the green of the previous coat of paint showed through cracks and chips in the current white coat, which was none too current.

This was where Flip Goodloe lived? Lenny shook his head. Flip could have had it all.

Building seven, apartment 4-D. Lenny rang the bell but heard no ring within. He did hear an acoustic guitar plunking away on the other side of the door, so he knocked. No answer. He knocked again, louder. The guitar kept playing, but not loud enough to drown out Lenny's pounding on the door. The player obviously heard Lenny; he was just ignoring him.

Typical.

He tried the doorknob. It turned. He went in.

A pigsty. That's what it was—a pigsty. Whopper boxes fluttered in the breeze from the door, tumbling among Styrofoam Big Mac containers and countless candy-bar wrappers littering the floor. Dust everywhere. The rug had once been red—possibly; it was hard to tell in the dim light. Cobwebs in all the ceiling corners. Clothes strewn everywhere. Acrid smoke layered out at three distinct levels in the air of the room, undulating sensuously in the draft.

And there in the middle of the room, sitting cross-legged like some black-skinned maharishi, his emaciated body naked but for a stained pair of jockey shorts, was Flip Goodloe, staring off into space while he picked and chorded an aimless melody from the Martin clutched before him. His hair was a rat's nest, looking as though he had tried to weave a natural into dreadlocks but had given up halfway along.

"Flip," Lenny said, raising his voice to break through the noise. *"Flip!"*

Rheumy, red-rimmed eyes focused on Lenny through pinpoint pupils. A slow smile spread across Flip's features.

"Well, if it ain't my old friend, Lenny. Been seeing you on TV pushing those moldy oldies collections. You've gotten fat, man. You look like Porky Pig on the tube. Yeah. L. Weinstein, a.k.a. Daddy Shoog, a.k.a. Lenny Winter, former DJ, former owner of countless tiny record companies—bankrupt record companies—and now known as Mr. Golden Oldies."

Lenny bowed—not an easy trick with his girth—more to escape the naked hostility in Flip's eyes and voice than to accept the sarcastic approbation.

"Oh, yeah. I almost forgot: former collaborator. I must be the only guy in rock who collaborated with someone who's never written a single lyric or note of music in his life."

Not the only, Lenny thought. *Plenty of others.*

Flip switched to his best Kingfisher voice: "Ah guess dat makes yo' de collabora*tor,* an' me de collabora*tee.*"

"That's all water under the bridge, Flip," Lenny said, acutely uncomfortable. This man had no class—no class at all. "Whatever disagreements we had in the past, we can bury now. I've got a deal for you. A great deal. It'll mean your comeback. Chuck Berry came back. You can, too—bigger than ever!"

Flip's smile finally faded. "What makes you think I want a comeback?"

Lenny ignored the remark. Every has-been wants a comeback. He went on to explain the details of the ninth annual "One Mo' Once Golden Oldies Revival" tour, how it was going to be the biggest and best ever of its kind. And how he, Lenny Winter, out of the goodness of his heart, had decided to let Flip Goodloe headline the tour.

What he didn't say was that he needed Flip as headliner to put the icing on the cake, so to speak. The back-to-basics influence of the punk and new-wave groups over the past few years was having its effect, and Lenny was going to cash in on it. Lenny had always been able to pick up trends. It was his big talent. It was what had made him Daddy Shoog back in the fifties. He sensed new interest growing in old-time rock 'n' roll, especially in the unpretentious, down-and-dirty, no-holds-barred guitar style of someone like the Flipper. Lenny could feel it in his gut—Flip Goodloe leading the bill would turn a successful, reasonably profitable tour into a gold rush.

He needed Flip. And he was going to get him.

"Not interested," Flip said.

"You don't mean that. What else have you got going for you?"

"Religion, Lenny. I got religion."

Lenny kept his face straight but mentally rolled his eyes. *Who's the guru this time?*

"Born again?" he said.

"No way. I worship the great god Doolang."

"Doolang." *Swell.*

"Yeah." Flip pointed toward the ceiling. "Behold His image."

Lenny squinted into the hazy air. Hanging from a thread thumbtacked to the ceiling was a wire coathanger twisted into an "S"-like configuration . . . like a cross between a G clef and a dollar sign.

"Doolang?"

"You got it. The God of Aging Rockers. I already burned my offering to Him and was just warming up to sing His favorite hymn."

"Is that what I smell? What did you burn?"

"An Air Supply record." He giggled. "Know what hymn he likes best?"

Lenny sighed. "I'll bite—what?"

" 'He's So Fine.' By the Chiffons. Remember?"

Lenny thought back. Oh, yeah: *Doolang-doolang-doolang.* He laughed. "I get it."

Flip began to laugh, too. "You can also sing 'My Sweet Lord.' I'm not sure ol' Doolang knows the difference." He laughed harder. He flopped back on the floor and spread his arms and laughed from deep in his gut.

Lenny saw the tracks on Flip's arms and his own laughter died, strangled in coils of pity and revulsion. Flip must have noticed the direction of his gaze, for he suddenly fell silent. He sat up and folded his arms across his chest, hiding the scars.

"Doolang doesn't mind if someone shoots up once in a while. Especially if they've been blackballed out of the industry."

"Don't give me this Doolang crap!" Lenny shouted, angry with the knowledge that a hopped-up Flip Goodloe would be a liability rather than an asset. There'd be a constant risk of his getting busted making a score in K.C. or Montgomery or some other burg, and that would be it for the tour. Finis. Caput. Dead. "You're screwing up your—"

Flip was on his feet in a flash, his face barely an inch from Lenny's.

"Don't you *dare* take the name of the great god Doolang in vain! Your lips aren't even worthy to speak His name in praise! You'd better watch out, L. Weinstein. Doolang's pretty pissed at you. You've screwed more rockers than anybody else in history. One day He may decide to get even!"

That did it! The Flipper was completely *meshugge*. His brain was fried. He'd mainlined once too often. Lenny pulled five C-notes from his wallet and threw them on the floor.

"Here! Buy yourself a nice load of smack, a bunch of Air Supply records, and a truckload of coat hangers. Twist the hangers into cute little curlicues, burn the records, and shoot up to your heart's content. I don't want to hear about it!"

He spun and lurched out the door, away from the stink, away from the madness, away from the sight of the man he had ruined twenty years before.

Twenty years . . . had it been that long?

A third Goodloe song, "Goin' Home," immediately followed the second. Flip's music was starting to get on his nerves. He went back to where he had left his cigar. Smoke ran straight up in a thin, wavering line from the tip. Near the ceiling it curled into a twisted shape almost like a G clef. Lenny gave it passing notice as he knocked off the ash, then wandered around the trophy room in a pensive mood.

Flip had accused him of screwing more rockers than anyone else in history. A rotten thing to say. Sure, a lot of them *felt* screwed, but in truth they owed Lenny Winter a debt of thanks for giving them a chance in the first place. He'd pulled some fast ones—no use kidding himself—but he felt no guilt. In fact, he could not help but take a certain amount of pride in his fancy footwork.

He had realized early on the power wielded by a New York City DJ. He could make a new artist by raving about the record and playing it every half hour, or he could abort a career simply by losing the record. Those were heady days. Every agent, every manager, every PR man for every label was pushing gifts, trips, girls, and cash at him. He took everything they offered—except the cash.

Not to say he didn't want the dough. He wanted that most of all. But he saw the dangers from the start. For obvious reasons you couldn't declare the money as income; but that left you open to a federal charge of income-tax evasion if a scandal arose. You wouldn't just lose your job then—you could be headed for Leavenworth if the IRS boys built up a good case against you.

So cash was out for Lenny unless it could be laundered and declared. It nearly killed him to say no to all the easy money being pushed at him . . . until the spring of '55, when he came up with a revolutionary scam. It happened the day a portly black—they were called Negroes then—from a small Washington, D.C., label brought in a regional hit by someone named Flip Goodloe. It was called "Georgia-Mae" and it was special. Lenny had never heard a guitar played quite that way. It seemed to feed directly into his central nervous system. His sixth sense told him this artist and this record had almost everything needed for a big hit. Almost.

"There's just one problem," Lenny had told the company rep. "That name won't play around here."

"Y'mean 'Flip'?" the black had said.

"No. I mean 'Georgia-Mae.' It's too hick, daddy. City kids won't dig it." (Hard to believe now that he actually talked that way in those days.)

"He wrote it, he can change it. What's in a name?"

"Everything, as far as this record's concerned. Tell him to change it to something more . . . American-sounding, if you get my drift." The message was clear: Change it to a *white*-sounding name. "Then I can make it a biggie."

The black guy had been sharp. *"Can? Or will?"*

Lenny had been ready to do his silent routine and see what was offered when it struck him that he had just made a significant contribution to this Flip Goodloe's song. Fighting a burst of excitement that nearly lifted him from his chair, he spoke calmly, as if making a routine proposal.

"I want to go down as co-composer of this song and of the B side as well. And if I make it a hit—which I will—I want half credit on his next ten releases."

The company rep had shaken his head. "Don't know about that. I don't think the Flipper will go for it."

Lenny had written "L. Weinstein" on a slip of paper, then stood up and opened the door to his office. "He will if he wants to get out of D.C.," he said as he handed the slip to the rep. "And that's the name of his new songwriting partner."

Lenny never did find out what transpired back in the offices of Backgammon Records, but four weeks later he received a promo 45 by Flip Goodloe called "Mary-Liz"— exactly the same song but for the name. And under the title was "(P. Goodloe–L. Weinstein)." Lenny began to play it two or three times an hour that very night. The record went gold before the summer. Half of all composer royalties went to Lenny. It was all legal, all aboveboard. It was, he knew, utterly brilliant.

It was not a stunt he could pull if the song came from the Brill Building or one of the Tin Pan Alley tune mills, but it became a standard practice for Lenny with new artists who wrote their own material. The trouble was there weren't enough of them.

Then it occurred to him: He had struck gold at the composer level. Why not get in on other levels? So he did. He started a record company and a publishing company, found an a cappella group with a few songs of their own, recorded them with an instrumental backup, and published their music. All without anyone's having the slightest notion that the famous Lenny Winter was involved in any way at all. The record was then pushed on Lenny's show and more often than not became a hit. Lenny knew nothing about music, could not sing a note. But he knew what would sell.

When sales of the record had dried up and all the royalties were in, Lenny closed up his operation and opened up down the street under a different name. The artists came looking for their money and found an empty office.

Lenny followed the formula for years, funneling all profits through Winter Promotions, the company he had set up to finance his plans for live rock 'n' roll shows, the kind with which Alan Freed was doing hand-over-fist business in places like the Brooklyn Paramount.

"Down the Road and Around the Bend," another Flip Goodloe hit, started through the speakers. Come *on!* Too bad about Flip being dead and all, but enough was enough. Lenny went over to the tuner. He noticed some wires had fallen out from behind the stereo system. They were twisted into a configuration that looked something like a dollar sign. He kicked them back out of sight and twisted the tuner dial a few degrees to the left until he caught the neighboring FM station. The opening chords of "You're Mine Mine Mine" by the Camellows filled the room.

Lenny smiled and shook his head. This must be oldies night or something. He had recorded The Camellows on his Landlubber label back in '58. This was their only hit. Unfortunately, Landlubber records folded before any royalties could be paid. Such a shame.

He moved along the wall to a poster from the fall of '59 proclaiming his first rock 'n' roll show. His own face—younger, leaner in the cheeks—was at the top, and below ran a list of his stars, some of them the very same acts he had recorded and deserted during the preceding years. A great lineup, if he did say so himself.

The shows—that was where the money was! Continuous shows 10 A.M. till midnight for a week or two straight! One horde of pimplepussed kids after another buying tickets, streaming in with their money clutched in their sweaty fists, streaming out with programs and pictures and records in place of that money. Lenny had wanted a piece of that action.

But he had to start small. He didn't have enough to bankroll a really big show the first time out, so he found the Bixby, a medium-sized theater in Astoria, whose owners, what with the movie business in a slump and all, were interested in a little extra revenue. The place was a leftover from those Depression-era movie palaces and wasn't adequately wired for the lighting needed for a live show. No matter: A wad of bills stuffed into the pocket of the local building inspector took care of that permit. From then on it was full speed ahead. The acts were lined up, and he began the buildup on his radio show.

Opening night was a smash. Every show was packed for the first three days. He should have known then it couldn't last. Things were running too smoothly. A screw-up was inevitable.

Lenny shifted his eyes right, to where a framed newspaper photo showed his 1959 self dashing wide-eyed and fright-faced from a smoking doorway carrying an unconscious girl in his arms. That photo occupied a place of honor in his trophy room, which it deserved: It had saved his ass.

She had wandered backstage after the fourth show to meet the great Lenny Winter, the Daddy Shoog of radio fame. She was a fifteen-year-old blonde but looked older, and she was absolutely thrilled when he let her sit in his dressing room. They had had a few drinks—she found Seven-and-Seven ''really neat-tasting''—and soon she was tipsy and hot and on his lap. As his hand was sliding under her skirt and slip and up along the silky length of her inner thigh, someone yelled ''Fire!'' Lenny dumped her on the cot and went to look. He saw the smoke, heard the screams from the audience, and knew with icy-veined certainty that even if he got out of here alive, his career as Daddy Shoog was dead.

He glanced back into his dressing room and saw that the kid had passed out. It wouldn't do to have a minor with a load of booze in her blood found dead of smoke inhalation in his dressing room. It wouldn't do at all. So he picked her up and ran for the stage door. By some incredible stroke of luck, a *Daily News* photog had been riding by, had seen the smoke, and snapped Lenny coming out the door with his unconscious burden.

A hundred and forty-six kids died in the Astoria Bixby fire—most of them trampled by their fellow fans. Fingers of blame were pointed in every direction—at rock 'n' roll, at the building inspectors, at the fire department, at teen-agers in general. Everywhere but at Lenny Winter. Lenny was safe, protected by that picture.

Because that picture made page one in the *News* and was picked up by the wire services. Lenny Winter, "known as 'Daddy Shoog' to his fans," was a hero. He had risked his life to save one of his young fans who had been overcome by smoke.

And when the payola scandal broke shortly thereafter in the winter of '60, that dear, dear photo carried him through. The Senate panels and the New York Grand Jury questioned everyone—even Dick Clark—but they left Daddy Shoog alone. He was a hero. You didn't bring in a hero and ask him about graft.

Looking back now, Lenny realized that it really hadn't mattered much what happened then. The whole scene was in flux. Alan Freed went down, the scapegoat for the whole payola scandal. Rock 'n' roll was changing. Even its name was being shortened to just plain "rock." Radio formats were changing, too. Lenny found himself out of the New York market in '62, and completely out of touch during the British invasion in the mid-sixties. Those were lean years, but he started coming back in the seventies with his series of "One Mo' Once Golden Oldies Revival" tours. He was no longer Daddy Shoog, but Mr. Golden Oldies. He sold mail-order collections of oldies on TV. He was a national figure again.

You can't keep a good man down.

A new song came on—"I'm On My Way" by the Lulus. A little bell chimed a sour note in the back of his brain. The Lulus had been one of his groups, too. Coincidence.

Lenny turned his attention back to the wall and spotted another framed newspaper clipping. He didn't know why he kept this one. Maybe it was just to remind himself that when Lenny Winter gets even, he gets *even*.

It was a 1962 UPI story. He could have cut it from the *Times* but he preferred the more lurid *News* version. The subject of the piece was Flip Goodloe and how he had been discovered *flagrante delicto* with a sixteen-year-old white girl. His career took the long slide after that, and by the time it had all blown over, he had messed himself up too much with heroin to come back.

Strange how one thing leads to another, Lenny thought. Shortly before the incident described in the article, Flip had refused to give Lenny any further composer credit on his songs. He had called Lenny all sorts of awful things, like a no-talent leech, a bloodsucker, a slimeball, and other more colorful street epithets. Lenny didn't get mad. He got even. He knew Flip's fondness for young stuff—young *white* stuff. He found a little teen-age slut, paid her to get it on with Flip, then sent in the troops. She disappeared afterward, so the case never came to trial. But the morals charges had been filed and the newspaper stories had been run and Flip Goodloe was ruined.

To think: If it hadn't been for the teenybopper incident during the fire at the Bixby, Lenny might never have dreamed up the scam he pulled on Flip. Yes . . . strange how one thing leads to another.

But Flip's overdose. Maybe that was really Lenny's fault. Maybe the five hundred he had left the Flipper last week—guilt money?—had been too much cash at once. Maybe it had let him go out and get some really pure stuff. A lot of it. And maybe that's why he was dead—because of the money Lenny had left him.

The Lulus faded out, followed without commercial interruption or DJ comment by the Pendrakes' "I'm So Crazy for You."

Another of Lenny's groups from the fifties!

He felt a tingle crawl up from the base of his spine. What was going on here? Coincidence was one thing, but this made seven songs in a row that he was connected with. Seven!

Lenny strode back to the tuner and spun the knob. Stations screeched by until the indicator came to rest in the nineties. Flip Goodloe once again shouted the chorus of "Little Rocker" from the speakers. Lenny gasped and gave the knob a vicious turn. *Another* screech and then the Boktones—another group on one of Lenny's short-lived labels—were singing "Hey-Hey Momma!"

Sweat broke out along Lenny's upper lip. This was crazy! It was Lenny Winter night all over the dial!

One more chance. Steadying his hand, he guided the indicator to the all-news station. The only tunes you ever heard there were commercial jingles. He found the number—

—and reeled away from the machine as the familiar opening riffs of "Mary-Liz" rammed against him.

With a quaking index finger stretched out before him, he forced himself forward and hit the power button.

Silence. Blessed silence.

He realized he was trembling. Why? It was all just a coincidence, nothing more. The Flipper's death had put the stations into a retrospective mood. They were playing old Goodloe tunes and other stuff from his era. And the all-news station . . . it was probably doing a feature on Goodloe and Lenny had tuned in just as they were airing a sample of his work.

Sure. That was it. So why not turn the radio back on?

Why not indeed?

Because he had to go out now. Yes. Out. For some air.

Lenny fled the trophy room and went to the front hall. It was January and he'd need a coat. He pulled the closet door open and stopped.

At first glance he thought the closet was empty. Then he saw all the coats and jackets on the floor. They'd all fallen off their hangers.

And those hangers . . . they didn't look like hangers anymore.

They hung on the closet pole in a neat row, but they had been twisted into an odd shape that was becoming too familiar . . . something like a cross between a G clef and a dollar sign. They hung there, swaying gently, the light from the hall gleaming dully along their contorted lengths of wire. Lenny stared at them dumbly, feeling terror expand with the memory of where he had first seen that shape.

Goodloe's apartment.

Flip had been squatting under a hanger shaped just like these when Lenny had last seen him. He'd called it the great god Doolang or some such nonsense. Just a junkie fever dream—but what had happened to these?

Someone was in the house! That was the only explanation. Some buddy of Flip's had come here to twist these things up into knots and scare him. Well, it was working. Lenny was terrified. Not of any supernatural mumbo-jumbo, but of the very idea of one of Flip's junkie friends in his house. Probably upstairs right now, waiting. He had to get out!

Lenny snatched a coat from the floor and stumbled toward the front door. He'd be safer outside. He could run around to the garage and take the car. Then he'd phone the police and have them go through the house. That was the best way, the safest way.

As the door slammed behind him, he tensed for a cold blast of January air. It never came. Instead, it was warm out here. The air was stale, heavy with the smell and humidity of packed bodies. And it was dark . . . darker than it should be.

Pain shot through Lenny's abdomen as his intestines twisted in fear. This wasn't his front yard! This was someplace else! He turned back to his front door. It was gone, replaced by a pair of wide, flat, swinging panels, each with a small glass rectangle at eye level. Through the glass he could see what appeared to be a lighted theater lobby with Art Deco designs on the walls, popcorn machine and all. But deserted. He pounded on the doors, but it was like pounding against the base of a skyscraper; they didn't even rattle.

He turned. A light was growing out where the apron of his driveway should have been. Something was moving in the glow. As his eyes adjusted, he could see rows of

theater seats stretching away on either side, and a filthy
carpet leading down to a stage where the light continued to
grow.

Noise filtered in like someone turning up the volume of
a record player. Music: the driving rhythm of "Mary-Liz"
and Flip Goodloe himself shouting the lyrics.

With his tongue cleaving to the roof of his mouth,
Lenny took a faltering step or two toward the stage. It
couldn't be!

But it was. No mistaking those gyrations, or the voice,
or the riffs: the Flipper.

He heard crowd noises—cheers, hoots, shouts, hands
clapping—and tore his gaze from the stage. The seats
around him were filled with kids jumping up and down
and gyrating wildly as they listened to the music. But
there was no excitement in their slack faces, nor in their
cold eyes. Lenny knew this place. And he recognized
those kids.

It was the Bixby in Astoria! But that was impossible—
the Bixby was gone—burned out back in '59 during his
first rock show and torn down a few months later!

Lenny ran back to the swinging doors and slammed
against them. They still wouldn't budge. He pounded on
the glass but there was no one in the outer lobby to hear.
There had to be another way out, another exit. He was
halfway down the aisle when he smelled it.

Smoke.

A cough. Another. Then someone shouted "Fire!" and
the panic began. The crowd leaped out of its seats and
surged into the aisle, enveloping Lenny like a hungry
amoeba. As he went down under the press of panicked
bodies, he caught a glimpse of the stage. Flip Goodloe was
still up there, hurling his wild riffs into the smoky air,
oblivious to the flames that ringed him. Flip smiled fiercely
his way, and then Lenny was down, his back slamming
against the filthy carpet.

Pain. Shoes kicked at him, heels high and low dug into
his face and abdomen in frantic effort to get by. Bodies
fell on him. The weight atop him grew until he heard his

ribs crack and shatter; but the lancinating pain from the bone splinters was overwhelmed by his hunger for air. He couldn't breathe! Stale air clogged in his lungs. The odor of old popcorn and dried chewing gum from the carpet was becalmed in his nasal passages.

Vision dimmed, tunneling down to a narrow circle of hazy light filtering through the chaos that swirled around him. And there on the ceiling of the theater he saw a chandelier. But this was not the punchbowl affair that had hung in the old Bixby. This was a huge fluorescent tube, glowing redly, twisted into that same shape . . . the Doolang shape . . .

A COUNTRY HOME
Wade Kenny

There is nothing more peaceful than a country home. Perhaps that was why the Casselmans had decided to live in the house which Doug's grandfather had left him. Neither regretted the decision. They loved farm life, and they were well suited to it. Gathering the eggs, milking the cow, repairing the old broken wagon; they went from chore to chore without even realizing that they were working. And when Katie was born their fulfillment was complete. She kept them busy with her mischievousness; her roaming from room to room, exploring every nook and cranny.

Yes, Casselman farm was very happy.

Until the day Doug had to drown the kittens.

They were Tabatha's kittens. Tabatha was a large brown stray they'd found in the barn and kept because she was such a good mouser. This was her first litter; a month old—very playful and very soft. But none of the neighbors wanted more cats. And the Casselmans certainly couldn't keep all of them. There was only one thing to do. In the

61

city they're sent to the SPCA. In the country they're
drowned.

"I think I'll drown those kittens today," he said to his
wife over breakfast.

"All right. But I'd rather not be around.—Katie, come
out from under the table.—Maybe I'll go in for groceries."

"Fine." They finished their breakfast in silence.

Outside it was raining and cold. Doug put on two pairs
of heavy woolen pants and his big brown boots with the
felt liners. Also his storm jacket and his wool-lined neo-
prene gloves. He rummaged around till he found two
burlap bags. They had been used for the potatoes last fall.
Now they were empty. He stuffed one inside the other and
threw them on the pantry floor. Then he went outside to
dig the pit.

He chose a spot near the brook. There the soil was soft
and easy to work. With the point of his shovel he cut back
the sod. Then he began shoveling out the dirt and piling it
in a mound.

While he was working his wife came out. She held her
coat together with her hand and shouted through the wind.
"I'm leaving now."

"What time will you be back?"

"I shouldn't be too long."

Then she went to the car and drove off. He continued
digging, until the hole was three feet deep. Then he thrust
the shovel into the black pile beside it and headed back to
the house.

This would be the hard part—picking up the kittens and
putting them into the bag. Maybe he would close his eyes.
And with those thick gloves on he'd hardly feel the fragile
bodies. Still, it would be an uncomfortable experience.
Even if he didn't look, he would still know what was in
that bag. He would still know that six little fur balls were
suffocating inside the heavy burlap. He took ear plugs
from his pockets and stuffed them into his ears. At least he
wouldn't have to hear the kittens' cries. He left the door
open when he went inside.

The sack was on the pantry floor. "That was good of

Nancy,'' he thought as he tied the end, ''putting the kittens into the sack for me.'' He hoisted the bag and holding it in one hand, away from his body, went out the door and to the brook.

It was surprising how much they struggled. Even when he threw the bag in the brook he had to put his heavy brown boot on it to hold it under. He stood like that, counting slowly for a full five minutes. Then he hoisted the bag, heavy now with water and with the dead weight, and carried it to the pit.

He tossed it in and began covering it with shovel after shovel of the black soil. The rain continued. It was very cold. At last he scraped in the last of the dirt and pounded the sod back in place. He checked his watch. Two hours was all it had taken. Two hours from beginning to end.

Nancy turned into the driveway as he started back to the house. ''Mrs. Long didn't open the store today because of the rain,'' she told him, ''I'll go start lunch.''

Doug held the door for her. He watched her as she went into the kitchen. Then he turned and went into the baby's room. He reached over the crib rail to hoist her out . . .

. . . But she wasn't there.

''Katie,'' he called. No answer. He checked the floor. He looked through the other rooms. No sign of her.

''I'll go ask Nancy,'' he thought, and he was on his way to do just that when Nancy called to him, ''I thought you'd've drowned these kittens by now, Doug.''

The room swam. He heard his wife calling, ''Why don't you bring Katie through.'' But he didn't answer. He just reached behind the couch for his shotgun and went out the living-room door.

''Doug? Doug, why don't you answer?'' As soon as she finished peeling potatoes, Nancy went into the living room. ''Now where could he have gone?

''And where is Katie? Katie? Katie? Oh, there you are! Naughty girl! Katie mustn't go in places like that.'' Nancy reached down and picked Katie up from behind the space heater. On their way to the kitchen they heard a shot coming from over the hill. "Now, who could be out hunting on a day like this!"

The kittens were gathered around her feet, meowing loudly. "Oh, you'll be all right," she said. "Your mother will be along any minute and she'll feed you. I can't imagine why she'd go out during a storm like this, in the first place."

Bill Nolan is one of the field's most revered authors, and one of its most versatile talents: He has written novels and biographies, film scripts and television plays. "Of Time and Kathy Benedict" is a time-travel fantasy that is historically accurate, spins an intriguing web of mystery, and tells the simple tale of two people destined to be lovers.

OF TIME AND KATHY BENEDICT
William F. Nolan

Now that she was on the lake, with the Michigan shoreline lost to her, and with the steady cat-purr of the outboard soothing her mind, she could think about the last year, examine it thread by thread like a dark tapestry.

Dark. That *was* the word for it. Three dark, miserable love affairs in twelve dark, miserable months. First, with Glenn, the self-obsessed painter from the Village who had worshiped her body but refused to consider the fact that a brain went with it. And Tony, the smooth number she'd met at the new disco off Park Avenue, with his carefully tailored Italian suits and his neurotic need to dominate his women. Great dancer. Terrific lover. Lousy human being. And, finally, the wasted months with Rick, God's gift to architecture, who promised to name a bridge after her if she'd marry him and raise his kids—three of them from his last divorce. She had tried to make him understand that as an independent woman, with a going career in research, she wasn't ready for instant motherhood at twenty-one. And there was the night, three months into their relationship, when Rick drunkenly admitted he was bisexual and actually preferred males to females. He'd taken a cruel pleasure in explaining this preference to her, and that was the last time they'd seen each other. Which was . . . when? Over two months ago. Early October now, and they'd split in late July.

She looked ahead, at the wide, flat horizon of the lake as the small boat sliced cleanly through the glittering skin of water.

Wide. Timeless. Serene.

What had Hemingway called it? The last "free place." The sea. She smiled. Lake St. Clair wasn't exactly what he'd been talking about, but for her, at this moment, it would do just fine. She did feel free out here, alone on the water, with the cacophonous roar of New York no longer assaulting her mind and body. The magic peace of the lake surrounded her like a pulsing womb, feeding her hunger for solitude and silence. This assignment in Michigan had been a true blessing, offering her the chance to escape the ceaseless roar of the city . . .

"Dearborn? Where's that?"

"Where the museum is . . . in Detroit. You can check out everything at the museum. They've got the car there."

Her boss referred to "999"—the cumbersome, flat-bodied, tiller-steered vehicle designed by Henry Ford and first raced here at Grosse Pointe, just east of Detroit, late in 1902. The newspaper she worked for was planning a special feature piece celebrating the eighty-year anniversary of this historic event. Old 999 was the car that launched the Henry Ford Motor Company, leading to the mass-production American automobile.

"The museum people restored it, right down to the original red paint. It's supposed to look exactly like it did back in 1902," Kathy's boss had told her. "You go check it out, take some shots of it, dig up some fresh info, then spend a few days at Grosse Pointe . . . get the feel of the place.''

She'd been delighted with the assignment. Autumn in Michigan. Lakes and rivers and hills . . . Trees all crimson and gold . . . Sun and clear blue sky . . . Into Detroit, out to the Henry Ford Museum in Dearborn, a look at Ford's birthplace, a long talk with the curator, some pictures of ridiculous old 999 (''. . . and they named her after the New York Central's record-breaking steam locomotive'') and on out to Grosse Pointe and this lovely, lonely, soothing ride on the lake. Just what she'd been needing. Balm for the soul.

As a little girl, she'd vacationed with her parents in Missouri and Illinois, in country much like this—and the odors of crushed leaves, of clean water, of hills rioting in autumn colors came back to her sharply here on the lake. It was a reunion, a homecoming. Emotionally, she *belonged* here, not in the rush and rawness of New York. Maybe, she told herself, when I save enough I can come here to live, meet a man who loves lakes and hills and country air . . .

Something was wrong. Suddenly, disturbingly wrong.

The water was gradually darkening around the boat; she looked up to see an ugly, bloated mass of gray-black clouds filling the lake sky. It seemed as if they had instantly materialized there. And, just as suddenly, a cold wind was chopping at her.

Kathy recalled the warning from the old man at the boathouse: ''Wouldn't go too far out if I was you, miss. Storm can build up mighty fast on the lake. You get some mean ones this time of year. Small boat like this is no good in a storm . . . engine can flood out . . . lotsa things can go wrong.''

The clouds rumbled—an ominous sound—and rain stung her upturned face. A patter at first, then heavier. The cold drops bit into her skin through her skirt and light sweater. Lucky thing she'd taken her raincoat along ''just in case.'' Kathy quickly pulled the coat on, buttoning it against the wind-blown rain.

Time to head back, before the full storm hit. She swung
the boat around toward shore, adjusting the throttle for
maximum speed.

The motor abruptly sputtered and died. Too much gas.
Damn! She jerked at the start rope. No luck. Again. And
again. Wouldn't start. Forget it; she was never any good
with engines. There were oars and she could row herself
in. Shore wasn't far, and she could use the exercise. Good
for her figure.

So row. Row, row, row your boat . . .

As a child, she'd loved rowing. Now she found it was
tougher than she'd remembered. The water was heavy and
thick; it seemed to resist the oars, and the boat moved
sluggishly.

The storm was increasing in strength. Rain stabbed at
her, slashing against her face, and the wind slapped at the
boat in ice-chilled gusts. God, but it was cold! Really,
really cold. The coat offered no warmth; her whole body
felt chilled, clammy.

Now the lake surface was erupting under the storm's
steadily increasing velocity; the boat rocked and pitched
violently. Kathy could still make out the broken shoreline
through the curtaining rain as she labored at the oars, but it
grew dimmer with each passing minute. Her efforts were
futile: She was rowing *against* the wind, and whenever she
paused for breath the shoreline fell back, with the wind
forcing her out into the heart of the lake.

She felt compelled to raise her head, to scan the lake
horizon. Something huge was out there. Absolutely mon-
strous! Coming for her. Rushing toward the boat.

A wave.

How could such a mountain of water exist here? This
ravening mammoth belonged in Melville's wild sea—not
here on a Michigan lake. Impossible, she told herself; I'm
not really seeing it. An illusion, created by freak storm
conditions, unreal as a desert mirage.

Then she heard the roar. Real. Horribly, undeniably
real.

The wave exploded over her, a foam-flecked beast that

tossed her up and over in its watery jaws—flinging her from the boat, taking her down into the churning depths of the lake.

Into blackness.

And silence.

"You all right, miss?"

"Wha—what?"

"I asked if you're all right. Are you hurt? Leg broken or anything? I could call a doctor."

She brought the wavering face above her into focus.

Male. Young. Intense blue eyes. Red hair. A nice, firm, handsome face.

"Well, ma'am, *should* I?"

"Should you what?" Her voice sounded alien to her.

"Call a doctor! I mean, you were unconscious when I found you, and I—"

"No. No doctor. I'm all right. Just a little . . . dizzy."

With his help, she got to her feet, swayed weakly against him. "Oops! I'm not too steady!"

He gripped her arm, supporting her. "I've gotcha, miss."

Kathy looked around. Beach. Nothing but water and beach. The sky was cloudless again as the sun rode down its western edge, into twilight.

"Guess the storm's over."

"Beg your pardon, miss?"

"The wave . . . a really *big* one . . . must have carried me in."

For the first time, she looked at this young man clearly—at his starched shirt with its detachable collar and cuffs, at his striped peg-top trousers and yellow straw hat.

"Are they doing a film here?"

"I don't follow you, miss."

She brushed sand from her hair. One sleeve of her raincoat was ripped, and her purse was missing. Gone with the boat. "Wow, I'm a real mess. Do I look terrible?"

"Oh . . . not at all," he stammered. "Fact is, you're as pretty as a Gibson Girl."

She giggled. "Well, I see that your compliments are in keeping with your attire. What's your name?"

"McGuire, ma'am," he said, removing his hat. "William Patrick McGuire. Folks call me Willy."

"Well, I'm Katherine Louise Benedict—and I give up. If you're *not* acting in a film here then what *are* you doing in that getup?"

"Getup?" He looked down at himself in confusion. "I don't—"

She snapped her fingers. "Ha! Got it! A party at the hotel! You're in *costume!*" She looked him over very carefully. "Lemme try and guess the year. Ummmm . . . turn of the century . . . ah, I'd guess 1902, *right?*"

Young McGuire was frowning. "I don't mean to be offensive, Miss Benedict, but what has this year to do with how I'm dressed?"

"This year?"

"You said 1902, and this *is* 1902."

She stared at him for a long moment. Then she spoke slowly and distinctly: "We *are* on the beach at Lake St. Clair, Grosse Pointe, Michigan, United States of America, right?"

"We sure as heck are."

"And what, exactly, is the month and the year?"

"It's October 1902," said Willy McGuire.

For another long moment Kathy didn't speak. Then, slowly, she turned her head toward the water, gazing out at the quiet lake. The surface was utterly calm.

She looked back at Willy. "That wave—the one that hit my boat—did you see it?"

"Afraid not, ma'am."

"What about the storm? Was anyone else caught in it?"

"Lake's been calm all day," said Willy, speaking softly. "Last storm we had out here was two weeks back."

She blinked at him.

"You positive *certain* you're all right, ma'am? I mean, when you fell here on the beach you could have hit your head . . . fall could have made you kinda dizzy and all."

She sighed. "I *do* feel a little dizzy. Maybe you'd better walk me back to the hotel."

What Kathy Benedict encountered as she reached the lobby of the Grosse Pointe Hotel was emotionally traumatic and impossible to deny. The truth of her situation was here in three-dimensional reality: the clip-clopping of horse-and-carriage traffic; women in wide feathered hats and pinch-waisted floor-length skirts; men in bowlers with canes and high-button shoes; a gaudy board-fence poster announcing the forthcoming Detroit appearance of Miss Lillian Russell—and the turn-of-the-century hotel itself, with its polished brass spittoons, ornate beveled mirrors, cut-velvet lobby furniture and massive wall portrait of a toothily grinning, walrus-moustached gentleman identified by a flagdraped plaque as "Theodore Roosevelt, President of the United States."

She knew this was no movie set, no costume party.

There was no longer any doubt in her mind: The wave at Lake St. Clair had carried her backward eighty years, through a sea of time, to the beach at Grosse Pointe, 1902.

People were staring. Her clothes were alien.

Had she not been wearing her long raincoat she would have been considered downright indecent. As it was, she was definitely a curiosity standing beside Willy McGuire in the lobby of the hotel.

She touched Willy's shoulder. "I—need to lie down. I'm really very tired."

"There's a doctor in the hotel. Are you sure you don't want me to—"

"Yes, I'm sure," she said firmly. "But you *can* do something else for me."

"Just name it, Miss Benedict."

"In the water . . . I lost my purse. I've no money, Mr. McGuire. I'd like to borrow some. Until I can . . . get my bearings."

"Why, yes, of course. I surely do understand your plight." He took out his wallet, hesitated. "Uh . . . how much would be required?"

"Whatever you can spare. I'll pay you back as soon as I can."

Kathy knew that she'd have to find work—but just where did a 1982 female research specialist find a job in 1902?

Willy handed her a folded bill. "Hope this is enough. I'm a mechanic's helper, so I don't make a lot—an' payday's near a week off."

Kathy checked the amount. Ten dollars! How could she possibly do *anything* with ten dollars? She had to pay for a hotel room, buy new clothes, food . . . Then she broke into giggles, clapping a hand to her mouth to stop the laughter.

"Did I say something funny?" Willy looked confused.

"Oh no. No, I was just . . . thinking about the price of things."

He shook his head darkly. "Begging your pardon, Miss Benedict, but I don't see how *anybody* can laugh at to-day's prices. Do you know sirloin steak's shot up to twenty-four cents a pound? And bacon's up to twelve and a half! The papers are calling 'em 'Prices That Stagger Humanity!' "

Kathy nodded, stifling another giggle. "I know. It's absolutely frightful."

In preparing the Henry Ford story, she'd thoroughly researched this period in America—and now realized that Willy's ten dollars would actually go a long way in a year when coffee was a nickel a cup, when a turkey dinner cost twenty cents and a good hotel room could be had for under a dollar a night.

With relief, she thanked him, adding: "And I *will* pay it back very soon, Mr. McGuire!"

"Uh, no hurry. But . . . now that I've done you a favor, *I'd* like to ask one."

"Surely."

He twisted the straw hat nervously in his hands. "I'd mightily appreciate it—if you'd call me Willy."

It took her a long while to fall asleep that night. She

kept telling herself: Believe it . . . it's real . . . it isn't a dream . . . you're really here . . . this *is* 1902 . . . believe it, believe it, *believe* it . . .

Until she drifted into an exhausted sleep.

The next morning Kathy went shopping. At a "Come in and Get to Know Us" sale in a new dry-goods store for ladies she purchased an ostrich-feather hat, full skirt, chemise, shoes, shirtwaist, and a corset—all for a total of six dollars and twenty-one cents.

Back in her hotel room she felt ridiculous (and more than a little breathless) as a hotel maid laced up her corset. But every decent woman wore one, and there was no way she could eliminate the damnable thing!

Finally, standing in front of the mirror, fully dressed from heels to hat, Kathy began to appreciate the style and feminine grace of this earlier American period. She had coiled her shining brown hair in a bun, pinning it under the wide-brimmed, plumed hat and now she turned to and fro, in a rustle of full skirts, marveling at her tiny cinched waist and full bosom.

"Kathy, girl," she said, smiling at her mirror-image, "with all due modesty, you are an *elegant* young lady!"

That same afternoon, answering a no-experience-required job ad for office help in downtown Detroit, she found herself in the offices of Dodd, Stitchley, Hanneford, and Leach, Attorneys at Law.

Kathy knew she could not afford to be choosy; right now, any job would do until she could adjust to this new world. Later, given her superior intelligence and natural talents, she could cast about for a suitable profession.

"Are you familiar with our needs, young lady?" asked the stout, matronly woman at the front desk.

"Not really," said Kathy. "Your ad specified 'Office Help Female.'"

The woman nodded. "We need typewriters."

"Oh!" Kathy shrugged. "Maybe I copied the wrong address. I don't sell them."

"You don't sell what?" The woman leaned forward, staring at Kathy through tiny, square glasses.

"Typewriters," said Kathy. Suddenly she remembered that in 1902 typists were called "lady typewriters." There was so *much* to remember about this period!

"Frankly, miss, I do not understand what you are talking about." The buxom woman frowned behind her glasses. *"Can* you operate a letter-typing machine or can't you?"

"Yes, I can," nodded Kathy. "I really can." She smiled warmly. "And I *want* the job!"

Which is how Kathy Benedict, a $28,000-a-year research specialist from New York City, became an $8.00-per-week office worker with the firm of Dodd, Stitchley, Hanneford, and Leach in Detroit, Michigan, during October of 1902.

With her first week's pay in hand, Kathy marched up the steps of Mrs. O'Grady's rooming house on Elm Street and asked to see Mr. William McGuire.

"Why, Miss Benedict!" Willy seemed shocked to see her there in the hallway outside his room. He stood in the open door, blinking at her. The left half of his face was covered with shaving cream.

"Hello, Willy," she said. "May I come in?"

"I don't think that would be proper. Not after dark and all. I mean, you are a single lady and these are bachelor rooms and it just isn't done!"

Kathy sighed. Again, she had failed to consider the period's strict rules of public conduct for unaccompanied females. She didn't want to cause Willy any embarrassment.

"Then could we meet downstairs . . . in the lobby?"

"Of course." He touched at his lathered cheek. "Soon as I finish shaving. I do it twice a day. Heavy beard if I don't."

"Fine," she said. "See you down there."

Waiting for Willy McGuire in the lobby of the Elm Street rooming house, Kathy reviewed the week in her mind. A sense of peace had entered her life; she felt cool and tranquil in this new existence. No television. No rock concerts. No disco. Life had the flavor of vintage wine.

The panic and confusion of the first day here had given way to calm acceptance. She was taking this quaint, charming period on its own terms.

Willy joined her and they sat down on a high-backed red velvet couch. Willy looked fresh-scrubbed and glad to see her.

"Here's the first half of what I owe you," she told him, handing over the money. "I'll have the rest next week."

"I didn't expect any of it back this soon," he said.

"It was very kind of you to trust a stranger the way you did," Kathy smiled.

"I'd surely like to know you better, Miss Benedict. I hope we can be friends."

"Not if you keep calling me Miss Benedict."

"All right, then . . ." He grinned. "Kate."

"*Kate?*"

"Aye," said Willy. "Or would you prefer Katherine?"

"Nope. Kate will do fine. It's just that—nobody's called me that since I was six. Hmmmmm . . ." She nodded. "Willy and Kate. Has a certain *ring* to it!"

And, at that precise moment, looking at the handsome, red-haired young Irishman seated beside her, she realized that she had met a totally decent human being, full of warmth and honesty and manly virtue.

She decided to investigate the possibility of falling in love with him.

They rode in Willy's carriage through the quiet suburbs of Detroit that Sunday, savoring the briskness of the autumn air and the fire-colored woods. Sunlight rippled along the dark flanks of their slow-trotting horse and the faint sounds of a tinkling piano reached them from a passing farmhouse.

"I love horses," said Kathy. "I used to ride them all the time in Missouri."

"They're too slow for my taste," Willy declared. "I like to work with machines . . . Cycles, for instance. That's how I got started in this business. Bought me a motor-tandem last year. Filed down the cylinder, raised the compression, then piped the exhaust around the carburetor. She went like Billy Blue Blazes!''

"I don't much care for motorcycles. People get hurt on them.''

"You can fall off a horse, too! Heck, I admit I've had me some spills on the two-wheelers, but nothin' serious. Hey—how'd you like to see where I work?''

"Love to,'' she said.

"Giddy-up, Teddy!'' Willy ordered, snapping the reins. He grinned over at Kathy. "He's named after the President!''

Willy stopped the carriage in front of a small shop at 81 Park Place—where she was introduced to a gaunt, solemn-faced man named Ed "Spider'' Huff.

"Spider's our chief mechanic, and I'm his assistant,'' Willy explained. "We work together here in the shop.''

"On cycles?''

"Not hardly, ma'am,'' said Huff in a rasping, humorless voice. "This here is the age of the horseless carriage. Do you know we've already got almost two hundred miles of paved road in this country? In New York State alone, they got darn near a thousand automobiles registered.''

"I assume, then, that you are working on automobiles?''

"We sure are,'' Huff replied. "But the plain truth of it is there ain't no other automobile anywhere on this whole round globe to match what we got inside—a real thoroughbred racing machine!''

"Spider's right for dang sure!'' nodded Willy.

She was suddenly very curious. "Could I see it?''

Huff canted his head, squinting at her. He rubbed a gaunt hand slowly along his chin. "Wimminfolk don't cotton to racing automobiles. Too much noise. Smoke. Get grease on your dress.''

"Truly, I'd *like* to see it.''

Willy clapped Huff on the shoulder. "C'mon, Spider—she's a real good sport. Let's show her.''

"All rightie,'' nodded Huff, "but I'll wager she won't favor it none.''

They led Kathy through the office to the shop's inner

garage. A long bulked shape dominated the floor area, draped in an oil-spattered blanket.

"We keep her tucked in like a sweet babe when we ain't workin' on her," Huff declared.

"So I see," nodded Kathy.

"Well, dang it, Willy!" growled Huff. "If you're gonna show her, then *show* her!"

Willy peeled off the blanket. "There she is!" he said, with obvious pride in his tone.

Kathy stared at the big, square, red-painted racing machine, with its front-mounted radiator, nakedly exposed engine, and high, wire-spoked wheels. In place of a steering wheel an iron tiller bar with raised handgrips was installed for control—and the driver sat in an open bucket seat. There was no windshield or body paneling.

"It's 999!" Kathy murmured.

The two men blinked in shock.

"How'd *you* know we call her that?" Huff demanded.

"Uh . . . rumor's going around town that there's a racing car here in Detroit named after the New York Central's locomotive. Some of the typewriters were talking about it at work."

"Good thing she's about ready to race," declared Willy. "Guess when you got a rig this fast word just leaks out."

"Anyway, it's a wonderful name for her. Who's the owner?"

"Our boss, Tom Cooper," said Huff. "Had a lot of troubles with 999 out at the track on the test runs an' old Hank got fed up and sold out to Tom. They came into this as partners—but Hank's out now."

"Hank?"

"Yeah," said Willy. "Hank Ford. Him an' Tom designed her together."

"And not an extra pound of weight anywhere on 'er," said Huff. "That's why the engine's mounted on a stripped chassis. She's got special cast-iron cylinder walls, giving a seven-inch bore and stroke. And that, ma'am, is *power!*"

"Yep," nodded Willy. "She's the biggest four-cylinder rig in the States. Separate exhaust pipes for each cylinder.

We can squeeze upward of seventy horse out of her! That means, with the throttle wide open, on a watered-down track, she'll do close to a mile a minute—better'n *fifty* miles an hour!''

Kathy was excited; her assignment to research a race eighty years in the past had become a present-day reality. ''And you've entered her against Alex Winton for the Manufacturers' Challenge Cup at Grosse Pointe on October 25!''

They both stared at her.

''But how—'' Willy began.

''Rumor,'' she added quickly. ''That's the rumor I heard.''

''Well, you heard right,'' declared Huff. ''Ole Alex Winton thinks that Bullet of his can't be beat. Him with his big money and his fancy reputation. He's got a surprise comin' right enough!''

Kathy smiled. ''Indeed he has, Mr. Huff. Indeed he has.''

Each afternoon after work Kathy began dropping by the shop on Park Place to watch the preparations on 999. She was introduced to the car's owner, Tom Cooper—and to a brash, dark-haired young man from Ohio named Barney, an ex-bicycle racer who had been hired to tame the big red racing machine.

Of course she recognized him instantly, since he was destined to become as legendary as 999 itself. His full name was Berna Eli ''Barney'' Oldfield, the barnstorming daredevil whose racing escapades on the dirt tracks of America would earn him more fame and glory than any driver of his era. In March of 1910, at Daytona Beach, he would become the official ''Speed King of the World'' by driving a ''Lightning'' Benz for a new land speed record of 131 miles per hour. But here, in this moment in time, he was just a raw-looking twenty-four-year-old youth on the verge of his first automobile race.

Kathy asked him if he smoked cigars.

''No, ma'am, I don't,'' said Oldfield.

And the next day she brought him one. He looked confused; ladies didn't offer cigars to gentlemen.

"Barney," she said. "I want you to have this for the race. It's important."

"But I told you, ma'am, I don't smoke cheroots!"

"You don't have to smoke it, just *use* it."

"You've lost me, ma'am."

"Horse tracks are bumpy, full of ruts and potholes. A cigar between your teeth will act to cushion the road shocks. Just do me a personal favor . . . try it!"

Oldfield slipped the fat, five-cent cigar into his coverall pocket. "I'll try it, Miss Benedict, because when a pretty lady asks me a favor I don't say no."

Kathy felt a current of excitement shiver along her body. When she'd been researching Oldfield, as part of her 999 assignment, she had difficulty in tracing the origin of Barney's cigar, his famed trademark during the course of his racing career. Finally, she'd uncovered an interview with Oldfield, given a month before his death in 1946, in which a reporter had asked: "Just where *did* you get your first cigar?"

And Barney had replied: "From a lady I met just prior to my first race. But I'll tell you the truth, son—I don't recall her name."

Kathy now realized that *she* was the woman whose name Barney had long since forgotten. The unique image of Barney Oldfield, hunched over a racing wheel, a cigar clenched between his teeth, began with Kathy Benedict.

They arrived at the Grosse Pointe track on Friday, October 24, a full day before the race, for test runs: Willy, Spider Huff, Cooper, and Oldfield. Kathy had taken sick leave from the office to be with them.

"We'll need all the practice time we can get," Willy told her. "Still some bugs to get out."

"McGuire!" yelled Tom Cooper. "You gonna stand there all day gabbin' your fool head off—or are you gonna crank her up? Now, *jump!*"

And Willy jumped.

Cooper was a square-bodied, gruff-looking man wearing a fleece-lined jacket over a plaid cowboy shirt—and he had made it clear that he didn't think women belonged around racing cars. Privately, Cooper had told Willy that he felt Kate Benedict would bring them bad luck in the race, but that he'd let her hang around so long as she "kept her place" and stayed out of their way.

Tom Cooper had always had strong ideas about what a "good woman" should be: "She ought to be a first-rate cook, be able to sing and play the piano, know how to raise kids and take care of a house, mind her manners, dress cleanly, be able to milk cows, feed chickens, tend the garden—know how to shop, be able to sew and knit, churn butter, make cheese, pickle cucumbers and drive cattle."

He had ended this incredible list with a question: "And just how many of these talents do *you* possess, Miss Benedict?"

She lifted her chin, looking him squarely in the eye. "The only thing I'm really good at, Mr. Cooper, is independent thinking."

Then she'd turned on her heel and stalked away.

In practice around the mile dirt oval, Barney found that 999 was a savage beast to handle at anything approaching full throttle.

"She's got the power, all right, but she's wild," he said after several runs. "Open her up and she goes for the fence. Dunno if I can keep her on the track."

"Are you willing to try?" asked Cooper. "You'll have to do better than fifty out there tomorrow to beat Winton's Bullet. Can you handle her at that speed?"

Oldfield squinted down from his seat behind the tiller. "Well," he grinned, "this damn chariot may kill me—but they will have to say afterward that I was goin' like hell when she took me through the rail!" He looked down sheepishly at Kathy: "And I beg yer pardon for my crude way of expression."

The morning of October 25, 1902, dawned chill and

gray, and by noon a gust of wind-driven rain had dampened the Grosse Pointe oval.

The popular horse track had originally been laid out
over a stretch of low-lying marshland bordering the Detroit
River, and many a spirited thoroughbred had galloped its
dusty surface. On this particular afternoon, however, the
crowd of two thousand excited citizens had come to see
horsepower instead of horses, as a group of odd-looking
machines lined up behind the starting tape. Alexander
Winton, the millionaire founder of the Winton Motor
Carriage Company and the man credited with the first
commercial sale of an auto in the United States in 1898,
was the odds-on favorite in his swift, flat-bodied Winton
Bullet. Dapper and handsomely moustached, he waved a
white-gloved hand to the crowd. They responded with
cheers and encouragement: "Go get 'em, Alex!"

Winton's main competition was expected to come from
the powerful Geneva Steamer, Detroit's largest car, with
its wide wheelbase, four massive boilers, and tall stack—
looking more like a landbound ship than a racing automobile.
A Winton Pup, a White Steamer, and young Oldfield at
the tiller of 999 filled out the five-car field.

Kathy spotted Henry Ford among the spectators in the
main grandstand, looking tense and apprehensive; Ford
was no longer the legal owner of 999, but the car *had* been
built to his design, and he was anxious to see it win. In
1902, Ford was thirty-nine, with his whole legendary
career as the nation's auto king ahead of him. His empire
was still a dream.

Kathy's heart was pounding; she felt flushed, almost
dizzy with excitement. The race she'd spent weeks reading
about was actually going to happen in front of her; she was
a vital, breathing part of the history she'd so carefully
researched. At the starting line, she overheard Tom Cooper's last-minute words to Oldfield.

"All the money's on Winton," he was saying. "But
we're betting you can whup him! What do you say, lad?"

"I say let him eat my dust. Nobody's gonna catch me
out there on that track today."

"Do you think he can do it, Kate?" asked Willy, gripping her elbow as they stood close to the fence. "Do you think Barney can beat Winton? The Bullet's won a lot of races!"

"We'll just have to wait and see," she said, with a twinkle in her eyes. "But I can guarantee one thing—this race will go down in history!"

At the drop of the starter's flag all five cars surged forward, the high, whistling kettle-boil scream of the steamers drowned by the thunder-pistoned roar of 999 and the Winton Bullet.

Sliding wide as he throttled the bouncing red hell wagon around the first turn, Barney immediately took the lead away from Winton. But could he *hold* it?

"Winton's a fox!" declared Willy as they watched the cars roar into the back stretch. "He's given Barney some room just to find out what 999 can do. See! He's starting his move now!"

Which was true. It was a five-mile event, and by the end of the first mile Alex Winton had Oldfield firmly in his sights, and was closing steadily with the Bullet as the two steamers and the Pup dropped back.

It was a two-car race.

Barney knew he was in trouble. He was getting a continuous oil bath from the exposed crankshaft, and almost lost control as his goggles filmed with oil. He pushed them up on his forehead, knowing they were useless. But there was a greater problem: Bouncing over the ruts and deep-gouged potholes, the car's rigid ashwood-and-steel chassis was giving Oldfield a terrible pounding, and he was losing the sharp edge of concentration needed to win. On some of the rougher sections of the track the entire car became airborne.

Watching the Bullet's relentless progress, as Winton closed the gap between himself and Oldfield, Kathy experienced a sharp sense of frustration. At this rate, within another mile the Bullet would overhaul 999 and take the lead.

But that must not happen, she told herself. It *could* not happen. The pattern of the race was already fixed in history!

Suddenly, she had the answer.

"He forgot it!" she yelled to Willy.

"Forgot what?"

"Never mind! Just wait here. I'll be back."

And she pushed through the spectators, knocking off a fat man's bowler and dislodging several straw boaters; she had a destination and there was no time to waste in getting there.

When Oldfield neared the far turn, at the end of the back stretch, each new wheel hole in the track's surface rattling his teeth, he saw Kathy Benedict straddling the fence.

She was waving him closer to the rail, pointing to something in her hand, yelling at him, her voice without sound in the Gatling-gun roar of 999's engine.

Closer. And yet closer. What in the devil's name did this mad girl want with him?

Then she tossed something—and he caught it. By damn! The cigar!

It was *just* what he needed—and he jammed the cushioning cheroot between his teeth, lowered his body over the iron control bar, and opened the throttle. In a whirling plume of yellow dust, 999 hurtled forward.

Now let ole Winton try and catch him!

"Look at that!" shouted Willy when Kathy was back with him at the fence. "He's pullin' away!"

Oldfield was driving brilliantly now, throwing the big red wagon into each turn with fearless energy, sliding wide, almost clipping the fence, yet maintaining that hairline edge of control at the tiller. The blast from the red car's four open exhausts was deafening—and the crowd cheered wildly as 999 whipped past the main grandstand in a crimson blur.

By the third mile, Alex Winton was out, his overstrained

engine misfiring as the Bullet slowed to a crawl in Barney's dust.

And when Oldfield boomed under the finish flag, to a sea of cheering from the stands, he had lapped the second-place Geneva Steamer and left the other competitors far, far behind.

Willy jumped up and down, hugged Kathy, lifting her from the ground and spinning her in a circle, yelling out his delight.

Sure enough, just as she'd promised it would be, this one had been a race for the history books.

The morning papers proclaimed 999's triumph in bold black headlines: WINTON LOSES! OLDFIELD WINS! And the lurid copy described Barney as "hatless, his long, tawny hair flying out behind him with the speed of his mount, seeming a dozen times on the verge of capsize, he became a human comet behind the tiller of his incredible machine."

Reporters asked Barney what it was like to travel at a truly astonishing fifty miles per hour! How could mortal man stand the bulletlike speed?

Oldfield was quoted in detail: "You have every sensation of being hurled through space. The machine is throbbing under you with its cylinders beating a drummer's tattoo, and the air tears past you in a gale. In its maddening dash through the swirling dust the machine takes on the attributes of a sentient thing . . . I tell you, gentlemen, no man can drive faster and live!"

Henry Ford was quick to claim credit for the design and manufacture of 999, and the nation's papers headlined his name next to Oldfield's, touting the victory at Grosse Pointe as "the real beginning of the Auto Age."

Within a month, riding the crest of public acclaim, Hank Ford laid the foundations for his Ford Motor Company—already planning for the day when his "tin lizzies" would swarm the highways of America.

The victory of 999 also benefited Willy McGuire. "I want you and Spider to work for me from now on, Willy,"

Hank Ford had told him. "Cooper just doesn't appreciate you. And, for a start, I'll *double* your salary!"

During the days following the race at Grosse Pointe, Kathy fell deeply in love with the happy, red-haired Irishman. He was totally unlike any man she'd ever known: honest, kind, strong, gentle and attentive. And he loved her as a *complete* woman—mind and body. For the first time in her life, she had found real emotional fulfillment.

His question was inevitable: "Will you marry me, Kate?"

And her reply came instantly: "Yes, yes, yes! Oh, *yes,* Willy, I'll marry you!"

As they embraced, holding one another tightly, Kathy knew that she was no longer afraid of anything. The old life was gone.

"Nothing frightens me now that I'm with you," she told him.

"Not even the lake?" he suddenly asked, his blue eyes intense.

She was startled by the question. "I never said that I was afraid of the lake."

"It's been obvious. We do everything together. Ride . . . skate . . . picnic . . . attend band concerts. But you never want to go boating with me on the lake."

"I don't like boating. I told you that."

His eyes were steady on hers. "Then why were you on the lake alone the day I found you? What made you go out there?"

She sighed, lowering her eyes. "It's a long, long story and someday, when I'm sure you'll understand, I'll tell you all about it. I swear I will."

"It's a fine day, Kate. Sky's clear. No wind. No clouds. I think we ought to go out on the lake. Together."

"But why?"

"To put that final fear of yours to rest. It's like climbing back on a horse once he's bucked you off. If you don't, you never ride again. The fear is always there."

A strained moment of silence.

"I'm *not* afraid of the lake, Willy," she said in a measured tone.

"Then prove you're not! Today. Now. Show me, Kate!"

And she agreed. There was nothing to fear out there on the quiet water. She kept telling herself that over and over . . . Nothing to fear.

Nothing.

Nothing.

Nothing.

The weather was ideal for boating—and Willy handled the oars with practiced ease, giving Kathy a sense of confidence and serenity.

She *did* feel serene out here on the placid lake. She enjoyed the pleasant warmth of the afternoon sun on her shoulders as she twirled the bright red parasol Willy had bought her just for this occasion.

The water was spangled with moving patterns of sunlight, glittering diamond shapes, shifting and breaking and re-forming in complex designs around the boat as Willy rowed steadily away from the shore.

In this calming aura of peace and natural beauty she wondered why she had been so afraid of the lake. It was lovely here, and there was certainly nothing to fear. The bizarre circumstances of that fateful afternoon in 1982 were unique; a freak storm had created some kind of time gate through which she had passed. And no harm had been done to her. In fact, she was grateful for the experience; it had brought her across a bridge of years to the one man she could truly love and respect.

She reached out to touch his shoulder gently. "Mr. McGuire, I love you."

He grinned at her. "And I love *you*, Miss Benedict!"

Willy laid aside the oars to take her into his arms. They stretched out next to one another in the bottom of the easy-drifting boat. The sky above them was a delicate shade of pastel blue (like Willy's eyes, she thought) and a faint breeze carried the perfume of deep woods out onto the water.

"It's an absolutely perfect moment," she said. "I wish we could put it in a bottle and open it whenever we get sad!"

"Don't need to," said Willy softly. "We've got a lifetime of perfect moments ahead of us, Kate."

"No." She shook her head. "Life is never perfect."

"Ours will be," he said, running a finger along the side of her sun-warm cheek, tracing the curve of her chin. "I'll make it perfect—and that's a promise."

She kissed him, pressing her lips deeply into his.

He sat up.

"Hey," she protested, opening her eyes. "Where'd you go? We were just getting started." And she giggled.

"Sky's darkening," he said, looking upward, shading his eyes. "I'd better row us in. A lake storm can—"

"Storm!" She sat up abruptly, staring at him, at the sky and water. "No! Oh, God, no!"

"Whoa there, you're shaking!" he said, holding her. "There's nothing to get worried over. We'll be back on shore in a few minutes."

"But you weren't *there* . . . you don't understand!" she said, a desperate tone in her voice. "That's just how the other storm came along—out of nowhere. And the wind . . ."

It was there, suddenly whipping at the lake surface.

He was rowing strongly now, with the boat cutting toward the shoreline. "Be on the beach in a jiffy. You'll see. Trust me, Kate."

But the wind was building rapidly, blowing against them, neutralizing Willy's efforts.

Kathy looked fearfully at the sky. Yes, there they were, the same ugly mass of gray-black clouds.

It began to rain.

"Hurry, Willy! Row faster!"

"I'm trying . . . but this wind's really strong!"

She sat in a huddled position in the stern of the boat, head down now, hands locked around her legs as the rain struck at her in blown gusts.

"Never seen a storm build up this fast," Willy grunted, rowing harder. "Freak weather, that's for sure."

How could he understand that she'd seen it all before, in a world eighty years beyond him? Clouds, wind, rain and—

And . . .

She knew when she looked up, slowly raising her head, that it would be there, at the horizon, coming for them.

The wave.

Willy stopped rowing at her scream. He looked toward the horizon.

"God A'mighty!"

Then, in the blink of a cat's eye, it was upon them— blasting their senses, an angry, falling mountain of rushing water that split their boat asunder and pitched them into the seething depths of the lake.

Into blackness.

And silence.

Kathy opened her eyes.

She was alone on the beach. Somehow, without any visible proof, she knew she had returned to 1982.

And Willy was gone.

The thought tore through her, knife-sharp, filling her with desperate anguish.

Willy was gone!

She had lost him to the lake. It had given him to her and now it had taken him away.

Forever.

A husky lifeguard in orange swim trunks was running toward her across the sand.

I don't *want* to be saved, she told herself; I want to go back into the lake and die there, as Willy had died. There's no reason to go on living. No reason at all.

"You all right, miss?"

Same words! Same voice!

She looked up—into the face of her beloved. The blue eyes. The red hair. The gentle, intense features.

"Willy!" she cried, suddenly hugging him. "Oh, God, Willy, I thought I'd lost you! I thought you were—"

She hesitated as the young man pulled back.

"Afraid you've made a mistake," he said. "My name's Tom."

She stared at him, and then she knew who he was. No doubt of it. Kathy *knew*.

"What about your middle name?"

"It's William," he told her. And then grinned. "Oh, I see what you mean—but nobody ever calls me Willy. Not since I was a kid."

"I know your last name," she said softly.

"Huh?"

"It's McGuire."

He blinked at her. "Yeah. Yeah, it *is*."

"Thomas William McGuire," she said, smiling at him. "Please . . . sit down here, next to me."

With a small sigh, he did so. She intrigued him.

"When were you born?"

"In 1960."

"And who was your father? What was *his* name?"

"Timothy McGuire."

"Born? . . . The year?"

"My Dad was born in 1929."

"And your grandfather . . . What was *his* name and when was he born?"

"Patrick McGuire. Born in 1904."

Kathy's eyes were shining. She blinked back the wetness. "And his father, your great-grandfather—"

He started to speak, but she touched his lips with a finger to stop the words.

"He was William Patrick McGuire," she said, "and he was born in 1880, right?"

The young man was amazed. He nodded slowly. "Yeah. Right."

"And he survived a boating accident late in 1902, on *this* lake, didn't he?"

"He sure did, miss."

"Who was your great-grandmother?" Kathy asked.

"Her name was Patricia Hennessey. They met after the accident, that Christmas. They say he kind of—"

"Kind of what?"

"Kind of married her on the rebound. Seems he lost the girl he *was* going to marry in the boating accident. My great-grandma was what I guess you'd call a second choice."

Then he grinned (Willy's grin!), shaking his head. "I just can't figure how you knew about him . . . Are you a friend of the family?"

"No." She shook her head.

"And we've never met before, have we?"

She looked into the deep lake-blue of his eyes. "No, Willy, we've never met." She smiled. "But we're going to be friends . . . very, very good friends."

And she kissed him gently, softly, under the serene sky of a sunbright Michigan afternoon on the shore of a placid lake in the autumn of a very special year.

Dennis Etchison is probably the finest writer of short fiction in the field today. If there were justice in this world, he would be making millions of dollars and writing at his leisure, but . . . The West Coast Review of Books *reviewed one hundred titles one month and gave four-star ratings to books by Norman Mailer, Stephen King, and Gabriel García Márquez; it gave its highest rating, five stars, to only two books, and one of them was Dennis's* The Dark Country. *I have often compared Dennis to Ray Bradbury and Charles Beaumont, but "Deadspace" appears closer to the writings of the celebrated British writer Robert Aickman. This is a strange story of images, feelings, and . . . deadspace.*

DEADSPACE
Dennis Etchison

It was only his first morning there. But, very early, he was awakened by the ringing of a bell.

So soon? he thought.

Well, it was about time. . . .

He rolled over and fumbled the receiver out of its cradle.

The ringing continued.

He lay on his back for a moment while his senses reassembled. One of his legs tingled, as if he had slept with it twisted under him. He could hardly feel it. But he

swung his feet down, climbed out of bed as best he could
and went in search of the sound.

As soon as he opened the drapes and staggered outside,
it stopped.

He squinted and tried to clear his head.

From the balcony of his room at the Holmby Hotel, he
had an unobstructed view of a sea of evergreens rolling
away in tufted waves toward Sunset Boulevard and the
Palisades beyond. Above the treetops clouds parted like
curtains framing an electric blue proscenium, clean and
vibrant with promise. He stood with his hands on the
railing, his face tipped back, and awaited the warming rays
of the sun as it passed on its way to the Pacific.

Now the sound resumed, drawing his attention to the
driveway below, where it became the distant bleating of
an automobile security alarm.

He braced his arms and leaned forward. The alarm was
cut off as a door slammed and a desperate woman in a
white jumpsuit hurried to the carpet in front of the hotel,
swinging a bulging Sportsac like a stuffed armadillo. A
valet tipped his cap at her heels, opened the car door, slid
behind the wheel, closed the door and guided her black
Mercedes away from the curb and into the underground
garage. As the sedan glided out and turned into darkness,
the insignia of the hotel was revealed in the macadam
beneath. The roof of the carport covering the loading zone
was dull and weathered, but the inlaid coat of arms was
readable even through the yellowed plexiglass.

VAYA CON DIOS, read the circle of tiles. BEVERLY HILLS,
CALIFORNIA.

He had not noticed it before. *Go with God?* he thought.
Was that really what it said? Decipherable in its entirety
only from above, the message must have been designed
exclusively for visitors on high, like a mysterious hiero-
glyphic invitation to the gods of the Nazcas. Reeling from
a sudden rush of vertigo, he grasped the railing with both
hands and forced himself to step back.

He wondered if the management had considered the
possible effect such a logo might have on guests of suici-

dal inclination. It was conceivable that someone on the upper levels would see the emblem as a target. An image came to mind of a despondent man hurtling down, executing a perfect swan dive as he crashed through the panes to take the place of the Mercedes dead-center on the mosaic. From this height a body would fall like a stone, straight as a plumb line. The thought left him dizzy.

He took a deep breath and lifted his face again to the morning light. Somewhere a radio was playing a transient popular tune; it came from the other side of the building, from the high-priced bungalows or perhaps the pool. Was that the sound of another telephone ringing? No, only the whine of a power saw fading in and out like static on the breeze. On a nearby balcony glasses clinked. A scent of orange juice ripened the air. He opened his eyes.

The sky remained clear above the trees, though the expanse of blue invited some new pattern to take up the slack. If more clouds did move in to clot the horizon, he would not be surprised in the least.

He was sure of only one thing.

Once, a long time ago, someone had taken from him something irreplaceably valuable. He couldn't remember what it was. And no one would admit it.

But now, today, all that was about to change.

He finished dressing. The message light on the telephone was still dark. He dialed the desk. No calls for him yet. He took out a pack of cigarettes, picked it open, set it down, fingered it again and dropped it into his pocket, then put it away in the drawer and made himself leave it there. Trying to shake a vague feeling that he was forgetting something vital, he slipped into his sandals and rode the elevator down.

There were no messages waiting at the desk and the lobby was empty. The soft pink cushions on the antique divans were still undented, and a copy of *Architectural Digest* lay unread on the polished tabletop near the mock fireplace; the photograph on the cover showed a room remarkably like this one but without the vase of fresh flowers to add a tropical touch to the decor. He left word that any calls be directed to the wet bar, and stepped out through the French windows as carefully as a visitor to a closed and extremely restricted movie set. He reminded himself that the contract in his suitcase would serve as his pass to the Holmby and places like it from now on. As soon as he had taken care of one very simple formality.

He followed the signs that pointed the way to the pool.

He passed a Latin maid in a spotless white uniform, her cleaning cart color-coordinated to match precisely the green of the walkway and the trim around the doors. He noticed that she was munching a crisp snack of some sort. The dining room was open, but he was too edgy to hold down breakfast. The maid smiled at him familiarly. She knows, he thought. Already! Was that a copy of *Daily Variety* on top of her sheets and pillowcases? She must read the trades, he realized with satisfaction, and continued on under the stucco arches.

The walking path led him between discreetly-spaced cottages where the blinds were still drawn, heavy Spanish tile roofs ruddy and shimmering under the perpetual sun. Shamelessly large potted palms trembled in the belvederes, shading rows of shy hydrangeas that filled the dampened beds. In alcoves along the way photos of visiting dignitaries hung like icons; an oversized frame near a particularly isolated suite displayed signed glossies of Princess Grace of Monaco and her daughter Caroline, a memento of the final unpublicized stay. At once he recognized the haughty features of the former actress. He hesitated briefly to pay his respects, nodding and smiling back in reverence and complicity. Then he moved on, basking in the glow, his own chin elevated a few degrees.

Trusting the signs, he descended deeper into the most secluded portions of the grounds, levels he had never before penetrated without Joe Gillis at his side. The film star knew the junglelike terrain as intimately as a tour guide, and had stayed here so often at the height of his popularity that he was now venerated by the establishment as an old and valued friend. The front table in the dining room would be his for as long as he lived, the headwaiter would never forget to hold the salad for the final course. After the first few business lunches Wintner began to envy such treatment, and longed for the day when it would be his by association. Tonight, whether or not Gillis stayed on for dinner, he would at last dare to request the front table for himself as if it were a foregone conclusion.

He was no longer sure of his exact location, but pressed bravely ahead along the winding path.

At the bottom of a terraced embankment he came upon a workman carrying a load of lumber on his shoulders. The man was on his way toward a gazebo that overlooked the fish pond. Wintner passed him on the narrow footbridge without a word, pretending interest in the signs that labeled the subdivisions of flora. Handpainted lettering identified each variety with the care of a horticultural exhibit, white crosses marked with both popular and scientific names staked into the soil or nailed to the trunks of the oldest trees. He paused to study the placards, like a tourist intent on memorizing every detail of a long-awaited trip.

A few seconds later he was startled by the wail of a buzz saw. The back of his neck bristled as if a stranger had screamed his name. He shot a glance back through the foliage and saw the carpenter busy cutting a hole in the roof of the gazebo. A plywood circle dropped out of a spray of sawdust and a clear spot of sky shone down like a blue moon. Wintner could not imagine what the hole was for. He turned away, picking up the pace as he crossed the bridge to the other shore.

On the far side the path took him by a grouping of bungalows completely hidden from the other bank. Their separate doorways connected to an elevated wooden deck, where a long table was already set for lunch. Each crystal water glass was topped by a cloth napkin folded into the shape of a bird. Reflected in the facets of the cut glass were inverted images of the adjacent pond, where just now a cloud of white light seemed to be descending, the miniaturized movement of a napkin unfurling from the skies like wings. Wintner focused past the glasses to the pond. There an enormous white swan glided up out of hanging vines, tucking its feathers and neck back into a pose as graceful as an arrangement of folded linen.

Impatient, Wintner climbed the bank and cut through a glade of Italian cypress. He came out into a totally unfamiliar area, dense and overgrown. Here a cluster of redwoods filtered the light into bands of premature dusk. He made a mental note of the turns he had taken so that he would not make the same mistake after dark. Maybe Joe Gillis could draw him a map. But that wasn't necessary. There were guideposts all around, situated conspicuously along every route in the botanical gardens.

Everywhere except here.

Quietly the shrubbery closed like a wound behind him. Now it was all the same. He turned, turned again, trying to find the sun. The tops of the redwoods spun.

He was tempted to call out for help, to ask someone, the workman, perhaps, for directions. No. He would never be taken seriously on these premises after that. Word would get out. He visualized the headline in Army Archerd's column tomorrow morning: PRODUCER CAN'T FIND HIS WAY TO SWIMMING POOL. And the sidebar: *Can He Find Financing for Gillis Project?* He would never live it down. He had gotten this far on his own, hadn't he? He couldn't give up now.

"Is that anybody?"

A queue of tiger lilies whispered at his back. He faced them. Their hungry orange throats seemed to be speaking to him. There was a suggestion of movement, a silken rustling, close and yet separated from him.

"Hello?" he answered.

"Oh! I thought so. Ec-excuse me." The lilies stopped moving and a giant, waxy jade plant shook and murmured with a female voice.

"I hear you," he said. "Only I can't—"

"Are you the carpenter?"

"Sorry to disappoint you." He concentrated and zeroed in on her thin, reedy voice. He thrust his hand between bamboo stalks, took a chance and stepped through.

And there. He was out. It was easy, after all. He felt foolish. "I didn't mean to scare you." He shaded his eyes. "I just stopped to—to admire the orchids." Were there orchids? He hoped so. He was still disoriented.

Her eyes widened but she stood her ground. She tilted her head diffidently and he could almost see the wheels turning behind her forehead, clicking into place as she arrived at a decision. The pool enclosure began a few yards farther up the path, a white enameled fence; through its bars a bright oval of water sparkled like an azure teardrop.

"Buy you a drink?"

"Hm? Oh, no. Th-thank you."

"Well, think I'll have one. Today's a very important day. It's—"

"I know. But I think you'll have to wait awhile longer."

"What?"

"The bar. It's not open yet."

He sighted past her. She was right. The wet bar was bare. The glasses had not yet been set out and there was no bartender in view. At her back the water was still and crystalline. She pulled a string and loosened her outer garment; the top sloughed off one tender shoulder. He settled back into the chaise and extended his legs so that one foot nearly touched her. She did not move away.

"Do you stay here a lot?" he said, already guessing the answer. Her skin was pale as alabaster.

"Hm? Oh, for the winters mostly." She seemed distracted. "I had to come early this year. Sometimes everything takes so long. I wish it didn't."

"I know what you mean," he said sympathetically, choosing not to press her for details. When in Rome and all that. It was the way people spoke out here, a tantalizing game of one-upmanship. A game he must learn to play. A lazy breeze filtered through the windbreak, feathering the surface of the water. "I've been waiting a long time myself. I mean, I only checked in last night. But this deal has taken years to set up—longer, if you count finding the right script, lining up the backers . . .''

He let his voice trail off. No need to get ahead of himself. There was all the time in the world. She studied him impersonally, neither advancing nor retreating. He was sure he had said exactly the right things. He lay his head back against the white strands of the chaise and folded his hands confidently across his lap.

He felt at ease here. He had always known it would be this way. This place or something like it had been his destiny since the age of ten, when his life was changed irrevocably by so many glorious Saturday matinees. After that it was clear to him that film would be his life. He had never given up hope. And now it was as if this perfect setting had been arranged especially for his entrance. It had been a long time coming, but he was ready to assume his rightful place at last. The backwork was done; now he had taken the chair which was meant for him alone. It was right as rain. This empty position at poolside, this particular one and no other, had been waiting patiently all these years. He was here to stay.

The wafer of sun angled higher, warming the water. Ripples glinted through his eyelids like silver needles. He heard splashing and raised one hand to his forehead. Now she sat on the edge of the deep end and dipped water over her arms and legs. Her short robe lay nearby, deflated as a shedded skin. While he watched she mounted the board and jackknifed into the pool, displacing a high, transparent bell of water. A spatter of droplets fell across his ankles. It was cool and refreshing.

She arched to the center, where she broke the surface with a gasp and a fleeting grin. Was she performing for him? He was alone to witness the audition. As yet no other sunbathers had shown themselves; only an empty cabana tilted in one corner of the enclosure, its tent flap snapping like a flag in the drafts. He enjoyed the privilege.

He sat up as she ascended from the shallow end. The conservative one-piece suit adhered to her slender body, glittered and bled water into a growing spot on the cement.

He pushed out of the chair. She slicked her hair back from her narrow face; now, with darkened curls pasted to her skull, she appeared smaller, almost childlike. She clung there to the side bars, younger and more vulnerable than he had imagined. She could practically be my daughter, he thought. If my marriage had lasted. But then his life would have turned out altogether differently. For a while caring for Laurie had taken the place of his career. Now he was back on track. Without her he was free to resume the path that had led him here today. It was just as well this way—incomparably better, in fact.

"Where'd you learn to do that?" he asked. He left his sandals by the chair, approached the rim and squatted next to her.

She grimaced with embarrassment, as though afraid they would be overheard. Her eyes darted to the corner, where a clutch of hyacinths huddled in the shadow of an imposing queen palm. He was surprised at her shyness, and that made her even more appealing.

"You should see some of the girls who come here," she said self-consciously.

Was that why she was out so early? To avoid the competiton? He pictured her withdrawing to her room as soon as the pool filled up, then sneaking out at the end of the day when once again there was no audience.

"I've seen them," he said.

She trailed her feet in the water, hiding her toes. "How long are you staying?"

"Uh, well, that's hard to say. Until I close the deal, at least. But I'll be back. You can count on that."

"Are you an actor?"

"Me? No, no. I'm a—" He faltered; it was the first time he had dared to let the word pass his lips in casual conversation. "I'm a producer." Or I will be, he told himself, after today. "I'm here to sign my star."

"Your star?"

"My leading man." You know, he thought, the name, the one who brings the money into the box office. For my

movie. She did go to the movies, didn't she? He had an
urge to play his role to the hilt. It would be good practice.

"Joe Gillis," he said matter-of-factly. She blinked at
him; incredibly the name didn't seem to register. He forced
himself to go on, overriding his old insecurities. "The
picture's called *Is Anybody There?* It was written for him.
We start shooting in the spring—sooner, if we can find the
right leading lady." He neglected to mention that they
were already in contact with Susan Penhaligon's agent in
London. No need to burst any bubbles so early in the day.
Let her dream a bit, he thought. No harm in that.

He wondered if she could see his pulse speeding, the
vein standing out on his forehead. She showed no reaction.
The sun nicked the water in expanding circles. He remembered that he had forgotten his dark glasses. They were in
his room, packed in the suitcase. He needed them; he
needed to see the exact expression on her face.

"In fact," he went on, "I should be hearing from Joe
right about now. He knows I'm in town. You know how it
is with actors. They like to sleep late when they're not on
call."

"Do they?"

This was a rare moment. He would remember this day
for the rest of his life. The day it all came together.

"I could give him a call if I wanted to. I have his home
number." Memorized, he thought. "As soon as he can
make it over here to sign the contract, we're in business."

He didn't say anything about the answering machine.
For seventy-two hours or more Gillis had let his Duofone
take all calls. But surely that was to ward off distractions
during the last stage of negotiations. For an Academy
Award winner the phone must never stop ringing. But it
would be back on the hook today. Either that or Gillis
would show up here in person, pen in hand. He loved the
script as much as Wintner's guarantors. And why shouldn't
he? It would be the role of his career.

He looked over her head and savored the scene. The
setting was made to order. Now the morning was officially
beginning; a young latino with a Walkman dangling from

one white pocket entered the enclosure. Wintner watched him walk to the bar carrying a tray loaded with cocktail napkins and swizzle sticks. He didn't need to bring the telephone; it was already plugged in by the cash register. Wintner stood.

It was time.

She raised her head. Her eyes were deep and shining. Drops of water evaporated from her complexion in the rising heat, leaving tracks of chlorination on her cheeks. Suddenly he was reluctant to leave her. *What is it she wants from me?* he wondered. *Most likely nothing more than a few minutes of companionship before fleeing all the golden strangers. She's new to this, too,* he thought. *Like me, she's as pale as milk-fed veal. It takes one to know one. But for both of us all that will change in the next few hours.*

He checked his watch. *I can let her have a few more minutes,* he thought. *Besides, it will be better if I give Gillis a chance to call first.*

He considered stripping down to his trunks and joining her for a brief swim. But he was not quite ready. His body, trim though it was, might blind her with its Eastern pallor. Feeling the first uncomfortable pangs of self-doubt since he had arrived, he flashed her an uneasy smile and knelt once more, gripping the lip of cement with his sandals.

"Did you hurt yourself?" he said casually, to compensate for the empty pause, and instantly regretted it.

Her eyes reluctantly followed his to her legs. There on the inner surface of her thigh was a glistening birthmark a few inches wide. It formed a rough outline of the North American continent. He looked away.

"It's all right," she said quickly. "It's nothing."

But she inched forward and dropped feet first into the pool, moving out into the deeper water, covering herself to the neck.

"Sorry," he muttered.

She bobbed closer. "Did you say something? I can't hear you."

"I said, I think I'll make that call now." He showed her an all-purpose grin, unbent his legs and stood.

She treaded water, painfully alone in the pool.

"Look," he said on a last reckless impulse, "maybe we could have some lunch. Together." When she did not flinch he pressed it. "Let me see how long this takes. He probably won't be by till this afternoon. I'm going to try to get back to the room and catch a nap. You could meet me there later. Or I'll give you a call. My name's Stu Wintner, by the way."

"Maybe," she said uncertainly. She kicked and drifted closer. "It depends."

Here it comes, he thought. I should have known. "Are you here with someone?" He felt the compleat fool. "If you are," he added expansively, forced into playing it out, "I'd be pleased if you'd both join me."

"It's not that. But I don't know if I can get away."

"I understand."

"Do you?"

He backed off awkwardly and headed for the bar, where the young man in the white jacket was polishing a highball glass. "Nice talking to you," he called over his shoulder, and waved. "See you."

Good luck, he thought.

The young bartender took up a stainless steel tool and began curling the rind off a lemon. Wintner sidled up and exchanged nods with him, as if they were old friends. He ordered a margarita and asked to use the telephone.

The answering machine was still on.

The world-weary voice on the other end had not changed. Like Gillis's films it would never change, at least not until the oxide wore away on the millionth playing, around the time his photographic image, equally unchanged and locked in the amber of celluloid, finally disintegrated and burned away with the last remaining frame of his last preserved film. With any luck that film would be *Is Anybody There?* His greatest, most memorable performance and his legacy for generations yet unborn. When he was gone, who could take his place? A kind of immortality. Wintner was jealous.

He left another message, reminding Gillis that he was waiting at the hotel. He contemplated leaving word with Gillis's agent in case the actor was out and called there first. But it was still early. He started on his drink and turned back to the overexposed brightness of the pool.

The girl was no longer in the water. Neither was she anywhere else that he could see. Somehow she had stolen away while he was on the phone. He hadn't heard a sound. If she had left wet footprints on her way out they were dry by now. There was no clue. He caught the bartender's attention. "Did you see . . . ?" he began.

The young man glanced up, munching on something round and white. As he bit down, Wintner saw that it was hollow, like a shell.

"Never mind." For all Wintner knew she might be the daughter of an important guest. There was no need to make a total idiot of himself. He paid for the drink, laying down a nice tip.

Before he left the bar his curiosity got the better of him. "Can I ask you a question?"

The young man disengaged the tape player headphones from one ear. A faint cacophony of insect music hissed on the air.

"Where did you get that?" Wintner indicated the crisp snack. "At the restaurant? I've seen people walking around with them all morning. I guess I must be getting hungry."

The young man offered him a piece.

"No, no. I only want to know what it is."

"Día de los Muertos."

"I beg your pardon?" Does he speak English? Wintner wondered. He's not from around here; probably substituting for the regular man. He doesn't know—

Then he got a clear look at the object. It was a miniature skull, what remained of one, apparently made of spun candy. Most of the face had been eaten away, and the inner surface glimmered with loose granules of sugar.

"The Day of the Dead," explained the bartender. "You know, the second of November. It's a big celebration in Mexico. I have one more, sir, if you'd care to—"

Wintner held up his hand. "No, thanks."

The bartender shrugged, an expression of bemusement in his polished brown eyes.

California, thought Wintner, shaking his head.

Balancing the drink, he sauntered back to the deck chair. On the way he became aware of a muffled rustling. It was the cabana in the corner of the enclosure. The top billowed as the interior filled like an air sock. Then the breeze died and it collapsed inward and hung limp, nothing more than empty canvas, like the umbrellas over the white enameled tables. But the cabana was not anchored securely; when the wind came up again the pole creaked and the striped cloth puffed out in a simulation of breathing. At this angle the sun backlighted the upper half, transforming it into a glowing, translucent orange. Was that a distorted profile inside? Probably only a shadow of the fence rear-projected against the material. Still, it made him uneasy. He ignored it and returned to the chaise.

There, inserted between the plastic weave of the seat: a small square of paper. A cocktail napkin. He reached down to remove it, and noticed that it contained a handwritten note.

PLEASE HELP ME, read the shaky black letters.

He looked around.

Behind the bar, the attendant emptied his hands of the candy skull and resumed stripping the skin off a pungent lemon.

Now he was convinced that there was someone in the tent.

Holding his drink in one hand and the flimsy note in the other, he walked back along the edge of the pool.

Wind ballooned the tent once more and moved on, leaving the sides sunken as empty cheeks. In the interval that followed he heard the rustling quite clearly.

It definitely came from inside.

He approached the structure, aware of the bartender's watchful eyes. He fought down a compulsion to peek directly into the opening and get it over with. Instead he stood there stiffly and shifted his feet.

A groaning.

Was it only the supports? He couldn't be sure.

Just inside the orange slit, two eyes locked on him. Startled, he stepped backward and almost fell. The eyes rose higher and the tent opened. A large woman lunged out, glaring at him. Before she drew the flap shut behind her he got a glimpse of something bathed in the unnaturally warm glow of the interior, something pale and nearly shapeless laid out on a white towel.

"Yes?"

He cleared his throat. "Can I be of any help?"

The woman stood guard at the entrance. Her bathing suit stretched to enclose her massive form, rolled black straps cutting into her doughy shoulders.

"You're new," she said. Though her protruding eyes did not move he knew that every detail, every inch of his body was being examined.

"Forgive me for bothering you," he said evenly. "But I didn't know . . ." He looked to the note as though it would explain everything. Unaccountably his hand shook. Already sweat ran from his wrists and blurred the lettering. He crumpled it and tossed it away.

Behind her something groaned.

"He gets cramps when I leave him in one position too long." She regarded Wintner warily for another moment, then abruptly stood aside. "He says he'd like to meet you."

"Are you sure?" Wintner was at a complete loss. He felt as though he had stepped into a nudist colony without his papers.

The woman held out a wattled arm. The canvas curled open.

A man lay sweltering in the livid interior. Essentially he had no legs. One grew to the knee, one was a mere flipper. Ignoring Wintner, the woman sat and took the man's great gray head into her lap.

She proceeded to massage his temples. She wiped his forehead with a cloth. She took up a cotton swab and then, after she had painstakingly cleaned the whorls of one ear, used manicure scissors to snip at the salt-and-pepper hairs growing there. Wintner stood by, a spy observing a private ritual.

"We always come here this time of year," she said. "For the weather. We don't like the cold, do we, honey?" She kneaded his speckled shoulders, his jutting breastbone.

The old man rolled his head to the side, a mighty effort. His eyes were black as beads but with a tinge of blue-gray around the frayed pupils. His shortened body was scarred, folded in on itself at every joint and orifice. The stump ends where his hands should have been were sucked in like navels, as though sewn to a point inside. His eyes searched Wintner's vicinity.

"Can I bring you something?" Wintner offered. "A cold drink? A glass of water? Anything?"

The gray head lolled in a swoon. The interior was sweltering; the sun transformed the walls of the tent into incandescent screens, the stripes a pattern of bars. Wintner itched to be gone.

He backstepped, feeling for the opening.

As if on cue the woman recentered the head on the towel, put down her tools and followed Wintner out.

He was instantly cooler. It was a sweatbox in there. Didn't she realize that? With his circulation so drastically shortened, the poor man's natural body temperature would be abnormally high to begin with; such confinement would become unbearable by midday. Was the tent a last resort to shield his condition from prying eyes? But wouldn't they do better in their air-conditioned room? Surely the man didn't care that there was a pool a few feet away, on the other side of the canvas barrier.

"Such a beautiful day!" she said. She inhaled deeply and shook her hair free. Moist curls flung jewels of perspiration into the glare. "I dream about this place all year long."

"Yes," said Wintner. He found his voice. "I was just on my way—"

"But you can't go. I won't let you." Her mood became

generous, her lumpy face girlishly animated. "We must talk."

Wintner did not know whether he should feel flattered or threatened. Either attitude seemed absurd.

"Sure," he said. "But right now I'm expecting a call. I'll be back later, though. I—"and here he foundered—"I hope your husband feels better." How else to put it?

Her face sagged, the mere mention dragging her down like gravity. "It's Tachs-Meisner Syndrome," she said, her voice coarse again. "We thought he was safe from the bloodline. But since his fortieth birthday. . . . One can only try to be as comfortable as possible, until the end."

"I'm sorry."

"You shouldn't be. We are almost free."

He nodded and stared at the cement. His feet were as pale as they had been the first day of summer on the sidewalks of the town where he grew up. He had never before felt grateful for his strong arches, his well-shaped toes. But now he noticed that his fourth and fifth toes were no longer perfect; distorted by years of proper shoes, they had grown inward—now they were mere knobs, the nails squeezed down to slivers and all but vanished, suggesting evolution to a lower form. How could he not have noticed until now? He was aware of a tightening. The concrete heated under his delicate soles, which had been pampered for so long that they were hypersensitive, less able to protect him from the real world. The taut skin covering his insteps wavered in a rising heat mirage. He detected a smell that was dangerously like burning meat. He needed to get away, back to his sandals and a patch of shade. But there was no shade here except in the tent.

"I'll stop by later," he suggested. "Do you take your meals in the dining room? Perhaps I'll see you this evening. I won't be alone, but you might enjoy meeting a friend of mine."

She shook her head. "There's no time. He needs me. Always." Her eyes filled with tears. "Every hour, every minute, *every second!*" she said with shocking bitterness, almost spitting the words. She gazed longingly at the pool as though it were an impossible distance away.

He moved off. "Well, I'm sure I'll see you later. This afternoon, probably. Good luck, Mrs. . . . ?"

"I was like my mother. I believed the dream. Young girls always do. We marry, thinking what a joy it will be. But somehow it changes." Her eyes distended above her puffy cheeks. "And now, God help me, it's too much!"

She lumbered toward Wintner to prevent his leaving, but too late. She stood there sadly, her fat bosom heaving, then wheeled around wearily and stooped to re-enter the tent. Wintner could not avoid seeing the shapeless mass inside struggling to turn onto its side, the misshapen features, the ruined arms batting out for leverage. Resigned, the woman returned to her duties. She took up cotton and alcohol and began cleansing the pores on his neck.

Wintner retrieved his sandals and beat a hasty retreat.

The path was harder to follow than he remembered, but he hurried back faster than ever through the lush vegetation. Blood-red bougainvillaea dripped over arbors, huge ivy choked off plots of delphinium and quivered at the borders of the walk, eager to overgrow and split the painted cement. The table setting next to the hidden cottages remained immaculate and untouched. Below, in the botanical gardens, variegated plants were locked in a stalemate of symbiosis. He came to the gazebo, white as a lattice of crossed bones, and finally saw that the hole in the roof had been cut out to make room for a rapidly maturing tree; as he passed, heavily-pruned limbs were already thrusting upward to fill the empty circle.

He realized that he could not call the girl from the pool even if he wanted to; he had forgotten to ask her name.

Now he would never know.

He remembered the last image of the man in the cabana, face crawling with sweat, mouth open on darkness in a desperate rictus. Wintner lay sprawled on the bed in his room and tried to put the memory out of his mind, but could not.

The morning lagged, the afternoon slackened until the sun came to a standstill above a blanket of smog. He made the call twice in the first hour, then every twenty minutes, then every ten. Each time Joe Gillis's voice droned the same prerecorded message. The actor's presence projected through the telephone to an extraordinary degree; even on tape his dark power was immediately recognizable. By midafternoon Wintner gave up leaving any word at all on the machine.

He pitied the man in the tent, but soon felt nearly as confined himself. The walls of his room narrowed in the lengthening shadows. He rode the elevator down to the lobby, which now seemed nothing more than a fey decorator's wet dream, hand-rubbed and unlivable. When he returned with a newspaper and a sandwich, the ceiling had closed in even more dramatically.

He considered renting a car. He had Gillis's address. He could simply drive over.

Why not?

He picked up the phone directory.

There was a knock on the door.

At first he didn't recognize her. She had put on a blouse and skirt; the lapels of the blouse, slightly too large, hung wide over the bathing suit so that she appeared childishly small, half hidden in her loose clothes. She kept a reasonable distance and blinked at him from beneath dark curls.

"Were you sleeping? I can come back."

"No! No, please. I'm glad to see you. Come in."

"I got your room number from the desk." The young woman sidled in, visibly ill at ease. Did she notice what had happened to the walls and ceiling? "I hope you don't mind."

"Not at all. I could use some company." He moved his suitcase, pushed aside the unopened newspaper so she could sit on the bed.

"Have you heard from your friend yet?"

"I'll talk to him later. You know how it is in this business—hurry up and wait."

"Oh."

"Can I get you anything? I think there's a room-service menu somewhere."

She tossed her curls, inexplicably amused. "No, but I'll be glad to get *you* something." She eyed the bottle of MacAllan Single Malt in his open suitcase. He had brought it to celebrate with Gillis. She reached for it. Before he could stop her she twisted off the seal with a flourish, an exaggerated bit of business she might have seen in a movie once. If she went to the movies. "Do you like it plain or with water?" she asked sweetly.

"No, really, I don't need anything." Then again maybe he did. It was not such a bad idea. Yet he felt oddly guilty. "You don't have to serve me. This was my idea, remember?"

"Was it?" she said. "That's all right. I enjoy it."

He believed she meant it. He leaned one arm back against the pillow and waited.

She removed the paper cover from one of his sanitized glasses and poured what she estimated to be a couple of fingers. She was trying so hard to learn the moves, to get it all down. She wanted to make it true, the way it would be on a bad television show. He was touched. The clothes, for example, were not quite right; he wondered where she had got them. He thought: She still accepts everything she was taught. She probably forces herself to go to the right places, do the right things, like staying at this hotel. And why? Is it worth it? She thinks it is. It may be all she knows. But what's the payoff for her?

He drank the Scotch down to the vapors while she sat on the end of the bed, one leg half-concealed under her.

"Did you hurt yourself?" He pointed to a small circle of cauterized skin on her shinbone. He had not noticed it earlier.

She made an attempt to cover it but her shirt was not long enough. "Oh, it's nothing. I don't mind anymore. It's only—only scar tissue."

Now he saw another mark an inch or two below her kneecap. She repositioned her legs nervously and her skirt hiked up. There were three, four, several more spots scattered along her calves, irregular patches of tissue, nearly round as if burned into her flesh by heated coins. Each scar covered a small concavity, suggesting that abscesses or tumors of some kind had developed there and been removed. They had healed well, but the indentations remained.

He had a hunch. "You didn't grow up on the beach, did you?" he asked.

She tilted her head quizzically.

Of course not, he thought. She was definitely not from around here. "My nephew had something like that. He was raised in San Diego. Surfer's knots, they were called. Calcium deposits. He had them removed, too."

"Oh no," she said with forced casualness, "these were—were bone-marrow transplants. Afterward there's always an empty space." She smoothed the hollows with her hands. "They'll fill out, though. It takes time, but something else grows in. I'm sure that's what will happen with me. The doctor says you can't leave nothing where something used to be. Till then it's just deadspace."

"I see." He was careful not to show any revulsion. "Does it hurt?"

"It used to. After a while you don't notice it anymore. Now there's no feeling. There will be again, though. If not . . ."

Fascinated, he bent closer. He touched one of the spots with infinite care. It was softer than anything he had ever touched before. Her leg tensed, then relaxed slowly as if from an effort of will. He felt the silkiness of tiny hairs growing in around the scar.

She pressed his finger lightly into the gap and smiled with satisfaction. The fingertip filled it perfectly.

The sensation was unnerving. He was both attracted and repelled. He pulled away and sat back against the headboard.

"You look tired," she said.

He knew it was true. He hadn't slept well and the long day was taking its toll. His neck ached. His mouth was sour with the peaty taste of the Scotch and his eyes felt scorched. He wanted to close them. Until it was time.

"Why don't you put your feet up?"

"They are up."

"Oh. Then why don't you take off your shoes again? Here, I'll help you. Would you like another drink?"

"No." He felt himself slipping away. "I guess I am tired. All this waiting."

"I know."

How could she? She couldn't know what it was like. He didn't know what to do with her. To throw her out so soon would be rude. "Pour yourself one, if you like."

"I like your voice," she said. "And your face. It's gentle. Not like the other men who come here."

"Thanks."

"Are you very successful?"

"Sure," he said. "I will be. You'll see. You'll all see."

She came around and perched on the edge of the bed.

"You haven't read your newspaper yet," she said, as if acting out some women's magazine version of an idealized domestic scene. Why bother? Go home, he thought, to the small town you came from, marry some guy with a polyester suit and a regular income. You won't have any surprises, but you won't have any disappointments, either. Meanwhile practice on someone who can fill the bill. She could find someone else, couldn't she?

He was aware of her inching closer. He felt smothered, immobilized. What did she want from him? Somehow things had taken a turn toward the surreal. He didn't understand it. For now he felt too weary, too ineffectual to resist. That would have to change, of course. In another minute. As soon as she eased off. Then it would be time to call again.

She unfolded the newspaper and laid it across his lap.

He opened his eyes. "You're very kind," he began, "but you really don't have to—"

He saw the headline.

FILM GREAT FOUND DEAD

He snatched up the paper.

HOLLYWOOD (UPI) Joe Gillis, one of the screen's

most durable leading men for more than four decades, was found dead in his West Los Angeles apartment today, the apparent victim of a massive stroke.

"Jesus Christ," he said, "did you see this?"
"No."
He read on numbly.

A security guard discovered the body early this morning, using a passkey only after the actor's agent and friends became alarmed. Preliminary reports indicate that the star of such film classics as "Man Afire," "La Carcel" and "Hole in the Wall" had been dead for at least several days. Police say the corpse, sprawled on the floor near an empty whiskey bottle and with the telephone only inches from his hand, had already begun to partially decompose . . . .

Wintner's eyes followed the story to the bottom of the page, then returned blearily to the three-column photo at the top and began again. He read the words over but they did not make any sense. It was some kind of sick, twisted joke.

He grabbed the phone, dialed 393-9058.

The receiver clicked.

"Hi," said a reassuring voice.

"Hi, Joe," said Wintner, remembering to breathe again. "Listen, is this April Fool's Day or something? What's all that crap in the *Examiner* about . . . ?"

"This is Joe Gillis. I'm sorry but I'm not in right now. If you'd care to leave a message, wait for the beep and I'll get back to you as soon as I can. And thanks for calling. . . ."

"Hello?" said Wintner. The receiver began to shake in his hand. His fingers went cold, as though they were dying. The blood drained from the left side of his body and pounded in his ears. He could not hear whether or not anyone had picked up the other end. "Hello? Is anybody . . . ?"

She placed the glass in his right hand and poured.

The electronic beep sounded and, when he could not speak, clicked off into a dial tone.

She hung up the phone for him.

Dazed, he said, "I'm sorry, but something terrible's happened. I'll have to ask you to—"

"Is it so terrible?"

"*What?* Do you realize what this means?"

"Yes. I didn't think you knew."

"Why didn't you tell me?'

"That's partly why I came here."

"You did read it, then."

"No."

"Then how could you know?"

"I know he's dead." A maddening tranquillity passed over her features. "I went to the room to get my towel, and when I got back he was—gone. He waited for such a long time. We all did."

"What the hell are you talking about?"

"My father. I believe you met him. Mother said you did. She's very strict with me, by the way. That's why I told you I wasn't sure when you asked me if I could—"

"Who? You mean the man by the pool? You mean that he's dead, too?"

He spilled the drink as he drained the glass dry. It went down like sweet fire, but this time he could hardly taste it. She wiped the drops from his shirt, then poured herself a small one and sat sipping, watching him patiently.

It was too much. His head tilted back. His muscles were rubber. He felt his body, his legs, the bed and the floor dissolving and falling through while his mind continued to function, like the elusive Joe Gillis whose answering tape had stayed on as his stand-in even after he had gone, like the man in the cabana whose body, what was left of it, remained in place even as his mouth opened in a final wrenching paroxysm of terror.

"We all have to let go," she said, moving over him.

What would become of the actor after his tape was turned off? His number would be given to someone new, his furniture moved out and someone else's moved in. And then? Wintner was at sea, cast adrift.

"What happens now?" he said groggily, as the liquor anesthetized him.

"Now we're free," she whispered. He smelled the alcohol on her breath, close and sickeningly medicinal.

He saw the note in his mind, as if in a dream. It fluttered up on a dark wind. Was *he* the one, then? Wintner saw the man crawling like a living torso toward the opening and the light, struggling to speak, to scrawl one last plea before falling across the threshold to another country. HELP ME, PLEASE HELP ME . . .

"What did he want?" Wintner choked, as her hot breath filled the shrinking space around him. *"What?"*

"The same as anybody," she said. "The trouble was, Mother's too old to take care of him now. I couldn't help. She wouldn't let me. She says I've got myself to worry about. No one else could do it for her. It was her job, you see. You do see, don't you? Don't you . . . ?

"It's going to be easy from now on," she said, climbing higher, settling in. "You'll see. It's simple, so simple, I promise. . . . "

The morning sun was a burning penny in the sky. It blasted the canvas until the sides blazed with louvers of hot orange light.

She took down the top of her black bathing suit and lay prone on the bleached white towel, her elbows out and her small hands locked under her chin. When he glanced down it appeared at first that her arms were abnormally shortened, the bones already eaten away close to the body. But then she flipped her head to the other side and used one hand to touch a spot on the back of her neck.

"Here," she said, "between my shoulders. Can you get it, honey? It's starting to bother me."

So soon, he thought. He paused to peel off his T-shirt, then sat over her, kneading the hyaline flesh. He worked up slowly to a regular rhythm, soothing and mindless.

"Mmm," she moaned. "Feels so good. I love you to take care of me like this."

"Do you?" He didn't mind. It was easy, after all. So much easier. It gave him something to do now besides waiting.

A gust shook the tent. It was strong today, the first intimation of a full-blown wind, possibly even a rainstorm, what passed for winter here. The flap blew open. The sudden coolness raised bumps on his arms.

"Can you see my mother?"

He leaned back and peered through the gash of the opening.

"She's at the end of the pool, by the diving board. It doesn't look like she's ready to go in yet."

"It's been too long," said the young woman wistfully. "It's like she has to learn all over again."

The woman was standing like an overgrown child, afraid to get her feet wet. There was no one else out yet; that, he thought, might make it easier for her.

"She's finally going to have some fun," he said.

"Oh, is she? I hope so! She deserves it. She waited so long . . . ."

"Shall we join her?"

"Not today. I'm not feeling well at all."

Of course, he thought. He heard the distant chime of glasses being stacked. "Maybe she's going to have a drink first."

"Mmm. That would be nice."

He stopped moving his hands and sat back to take a breather while the cabana grew brighter, the sides vibrating with an unearthly intensity, the threads of the canvas shimmering in bas-relief like the veining of a translucent membrane, like the projection of his own retinas on the screen of his eyelids when the light became too harsh and he had to close his eyes.

She took the opportunity to raise to her elbows and crawl forward a few inches. She put on his dark glasses and lifted the flap.

"Hey," she called, "can you do me a favor?"

Her mother turned from the bar and looked back blankly.

"Can you bring me something to drink?"

The mother nodded and said something to the attendant.

"I could use one, too," said Wintner.

"What?"

"I don't care," he said. "But tell her to make it a double."

She did. Then she crawled back into position so that he could continue taking care of her.

He did.

It went on like that.

Jerry Sohl's writing credits go back more than thirty years to The Haploids, Costigan's Needle, *and* The Transcendent Man. *His television writing—over twenty years' worth—includes work for "Star Trek," "Alfred Hitchcock Presents," "The Twilight Zone," "Route 66," "Naked City," and "The Outer Limits." I have been working for many years to get him to do a story for* Whispers *and finally succeeded—in between two novels he was writing. It is a* Whispers-*type look at today's counseling techniques.*

CABIN NUMBER SIX
Jerry Sohl

In the afternoon Henry cleaned the cabin, made certain the refrigerator was working, the gas on, and that there was enough wood for the fireplace. He put clean sheets on the bed, fluffed up the pillows, swept the floor, and washed the windows.

Mother said they were getting ready to come, and Mother was never wrong. Lots of times reservations were made but people never showed up. It never came as a surprise to Mother because she always *knew*.

It wasn't until well into evening that Mother spoke again. She was in her chair and Henry was at the television laughing over an old Marx Brothers movie.

"They've left the city," she said, not even slowing her knitting, needles clicking, rocker rocking.

If Mother said it, it was true. Henry figured they had more than an hour. *Duck Soup* would surely be over by then.

"They have a gun in the glove compartment," Mother said.

That was bad. Mother didn't like firearms.

They were both in a vile mood, and it was hard enough finding the Flennery off-ramp on the Interstate, but when they went the wrong way on Route 457, which intersected Flennery, George nearly blew his top. Joan got out the map and looked at it under the dash light and told him what he'd done, which didn't help.

They found the Daisy Bell Motel just off 457 about three miles up, and they could see its flickering neon VACANCY sign through the encroaching fog before they saw the office.

They pulled up in front and sat in dismay, looking at the old place, which was weather-beaten and in the need of paint. The only thing alive about it was the ghastly vacancy sign and the lights in the two windows on the porch.

"This can't be the place!" Joan said in downright disgust.

George, a large-boned man in the need of a shave, peered through the windshield with bloodshot eyes. "It's got to be. Dr. Woodford said Daisy Bell and we're at the X-marked place on the map."

"His idea of a joke, maybe."

"Woodford never jokes."

"I don't see how spending a night here is going to save our marriage."

"You don't want it saved."

"I didn't say that. You always—"

"Just remember," George said, opening the car door, "this was Dr. Woodford's idea, not mine."

"Help you folks?"

They looked toward the office, were startled to see an old man in bib overalls standing there.

"Name's Henry Cobbs," the old man said. "You two must be the Hudsons."

"Dr. Woodford made the reservations," George said.

"Of course he did. Come on in."

They moved to the steps, the porch, and into the seedy old office, Joan cringing to see old flowered wallpaper, an ancient switchboard, and dust everywhere, even on the counter.

"This here's Mother," Henry said, indicating an incredibly old lady in a rocker in the shadows. To her he said, "The Hudsons, Mother. Right on time."

"How-de-do," Mother said in a high-pitched, grating voice, peering out at them from a wrinkled old face, never stopping her rocking or knitting.

George nodded perfunctorily as Henry went around to the other side of the counter and moved the register toward him.

"If you'll sign in . . ."

George, whose mood had worsened, turned to Joan to see if she felt about it the way he did, but she was arranging her hair in a cracked mirror on the wall. Jesus, always monkeying with her hair, or her nails, or her lips, her eyes. George wrenched around, snatched the offered pen and scrawled their names.

Henry reached for the key. "That'll be fifty dollars."

"Fifty dollars!"

Even Joan turned in surprise.

"Since they put the Interstate through we don't get many. Had to raise prices." Henry smiled and dangled the key.

Fuming, George counted out the money, grabbed the key with a snarl, turned and started for the door.

"It's Cabin Number Six."

They drove through the entranceway to find ten cabins, five on each side, facing an open area, each with its adjacent carport. There were no lights on in any of the cabins, nor were there cars in the carports.

They found Number Six, parked the car, and went in.

"Fifty dollars!" George grumbled after he turned on the

lights and tossed his suitcase on the bed. "Christ, we could've got a place in Vegas for that. Look at this dump!"

"We?" Joan said archly, putting her overnight case on the vanity. "You mean you. You never take me."

"You don't like the place."

"I never said that." She looked around at the old bed, table, broken-down lounging chair, frayed carpet. "Thank you, Dr. Woodford." She made a sour face. "Thanks for nothing."

"He must be soft in the head," George said, opening his suitcase and starting to rummage through it. "Don't tell me I forgot the bourbon! No, here it is." He held it up for her to see. "Here's the little beauty!"

"That's not going to help," Joan said, sitting down at the vanity and regarding her image in the mirror.

"I don't remember Dr. Woodford saying anything about not drinking."

"We're supposed to face each other here, thrash out our differences, not get drunk."

"We'll need several drinks if we're going to do that," George said from the bathroom, where he found two wrapped glasses.

"I can take it or do without it," Joan said airily.

"Where the hell's the ice bucket!" Now George was in the kitchen. He opened the refrigerator. "Not a goddamn thing in this." He opened the freezer section. "How d'you like that? No ice cubes."

"There's the phone," Joan said, nodding to an old-fashioned phone on the wall next to the front door. "You know what your trouble is? You can't stand yourself. That's why you drink, to get away from yourself. That's what Dr. Woodford says."

"If old Woodford would take a drink it might loosen him up a little." George jiggled the receiver bracket. "While we're at it, let me tell you what he said about you . . .Hello? This is Number Six. There's no ice here. Yeah, a whole bucket. Looks like it's going to be a long night." He slammed down the receiver.

Joan turned in her chair, buffing her nails. "Just what did he say about me?"

"He said you were in love with yourself, so much so that you would never be able to love anybody else. He said you were like a Kewpie doll. You know, one of those dolls—"

"I know what a Kewpie doll is."

George opened the door to look for the old man. "Here he comes—what's his name? Henry." He turned to her. "The doc's right, you know. Dolls can't love. They don't even have a heart."

"If I'm so awful, why do you stick around?"

"Don't think I haven't given that a lot of thought, sweetie."

"Love isn't something that just happens. You've got to *make* it happen. That's what Dr. Woodford said. Or didn't you catch that?"

"Here's your ice," Henry said, stepping up on the small porch. "And that will be five dollars."

"Five dollars!" George was outraged. "Ice is supposed to come with the room."

"Not here it doesn't."

George gave him a five-dollar bill. "No tip."

"Didn't think there'd be any," Henry said, turning and starting back to the office.

"No wonder the rest of the cabins are empty," George said, closing the door and moving to the kitchen with the ice bucket.

Joan strained to hear something through George's list of complaints, finally saying, "Shh!"

"Shush yourself," George said, bringing her her drink.

"I heard something. It was a woman. A woman laughing."

"Maybe it's the old lady. Jesus, five dollars for ice!"

"It was a young voice. Listen!"

George went to sit on the bed. "So all the cabins aren't empty. Somebody's having a good time. It's a cinch it's not us." He downed the drink, got up to make another.

"There's someone out there," Joan said, getting up and

moving to the window and pulling the curtains back.
Through the pane she saw two figures standing in the eerie
night, light fog swirling around them. She was so shocked
she froze.

"You didn't answer," George said, "so I brought the
bottle." He took her glass. "Hell, you haven't drunk any
at all. What the hell's the matter with you?"

"Those two people . . ."

"Stop rubbernecking."

" . . .seem to be waiting for something."

George joined her at the window. "Probably waiting for
you to stop gawking." He saw them and it didn't help his
mood. "Who the hell do they think they are?"

"They're like statues."

He reached over, pulled the curtains closed. "Come on.
We've got some serious drinking to do."

Joan was frightened. "I don't like this place. What if
we just left? Could we do that?"

"And throw our fifty dollars away? No way."

Joan wet her lips and sat on the vanity chair. "Those
two people . . . they didn't look—human."

"Oh, for God's sake!" George gulped down his second
drink. "You still haven't touched yours, for Christ's sake."
His eyes followed her as she got up. "What do you think
you're doing?"

She stopped at the phone. "I want to see if anybody else
is registered here." She jiggled the hook. "Hello? . . .
Hello?" She turned around, her face ashen. "There's
no answer."

"Women!" George said, getting up and tearing the
receiver out of her grasp. He tried rousing Henry, but there
was nothing. He slammed the receiver down. "I'm gonna
give that old fart a piece of my mind." He put his hand on
the doorknob.

"Wait! Not without me! I'm not staying in here by
myself!"

"Oh, all right. Come on."

Once outside on the porch, the door closed behind them,
they stopped, startled to see the two figures not twenty feet

from the house. Now they could see them through the light fog, a man and a woman standing as still as death, staring at them.

The woman was so pale her skin was almost white, her eyes so large they looked unreal, and her hair was so highly lacquered it reflected the dull effulgence of the night. Her fat cheeks were rouged, her full lips a deep cherry red. She wore a flowing robe that looked as sheer as marquisette, for it did not hide the voluptuous body beneath.

The man wore a suit, complete with white shirt and tie. His shoes were shined. But he was hirsute. His disheveled wild hair fell loosely from the crown of his head, his face was like a wolf's, his hands were hairy, his nails those of a cat. The most terrible feature about him was his eyes. They were red and seemed to glow.

The male beast opened his mouth, exposing long incisors and a lolling tongue. He emitted a low growl. The woman's lips curled into a sneer. She gave a little laugh.

It took the Hudsons no time at all to decide that these two things they saw were inimical. As one they turned and hurried back into the house, Joan shoving the door's bolt in place and then leaning against it, trying to get her breath. She saw her drink on the vanity, moved quickly to it to down it in one gulp as George brought in the bottle to refill his and hers with shaking hands.

"What do they want?" Joan asked in a quavering voice.

"I don't know."

"Who *are* they?"

"I don't know that either." George went to the phone and tried once more to raise Henry Cobbs, but he could not. "The son of a bitch has turned off the switchboard."

They both heard the sounds on the porch.

Joan moved to George. He put his arm around her.

"They're on the porch!"

George finished his drink, threw the glass on the bed, pulled away from Joan even as she said, "George!"

"I've had enough of this Halloween stuff. Let's see how they like a knuckle sandwich." George suddenly pulled

the bolt back and opened the door to attack, uttering a
hoarse, threatening cry, his arms raised.

The two outside stood silent, menacing in the face of
George's attack, the man-beast catching one of George's arms
and twisting it violently, George uttering a cry of pain even
as Joan, inside, watched, terrified, her hands to her face.

George wrenched away, turned to come back in, the
man-beast uttering a fierce growl and lunging after him,
the woman giving voice to a loud, cackling laugh. Even as
George managed to get through the doorway the beast's
claws raked his back.

The beast's momentum carried him halfway through the
door, but when George started to close it on him, the beast
withdrew, leaving only one hairy arm and hand inside to
claw at the air.

"Joan . . . *Joan!*"

But Joan was transfixed with terror, could only watch
the clawing hand and George's struggle to keep the beast
out.

"The poker—over there by the fireplace!"

Joan swallowed, came out of it, ran to the hearth for the
poker, came to the door with it where she could only
stand, helplessly watching George push against the door,
not daring to relax, and the hand that groped about, almost
touching George. The harder George pushed the more frantic became the clawed hand and the louder became the
beast's cries outside.

"Hit the arm—hit the arm, damn it! I can't hold him
much longer!"

Joan tried to hit the arm, but she didn't connect with
each blow, and the blows she did deliver were doing
nothing.

"Harder . . . *Harder!*"

Joan, her face twisted with fear and great effort, sobbed
and swung the poker in a wide arc, connecting solidly with
the arm. The creature cried out in great pain and withdrew
his arm.

George quickly slammed the door shut and shot the bolt
into place, leaning against the door, gasping for breath.

Joan let the poker fall to the floor and stared at it. There were spots of blood on it.

From the outside came the woman's shrill laughter and the beast's low grunts of pain and growls of menace.

"The chair," George said between breaths. "The chair at the dresser."

Joan saw what he meant, brought it to him. He placed it beneath the doorknob and wedged it there. Only then did he step back and wipe his forehead with a handkerchief.

"Will it hold?"

"It better."

Even as George said it they heard the man-beast's body hit the door, trying to break in. Joan put her hand to her mouth. George picked up the poker.

George called out, "What do you people want?"

The only answer was the woman's giggle and the beast's growls.

"I should have brought in the gun."

"Don't you dare try to go get it."

They listened, heard the boards on the porch creak. Then there was silence.

"Maybe they've gone away," Joan said.

"They're off the porch, that's for sure."

Joan stiffened. "Listen."

Together they heard the scraping sound along the wall of the cabin.

"It's going to the rear!" she cried out fearfully. "Is there a back door?"

George did not wait to answer but rushed off, Joan behind him, but just as they found the back door it opened and the man-beast, eyes glittering ferociously, came roaring in, the woman behind him.

Joan screamed, but George struck out and caught the beast in the shoulder with the poker, causing him to cry out in pain. George raised the poker again, but the beast was already retreating and through the door. George threw himself against the door and slid its bolt closed.

Joan, feeling weak and unable to face any more, leaned

against the refrigerator. When George tried to disengage her hands, she said, "What's the matter?"

"No time for that. Help me move this refrigerator."

Together they moved it to the back door, relaxing only after it was in place.

Joan leaned against the sink, breathing hard. "I wish we'd never come here."

"I'm going to skin that shrink alive."

"Listen!" Joan looked upward with frightened eyes. They both could hear the scrapings on the roof, the sound of feet.

"He'd need a saw to get through the roof," George said. "Or a sledgehammer."

"Look!" Joan pointed to soot falling into the fireplace from up the chimney. Looking frightenedly to George she said, "He's too big to come down the chimney . . . isn't he?"

"Can't take a chance," George said, moving to the fireplace and striking a match to the kindling set on the grate. In a moment it was burning. He took some of the pieces of wood that had been set out for that purpose and added them to the fire. Soon it was blazing, but it was not drawing, and the room started to fill with smoke and they started to cough.

They heard the grunts of dismay before George, breathing through his handkerchief, pointed to the hearth. "It's drawing! He's out!"

It was true, the fire was blazing merrily and smoke was leaving the room.

For a long time they stood ready to do battle if either of the creatures tried to come in again. When, after a time, they did not, they relaxed a little, and in the end they lay on the bed on top of the bedspread, not caring that they were a sight, dirty and sweaty, resting to be ready for any onslaught, their eyes open and the lights on. George had the poker handy. Joan had picked up the fire tongs to use if she had to.

She looked at her watch. "It's three o'clock. When does it get dawn?"

"I dunno. Two, two and a half hours perhaps."

"Maybe they're really gone this time."

"I should go out to the car for my gun."

"No."

"At least we'd have a weapon."

"If they'd let you get that far."

"Maybe it's as you said, they're not out there."

They heard a sound and both stiffened, turned to look at each other in alarm. Joan sat up, listened.

"It's coming from underneath us!" she said.

"The crawl space!" George jumped out of bed. "There's a trap door out in the kitchen."

Carrying the poker, George ran into the kitchen.

Joan screamed because she could see the hinged trap door coming up and the hideous face of the beast rising with it.

George rammed the poker into the face of the creature and it fell back with a terrible cry of pain. George jumped to stand on the door. "Joan, come here, stand on this thing." When she did, George moved the vanity across the floor. It wasn't easy, but adrenalin helped. He placed a leg of it in the middle of the trap door. Only then did he allow himself to relax.

With a ragged cry Joan staggered into the other room and fell on to the bed, putting her hands over her eyes, drawing her feet up and making whimpering sounds. "George . . . I can't stand any more of this."

Just at that moment the lights went out. Joan screamed and sat up. She turned toward a blossoming light in the kitchen.

"I expected something like that," George said, carrying the lighted lantern into the room where she was.

"Oh, George," she said, putting her arms around him as he sat on the bed with her, holding the lantern. "I'm sorry for all the things I've said to you."

He put the lamp down on the floor. Eerie shadows played over the walls and ceiling. "I've been pretty much of a shit myself."

"Whatever happens, I want you to know I do love you. Truly."

George turned to her, kissed her tenderly. "I love you, too, sweetie."

After a while she said, "What happens now?"

"We wait."

"For what?"

"I wouldn't want to guess."

"You *do* think they'll be back, then."

"I'd like to get the gun."

Joan shuddered, "You can't leave me!"

"I wouldn't do that. I mean it." George sat up. "There's a light! You can see it through the curtains from here. In the office."

"I see it! What would they be doing up?"

"I don't know. There's something funny about them."

Even as they looked their view was cut off by the man-beast who moved to stand just inches on the other side of the window.

"Oh God!" Joan said, burying her face in her hands.

George got up slowly from the bed, the poker in his hand. Now they saw that the doll-like woman had joined the beast just outside their window. The woman giggled.

Suddenly, with a fierce animal cry, the beast came crashing through the window, to be rushed by George who struck at him with the poker with all his strength. The two came together and rolled on the floor, the beast full of snarls and growls. The woman appeared at the window and began her cackling laugh.

Though George struggled valiantly, flailing his arms, pushing, gouging and biting, he was no match for the beast who now had hold of him by the throat.

Joan screamed and screamed.

The doll-woman laughed and laughed. Then she, too, leaped through the window and into the room.

"Joan! . . .The poker," George said in a strangled voice, struggling for breath, the beast snarling over him.

Joan forced herself to action, jumping off the bed and reaching for the poker George had dropped. She was too late. The shapely doll-woman had already picked it up and was brandishing it menacingly, laughing at the same time.

With a cry of anguish Joan rushed her, shoved her to one side, grabbed the poker from the surprised woman, and advanced on the man-beast, holding the poker high. With a cry of rage she sent the heavy end of it down on the beast's head.

With a great howl of pain the beast let go of George and tried to ward off more blows. But Joan, once started, found she could not quit but kept whacking away at the creature who finally rolled away, got to his feet, and went back through the window.

Joan dropped the poker and got down on her knees to reach George, taking his head in her hands. "George! . . . *George!*" She saw him open his eyes. "Oh, George! Thank God!" She embraced his head.

She sat with him, rocking with him, George recovering.

"Joan . . .?"

"They're gone, darling."

With effort and her help George got to his feet, massaged his neck, and saw the bloody poker on the floor. He turned to her. "I'm proud of you." He took her in his arms. She sobbed with joy and relief.

"They're coming," Mother said, her needles clicking as she rocked.

"Nearly dawn it is." Henry got up, stretched, yawned, and put his teeth in.

As expected, there was a loud pounding on the door. Before he got to it the pounding sounded again. "All right, all right."

As soon as he opened the door George and Joan came in, very fast.

"Call the police," George said.

"Well, now," Henry said, scratching his head, "why should I do a thing like that?"

"Two horrible creatures . . ." Joan shuddered and could not go on.

"What did they do?"

"We'll show you," George said.

"Put that gun away," Henry said. "It makes Mother nervous."

Mother nodded as she rocked.

The couple led Henry to the cabin explaining how the two terrible creatures came at them from all ways, the roof even, and the crawl space, and how they finally came crashing through the window.

As usual, when they got there there was nothing to see, the cabin was as it always was.

"There was blood on the poker on the floor," George said.

Henry had to smile the way George went over and picked up the poker and looked at it.

"The lights are on!" Joan said with some astonishment.

"That window," George said, but did not elaborate. He said to his wife, "Honey, let's get out of here."

Later, as Henry stood by one of the office windows watching the Hudsons' car disappear down the road, he said, "Well, there they go, Mother."

"Didn't last long," Mother said. "Longer than most, though."

"Sure is funny what people will do when they come face to face with theirselves, isn't it, Mother?"

Mother nodded as she put her knitting down and got up.

"Time for bed," she said with a yawn.

Steve Rasnic Tem has sold Whispers *several stories, all of them unusual. This is probably the most direct tale that he has sent to me. He just sets it down and lets things lead inevitably to their conclusion.*

FATHER'S DAY

Steve Rasnic Tem

"I'm not going, Amy! Why should I?"

"Because he's sick and it's Father's Day. Mark *needs* to meet his grandfather."

Amy exasperated him. Her need to "do the right thing" usually meant *he* was to do the right thing. "He's *my* father, Amy!"

Amy looked up at him with her brow slightly wrinkled, mouth tensed. "We're supposed to be a *family*."

Will looked away, sighed, and shook his head vigorously as if to clear it. "All *right*. We'll *go*."

"Don't go on my account. The decision's yours." She always said that.

"No, you're right. Maybe it won't be so bad with you and Mark there."

Will accepted her hug, but found himself looking past her, out the window to where Mark was playing in the backyard. He had a hammer and was pounding a stake into the grass. Will felt a sudden surge of anger. He started to say something but didn't.

Then he thought of his father lying on his sickbed, and

he began to shake. His vision blurred and he could no longer see his son.

They stopped off at a bookstore on the way to the airport. Will was a compulsive reader, a habit both Amy and Mark complained about. Of course, he'd compromised again and cut his reading almost in half, forcing himself to participate in family activities he had no interest in or talent for. But that much made them happy; they were so eager, both of them so naturally romantic, they could only see him as fully involved in their lives. They couldn't see the continual distraction, the faraway gaze he knew he constantly wore. It wasn't that he had no interest or that he didn't try; there were just so many things for him to think about.

He was working his way through a shelf of paperback mysteries when he realized he'd only been vaguely looking at the books, and focusing the rest of his attention on what Mark was doing. It was like that most of the time he took the boy into a store with him, as if he were waiting for Mark to do something, to make one false step.

Amy called it *pouncing*, like some great cat on a small deer. He usually exploded at what he saw to be her self-righteousness, her holier-than-thou attitude, but he often wondered if she had a point. He certainly seemed to notice more of Mark's little transgressions than she did, but couldn't that just be because she didn't *want* to notice, that she wanted *him* to be the bad guy?

Will heard a slapping noise and wheeled. Mark was walking up and down the aisle, patting the fronts of the books with his fingertips.

"Mark!" Will swooped down on the boy, thinking in irritation that Amy might be watching. He shook Mark by the shoulders. "That's *no way* to *act* in a *store!*"

Amy was at their side immediately. She looked at Mark, opened her mouth to say something, but then apparently thought better of it. Mark stood with his head down. Will could see that Mark had that angry set to his mouth he always got when reprimanded. It angered him instantly; he felt a flashing sensation behind his eyes, and had to blink them rapidly to regain control. He wanted to hit the boy, slap that mouth right off him.

Confused about what was happening to him, Will stepped back out of the aisle, away from his wife and son, carefully avoiding the faces of the other customers.

Amy found him later at the back of the store, down on the floor near a bookcase full of old Westerns.

"Will . . . I'm worried. You were pretty rough on him."

Will leaned back. "So you want him to run wild in the store?"

"I hardly think touching a few books is running wild, Will."

There it was, that self-righteousness again. "You haven't seen him in stores enough. I don't know what it is, maybe nervous energy, but he's always grabbing things, hitting them, rearranging them, like he has to handle everything he passes. I want to teach him that's not appropriate behavior."

"Okay, but be selective. You act as if he can't do anything right. I'm really worried."

"Hey . . ." He suddenly felt dizzy, eyes burning. "Hey, it's *our* relationship; you worry about your own, okay?"

Amy looked puzzled, and Will was afraid she'd seen through whatever had happened to him. How would he explain?

But she just stared at him, then turned and stalked away.

Will leaned back, knocking several books off into the aisle, but was unable to bend down and retrieve them. His head was pounding, circles of scarlet pressure beginning somewhere behind his eyes and expanding in repeated waves until he imagined his skull would first bulge out into his forehead, making him look like some brain-damaged maniac, then explode his head completely into fragments of bone, gray matter, and blood.

And within the core of those expanding waves he was seeing images: himself gone berserk, gleaming knife in his hand, stabbing Mark again and again, as if he would completely sever the boy's torso. And Mark staring at

him, feeling nothing, that angry set to his lips. And Will
crying, hysterical, each knife blow ripping into his own
gut, and the force, the alien power thrusting through the
knife-wielding arm, a power Will knew did not come from
him.

As the plane was circling the field at Will's hometown
airport, Mark fast asleep in his seat across the aisle, Amy
turned to him and clutched his arm. "You're a *good*
father; you *know* that?"

Will looked at her earnest face, and managed a brief
smile for her. She often said things like that to him; he
didn't know if it was her way of encouraging him, or if
she really believed it, that the troubles with Mark were
small exceptions, and that Will was generally doing a good
job.

Funny how he'd always thought that being a father
would be a breeze. He *had* to do a better job than his own
father did. The old man had stayed drunk most of the time,
and Will's mental picture of him was always that of a dirty
body wrapped in smelly clothes much too large for it,
lying crumpled by the sofa it had failed to reach, one
filmy, gray fish-eye staring at the young boy, its offspring.

Will's mother was the only one waiting for them in the
airport, as Will had expected. The old man was probably
home sleeping off a long bender, a bender that he knew
must have started when he heard he would be seeing his
only son again.

"Oh, such a *big* boy!" Will's mother exclaimed, catching Mark up in her plump arms, her white hair falling over
her face. Mark seemed to like the attention. He soon had
one arm around his grandmother.

Will had to admit his mother did well with the boy;
she'd always been good at showing affection for little
boys. Mark usually didn't take to anyone that quickly.

"Hi, Marie." Amy stepped up and kissed her on the
cheek.

His mother glanced over at Will with a worried look.
"Your dad hasn't felt well the last few days. But he can

hardly wait to see you; he's been talking about little else for days.''

"I'm sure," he replied from a tight mouth as she went over to kiss him. She could obviously feel his disapproval as she touched his lips, he thought, and he was suddenly embarrassed. "You're looking good, Mama. I'm glad to see you."

"Seven years . . ." she whispered into his ear.

"You should have visited us, left him at home," he whispered back.

He almost winced, seeing the great fatigue in her eyes. This bender must be a bad one. He had to admit he didn't feel terribly sorry for her. She'd made her choices, made them over and over again to stay with the old drunk. He'd always resented the fact that that decision had condemned him as well; he didn't know if he could ever forgive her for it.

His mother's eyes suddenly lifted excitedly; she reached over and pulled Mark to her side. "Look," she cried, lifting Mark's plump chin, stroking the boy's thick black hair, and looking at Will. "He looks almost *exactly* like you did as a boy."

Will's breath caught and he couldn't reply. The pain was beginning again behind his eyes.

The house Will grew up in was a small, two-story wooden affair in a valley just outside town. The white paint had begun to turn, and a couple of the shutters were broken. The grass had been left half-mowed, trimmed just around the front porch and walkway. The rest of the lawn had at least two months' growth. Will looked at his mother tensely, but she seemed to be avoiding his gaze.

The interior hadn't changed much, the furniture the same and in the same locations he remembered from childhood. Marie brought down a box of Will's old toys from the attic, and Mark was soon running around outside building small settlements and make-believe forts. He seemed to think the unmown grass was wonderful; it made for perfect jungle terrain.

They sat down to dinner without yet seeing the old man anywhere. No one had said anything, but halfway through the meal Mark asked, ''Where's Granddad?''

Will glanced up at the door at the top of the stairs and waited for his mother's reply.

''Your grandfather's quite ill, but I'm sure he'll be well enough to see us all tomorrow.'' She looked over at Will. ''He hasn't felt well for several months.''

With a shock, Will senses the alienness entering his arms and stares in horror as muscles appear to rearrange themselves, hair sprouts where it has never grown, finger-nails grow long and hard. He suddenly feels consumed by a rabid, hungry rage, eating away into his intestines, demanding that he quench it. He leaves Amy in bed and stalks out into the hallway. His mother's bedroom is at one end of the hall, his son Mark's room at the other, where he used to sleep as a child. An unexpected chuckle rises to his lips, startling him. He strides rapidly down the hall, his speed both thrilling and frightening to him, and is suddenly even stronger, bolder, angrier as he passes the dark walnut door at the center of the hall, across from the staircase. He is at the boy's door almost immediately, already imagining the breaking down, the terrified child's screams, the pleasure of rending and tearing, slashing, and smashing. But when he sees himself in the antique mirror on the wall, sees the wild hair and pale white face, bared teeth and hollow cheeks, he cannot even recognize himself.

And eyes he knows cannot be his own—terrible gray fish-eyes, cold and animalistic, eyes watching him from the mirror, eyes grimly amused by his disheveled appearance.

Will woke with a start, sweating profusely, and with the beginnings of a scream he could not quite release rattling around in the back of his throat. As Amy tossed and turned beside him, he thought at first they were home in their own bed but then he recognized it as one of the guest rooms of his parents' house. His old bedroom was at the end of the hall; he wasn't sure, but thought Mark was sleeping there. They did bring Mark with them this time, didn't they? And then at the middle of the hall, his father's door.

He left the bedroom quietly, deciding milk might help him sleep. He had already turned the corner to start down the stairs, when he realized the door to his father's bedroom was open.

Out of bravery, or anger, or a lack of caution born of too little sleep, Will started through the doorway immediately. He rubbed his left hand gently across the smooth walnut surface of the door, pushing it open further.

The bed as huge as he remembered it. The wallpaper darker. *He has stumbled in his headlong flight around the bed, whimpering. He hears the drunken shouts a few feet away but cannot bring himself to look.*

He remembered the sheets his mother bought special for his father, for a Father's Day some twenty years past, and still the old man was using them. *He wraps himself behind the fallen sheets, thinking the big bear won't see him. He's so close now, his snarling so loud, the long claws beginning to tear into the sheets . . .*

The bureau had clothes piled on top, clothes hanging out of open drawers, clothes piled on the floor in front. *He squeals as one hairy arm touches him, squirms out of the huge, gnarled hands, and runs wailing from the beast, the devil, through the piles of clothes before the bureau, to hide behind the easy chair beyond. If only he doesn't fall!*

He could smell the stench of stale liquor everywhere. He wandered around the bed, looking at the photos on the wall, glancing nervously into the hidden shadows by the bureau, almost ready to call the man's name, but afraid to, afraid not to . . . *He is screaming because the beast is slashing the chair with his claws, screaming because, as the creature's massive arm rises higher and higher over the back of the chair, he can see that it is a long silvery knife in the hairy hand, screaming because as the animal climbs over the chair, exposing the wild mane of hair, the enraged red face, he can see that it is his own father trying to kill him, his father's dark eyes with the beast's cold gleam . . .*

. . . The eyes with the animal distance. Inhuman eyes. His father was staring at Will from the chair, his head rigid, mouth clenched, hands locked on the arms. Will gasped. Those unnatural eyes . . .

"How dare you!" *Let me see you, son . . .*

"The door was . . . "

"No one comes in here!" *I said come out!*

"It's been years, Dad!" *Daddy . . .*

"I'll not have my privacy violated!" *I'll find you!*

"I wasn't trying to."

"I'll not stand for it, Will" *I'll get you!*

"I only wanted to check . . ." *Daddy, please!*

"I'll stop you, Will!" *I'll kill you, boy!*

His father suddenly began shivering violently, his hands shaking up off the chair arms, then clasping together over his belly. Will watched in fascination as the cold, bestial gleam seemed to leave his father's eyes, his father suddenly a confused old man, looking lost in the oversize chair.

"Hello, Dad. You know . . . you scare me when you're like that." Why had he said that? Never before had he . . .

"Why, why, hello, Will. Guess I didn't see you come in. Just sitting here, thinking too much."

"I heard you've . . . that you've been *sick.*"

The hard gleam returned momentarily, and Will stared as his father once again stiffened in his chair. "My business," he spat.

"Mark is anxious to meet you."

"So you brought the boy, did you?" Again the hard edge.

His father was rising from the chair; Will stepped back involuntarily. He followed the old man with his eyes, wary, unsure of himself. What was he worried about now? This was an old man in front of him. What could he do to Will now?

His father had stopped in front of the bureau and was staring into the shadows by the bed, apparently oblivious to Will's presence. Will could still see the faint gleam in the man's left eye, and it occurred to him that the eye just didn't belong in that body. It was from another man, another time. But still, he couldn't leave the old man alone with Mark, ever.

"Good night, Dad, see you in the morning."

The eye suddenly changed; his father turned and looked at Will as if he had forgotten who he was. Then an unknitting of the brow, a loosening of the stooped shoulders, and "Oh, yes. Good night, son."

Before Will turned to leave he glanced at the easy chair. His mother had done a good job, but he could still make out the traces where the slashed upholstery had been repaired, almost twenty years ago.

The next morning was Sunday, June 15. Father's Day. By the time Will got dressed and arrived downstairs, the entire family was eating breakfast, including his father.

"Will, Will my boy! *Good* to see you! They wanted to wake you up but I told them, I said 'Let the boy be, needs his rest!' You got a *fine* family, son. Real fine."

His father walked briskly over to Will and grasped his hand and arm tightly, then led him to the breakfast table. The old man was obviously in his glory. Will's mother beamed. Both Amy and Mark laughed at his jokes and seemed completely charmed by him.

It never ceased to amaze him, the way his father could pull things together when he needed to. All it seemed to take was a special occasion, the right excuse. Will had seen it all his life, but still found it difficult getting used to.

Will caught his father looking at him out of the corners of his eyes. Sober, the old man almost frightened him.

"Hey, Will. We've been talking about going down to the old park for a picnic today. But we need some food, paper plates, and things. How about if I stay here with Mark and you and the women pick us up after you stock up?"

Will examined his father's face, not sure what he was

looking for. The eyes . . . they looked all right, but how could he be sure? "That's okay, Dad. *You* go. I'll stay here with Mark."

His father pursed his lips wordlessly, then nodded curtly to Will. "Okay, let's get going, folks! Day's half over."

Mark followed his mother and grandmother into the kitchen, leaving Will and his Dad still at the table, watching each other.

"Will?"

"Yes?"

"You know we haven't always gotten along so well . . ."

"That happens sometimes."

"I know, I know. I just want you to understand that I know I made a few mistakes, let my . . . emotions get the better of me."

Will sat rigidly in his chair, unable to reply. He hoped his old man would talk about the attacks, the anger, even the animal eyes, but at the same time prayed he wouldn't, afraid he might cry out if his father revealed anything, maybe even scream. He couldn't believe his father was talking about this, and so calmly.

"Guess it's a family thing, Will. My father was the same way with me, and I've heard that was the way it was with my grandfather as well. A bit too much *spirit*, you know? So much . . . energy, I guess, that sometimes we're not even sure quite what we're doing." He paused, and for the first time Will noticed some nervousness. "How are things between you and your boy?"

"Fine." Will looked at his hands, the low burn beginning behind his eyes making it difficult to see; the hands appeared raw, swollen to his blurred vision. Then he felt a sudden shiver, as if something metal had slipped under his skin, and up into his spine. "I have . . . a *fine* relationship with Mark."

"Glad-to-hear-it. Glad-to-hear-it." His father spoke rapidly, finishing his coffee and rising from the table. "Now let's see if the women are ready!"

*   *   *

From the living room window Will watched his parents' sky blue station wagon pull slowly into the highway off their long gravel drive. He watched his father's head move about; he was obviously enjoying himself, being "entertaining." Mark was playing with some of Will's old trucks and cars on the front lawn.

Daddy . . .

"Better not break them, son. Don't mess up my things," he whispered.

Will walked around the kitchen, opening cupboards, sliding out drawers. The pain was moving out from his eyes, into the back of his head.

Daddy, please . . .

"You shouldn't touch so many things, Mark. You've got to learn to behave," he whispered.

He leaned a moment against the counter, feeling his forehead, wondering if it were beginning to expand.

I'll find you!

"I just want to help you, Mark. That's why I discipline you over these things," he whispered.

He looked at his reflection in the shiny kitchen table top. His eyes appeared to be receding away from him, becoming shadowy, darker, more distant.

I said come out!

"You have to learn to obey adults, Mark. You need to do what they want," he whispered.

His arms began to burn, the hair on his body tingling as if electrically charged. He walked to the kitchen window and pushed it open with an angry thrust.

"Mark! Come in here right now! I want to talk to you!" He shouted out the window.

He clutched his head and fell against the sink. He examined his arms: massive, hairy, the hands seeming larger than normal, his fingers burning, his muscles appearing to blur, seeking new positions along the bone of his arms. *I'll kill you, boy . . .*

"Mark!" he shouted at the ceiling.

Daddy . . .

He recognized his hands and arms. They were his father's. He was his father's son.

Daddy, please . . .

"Mark! Now!" He shouted at the top of his lungs.

Daddy, please . . .

He reached into the drawer by the sink and pulled out the heavy knife. He hefted it in his father's hands, noting the delicate balance. It felt good. It felt natural. He was thinking about how wonderful it was to be home again when Mark came breathlessly in.

"Daddy?"

Daddy, please . . .

"Daddy!"

"Daddy!"

Even Whispers *gets a story or two quite unlike anything it has published. And that is just about all I can say about the following. Its author, Alan Ryan, is best known for his novels* Panther!, The Kill, Dead White, *and* Cast a Cold Eye, *and his critically acclaimed anthology,* Perpetual Light.

THE EAST BEAVERTON MONSTER

Alan Ryan

Do not be deceived by the innocent and rural-sounding name of the community of East Beaverton. For one thing, there were not, never had been, and certainly never were going to be, any West, North, or South Beavertons. East Beaverton stood quite alone and quite grand by the clear, if slow-moving, waters of the languid Beaver River, nestled snugly in a remote fold of these green and luxuriant hills. For another thing, East Beaverton was a very comfortable little community, filled with very comfortable people, all of them happy and secure—some of them even a little smug—at the worldly success that had bought them a place within East Beaverton's soothing embrace.

The rest of the world, when it had occasion to refer at all to East Beaverton—which was not often, as only the proper sort of person in the world at large had even heard of the village—would have referred to it as a "bedroom community.'' This term was not in favor in East Beaverton itself, which, in the rare situations where it even had to trouble itself with such vexing matters of self-appellation, would more properly have described itself as a ''sitting-room community.''

Certainly it is true that the bedrooms of East Beaverton played a significant part in its social life—albeit only in its *clandestine* social life and only when a successful man-of-the-house-in-question was called away to another part of the country or compelled to remain in the city by the press of his successful and lucrative business enterprises—but such matters were never brought up in polite conversation. No, East Beaverton was a sitting-room community, most definitely, and only things that happened in the broad light of day were suitable topics for afternoon chitchat over tea between the ladies of the village. Unless, of course, the ladies happened to be the closest of friends and each felt safe taking the other into her confidence, and only then if the scandal involved a lady—or, on rare occasions, a man—who had incurred the disfavor of both parties to the conversation.

East Beaverton was, all in all, a place of comfort and security, filled with quiet, tidy streets, lovely old homes, all of them handsomely maintained, tasteful shops, and well-groomed ladies. The only thing noticeably missing was a male population, for the gentlemen of East Beaverton were all carried off to the city early each morning by the railroad (which had never been permitted to lay its tracks through East Beaverton itself, thereby necessitating an even earlier drive to the next village over) and returned—most of them—in the middle hours of the evening, wan from their taxing labors in the city but relaxed unto drowsiness by the alcoholic refreshment they had taken on board the train. On the weekends, most of these industrious gentlemen—those who could be spared from their desks for two consecutive days of the week—preferred to spend most of their time sleeping or taking further alcoholic refreshment, either at the club or before their handsome fireplaces (seldom soiled by an actual fire which, of course, would have involved such uncongenial things as wood and various implements and ashes) or, in fine weather, by the sides of their in-ground swimming pools.

The ladies of East Beaverton, every last one of them, were bored.

Indeed, they were excruciatingly bored, so that filling the time of their very comfortable lives presented an ever more wearisome challenge. Preparations for an afternoon hour of window shopping on East Beaverton's main street required two hours of careful makeup and rejection of a variety of outfits before a suitable one could be settled on, and a Charity Society luncheon required a minimum of four hours of preparation at the least.

In consequence of this terrible, crushing boredom, a number of the ladies of East Beaverton had been known, on occasion, to take a lover. This was universally thought to be a wonderfully rejuvenating experience, as invigorating to the heart and the spirit as it was marvelous for the skin.

Alas, lovers were not easily come by in East Beaverton. Shopkeepers and tradesmen, of course, were out of the question. Gardeners would have been valued highly, were it not for the lamentable fact that nowadays, it seemed, they were all oriental, which quite naturally left them out of the picture. And traveling salesmen, it need hardly be noted, were not encouraged to travel through a village the likes of East Beaverton. The occasional telephone repairman, however, so very male and exciting with his rolled sleeves and all his mysterious equipment dangling from his belt, was called into service out of desperation, but this was not a path, delicious though it was, that could be relied upon for either safety or continuity.

Yes, the ladies of East Beaverton, every last one of them, were bored.

It is not surprising, therefore, that news of the arrival in the vicinity of Dr. Armand Lavalette, and the further news of the imminent opening of a Ladies Clinic under his direction on the grounds of a small private school (closed a year earlier after a mysterious but fascinating scandal in-

volving the headmistress and four of her tender charges)
was greeted with breathless excitement by the ladies of
East Beaverton.

"Well, Beatrice, what do you think of it all?" asked
Mrs. Candace Burgess Forbes one afternoon as she and her
closest friend sat in her sitting room drinking tea.

It was only a month since the much talked about opening of Dr. Lavalette's clinic, but none of the ladies of East
Beaverton had so far availed themselves of the clinic's
services. They had adopted, by mutual consent, a wait-and-
see attitude. The clinic, it had been learned through reli-
able channels, specialized in caring for the unique problems
of ladies who, for their health, wished to reduce, as necessary, their weight. This was never actually formulated in
so many words, however, and the clinic was referred to
most commonly as a "health spa." And none of the ladies
of East Beaverton had as yet wished to confess publicly
that she thought herself to have that particular sort of
health problem.

Mrs. Beatrice Shaw Alexander replaced her teacup on
the table and directed her casual gaze out the window to
where Candace's oriental gardener was bending over an
edging of *floribunda* marigolds.

"Oh, do you mean Dr. Lavalette and his clinic?" she
said, as if it had only just now occurred to her what
Candace might have meant.

"Yes. What do you think of it all?"

Beatrice allowed that, well, she certainly thought it was
all very interesting, so long, of course, as it did not attract,
you know, the wrong sorts of persons, who might take a
notion to begin patronizing the shops of East Beaverton
and perhaps even aspire, assuming, of course, that they
were able, to purchase property in the village.

Candace agreed heartily on all of these points, but continued to press Beatrice for a more personal statement of
her feelings with regard to Dr. Armand Lavalette and his
Ladies Clinic.

After some mild prevaricating and avoiding of her friend's

eyes, Beatrice observed that she thought it just a trifle queer that the doctor had so far chosen not to show himself at all in the village itself.

"Yes, I'd noticed that myself," said Candace, a tiny smile threatening to reveal itself at the corners of her mouth.

"Yes," said Beatrice, and they considered the matter for a moment in silence.

Then Beatrice said, still avoiding Candace's eyes, "Don't you think his behavior just the slightest bit . . . well, just the tiniest bit . . . sinister?"

"Yes!" said Candace, and the smile bloomed as brightly as the flowers that edged the lawn.

"Candace!"

"I do!" said Candace. "I think it's terribly sinister of him, and terribly clever. Don't you see it?"

Beatrice did not, but her eyes were all eagerness and light.

Candace advanced the theory that the clever Dr. Lavalette had very deliberately held himself aloof from the social circles of East Beaverton so as to arouse curiosity about both his clinic and himself in the minds of the ladies of the village, to wit, themselves.

Beatrice thought it over. "Yes," she said after a moment. "Yes, you know, Candace, I think you're right. I must confess to being curious myself."

"Of course you are," said Candace. "So am I. And so are we all. Dr. Lavalette has planned his campaign well and has fully succeeded in piquing our interest." She fixed her eyes meaningfully on her friend's face and added, "I admire that in a man."

Five minutes later, it was all settled between them. They would take the daring step of being first among the ladies of East Beaverton to meet the mysterious Dr. Lavalette, to see the inside of his clinic, and to avail themselves of his treatment. The social value to be gained among their friends by their exclusive firsthand knowledge would more than eradicate any stigma attached to their assumed admission of a "health" problem.

* * *

They were going to be just on time for their scheduled noon arrival at the clinic on the following Monday. The instructions, given by an extremely pleasant male voice when Candace had made the fateful telephone call, had been clear and precise, and the ladies had followed them to the letter. They had one suitcase each, packed only with very light clothing to last them until four o'clock on Friday, when they would be leaving the clinic. "It's really only so you'll have something of your own with you," the very pleasant male voice had said. "We'll provide everything you'll need during your stay."

Both of their hard-working husbands, when informed of their wives' protracted stay away from home and hearth, had elected, with only perfunctory grumbling, to remain in the city for the week.

The clinic, when the ladies reached it, provided a most pleasing prospect. At the end of the long, curving, oak-edged driveway, a smooth expanse of neat green lawn stretched out in welcome. On either side of the main building's imposing entrance, a heart-shaped bed of flowers shimmered colorfully in the sun-warmed breeze. And the building itself was all that one could hope for: three stories tall, built solidly of local stone, with a handsome slate roof and gleaming, white-shuttered windows. Just beyond a hedge that extended out from one corner, the ladies caught a glimpse of brightly striped lawn umbrellas and a peal of merry feminine laughter, followed by a resounding splash of water that could only mean a pool, followed instantly by an even more merry peal of definitely masculine laughter.

"Oh my, yes," sighed Candace, her eyes wide with eagerness and delight, "this is going to be just lovely."

"Yes," agreed Beatrice softly, her voice holding just a bit on the sibilant as she stared hard in the direction of the male laughter.

A moment later, the front doors of the clinic were being pulled open for them by a quite attractive and muscular young man, whose pale blue T-shirt and white slacks displayed his physique to very good advantage, and whose smile rivaled the brilliance of the sun.

"Mrs. Forbes!" he cried, "Mrs. Alexander!" His eyes fixed on those of one lady, then the other, "Welcome to Dr. Lavalette's clinic! Please come right in! I'll have someone fetch your bags!"

Their heads whirling and their hearts pounding with the warmth of their welcome, the ladies, only a moment later, found themselves seated in a very nicely appointed office, its walls properly paneled and its floor comfortably carpeted.

"Are . . .? Are you Dr. Lavalette?" Beatrice managed to say.

"Oh no," the young man replied, his smile gentle. "Dr. Lavalette will be consulting with you in the morning, just before administering his treatment. Now, ladies, if you'd be kind enough to sign these forms"—he slid two sets of papers, already prepared, across the shining surface of the desk—"we can get the ball rolling for you at once. The, ah, last form you have there requests that we take care of all business matters right now." He had an absolutely lovely smile.

The last form in each set requested payment at once, and even these ladies of East Beaverton were startled by the cost of their four days' stay at the clinic and Dr. Lavalette's treatment. However, their surprise was considerably allayed by an unequivocal statement, at the bottom of that last form in the set, that Dr. Lavalette absolutely and unconditionally guaranteed that each of his patients— and the form, it must be stated, did not mince words here—would lose enough weight during her stay to bring her down to the medically approved body weight for her height, bone structure, and general physical condition. A further sentence made mention of "follow-up attention and supervision" at corresponding rates.

How discreet the doctor and his clinic were, with never a word spoken aloud. The ladies signed, fished multicolored checkbooks from their purses, scribbled as necessary, and silently added their checks to the sets of papers before them.

The smiling young man whisked the papers and the checks away into a drawer without so much as a glance. Then he leaned forward, positively beaming.

"May I call you Candace and Beatrice?" he asked.

"Of course!" the ladies replied in unison.

"Wonderful!" the young man said. "Call me Bob!"

"Bob!" they said together, as if no more apt name had ever been conferred on a handsome young man.

"I'll be working very closely with you during your stay," he said. "In fact, I'll be personally responsible for seeing to it that you enjoy your stay and that everything goes smoothly for you. And later, of course, I'll be in charge of your follow-up attention."

This all sounded very promising indeed, and the ladies beamed right back at his bright eyes, his dazzling white teeth, and the rippling muscles of his shoulders beneath the pale blue T-shirt.

"Won't you come with me and I'll show you where you'll be staying. I want to be certain everything is to your taste."

They followed him.

Bob led them through a long, silent corridor and out a side door of the building, where their path just happened to follow a walkway alongside a hedge that came exactly to shoulder height and on the other side of which they could see the people at the pool. While they themselves were concealed from sight by the hedge, they had an unobstructed view of a dozen or so extraordinarily attractive women frolicking in the blue waters of the pool and sunning themselves at its edge. Candace and Beatrice slowed their pace for a better look.

The women at the pool were all of about the same age as Candace and Beatrice, but oh, such marvelous bodies they displayed in such wonderfully revealing bathing suits of the very latest and skimpiest fashion! Each of them just glowed with brimming good health, gleaming taut skin, a glistening flat tummy, firm round buttocks, shapely thighs and ankles, a smooth slender neck, and jutting full breasts that yet took every advantage of what had been called in the two ladies' younger days "youthful separation." And there alongside them, smiling in open admiration, were half-a-dozen young men, each at least as attractive as their own Bob.

"These ladies have already had Dr. Lavalette's treatment," Bob told them casually over his shoulder. "Some of them had it only just this morning."

"This morning?" the ladies gasped together.

"That's right," said Bob. "You can join them any time you like, today or after your own treatment tomorrow. Well, here we are!"

In their wonder at the sight they'd seen, Candace and Beatrice had been lost in contemplation of their own images as viewed in their dressing mirrors at home, and of another, more Platonic, image, that seemed always to shimmer just beyond the edge of vision. Startled by Bob's exclamation, they now found themselves standing before a very pretty little cottage, set in a very private little arbor at the edge of the woods.

"You'll be staying here," Bob told them. "Let me show you around."

The inside of the cottage was as prettily designed as the outside, with a cozy living room and a bedroom for each of the ladies. But it was not the floral-patterned chairs and curtains that stopped the ladies in their tracks.

"Oh yes," said Bob, smiling, as if he'd only remembered upon actually seeing the sight. "We've laid in a few things for your refreshment. We want you to enjoy your stay before the treatment as much as after it."

The ladies stared.

On every flat surface in the living room were bowls and platters, all heaped with the loveliest of goodies: onion-and-garlic potato chips, nacho dip, cheese and peanut butter sandwich crackers, canapés of dizzying variety in color and design, Mars bars, M & M's, jelly beans, jujubes, marzipan in the shape of little fruits, strawberries covered with rich dark chocolate, Fig Newtons, Mallomars, salted peanuts, cashews, Brazil nuts, Almond Joys, Hostess cupcakes, Linzer tarts, and on and on, everywhere they looked.

And there was more in the kitchen: ice cream in a dozen flavors; chocolate and marshmallow and strawberry syrup; six kinds of sherbet, including boysenberry; pecan pie, Boston cream pie, and genuine Tennessee chess pie; carrot cake and cherry-topped cheesecake and brandy-soaked fruit cake; plum pudding, bread pudding, and rice pudding; flaky Napoleons; buttery croissants; and golden apricot tarts; and more and more and more.

The ladies were speechless.

Bob was smiling, even more broadly than before.

"I know just what you're thinking," he said softly. "But let me assure you, this is here for your pleasure and you can help yourselves as you wish. Tomorrow, after Dr. Lavalette's treatment, you won't have to give it a moment's thought." He glanced around at the myriad bowls and platters. "In fact," he said, "I wouldn't be at all surprised if you chose to spend the rest of the day here, then get a good night's sleep, which of course Dr. Lavalette recommends, and then tomorrow, after your treatment, you can join the other ladies at the pool."

Candace and Beatrice, without consulting each other by so much as a glance, nodded their heads in unison.

"Wonderful!" said Bob, his smile confirming the wisdom of their decision. "I'll leave you to yourselves, then. Have a lovely evening!"

He backed out the door and shut it with a gentle click.

The ladies, still breathless at the prospect of the wonderful new world opening up before them, and at the wonderful world spread out for their pleasure this evening, glanced briefly at each other, caught their breath sharply, then went at it with a will.

Bob, smiling, still in white slacks but with a lemon yellow T-shirt this time, fetched them at nine-thirty the next morning just as they were easing off from a breakfast of croissants and steaming hot chocolate.

Talking soothingly to them all the way, obviously eager to set at rest any fears they might have regarding the treatment they were about to undergo, he led them from the cottage—their route this time did not pass near the pool, but they could hear laughter and splashing even so—to a door at the back of the building. Inside, he escorted them into an elevator that carried them to the third floor, where they were greeted by an antiseptic white corridor and glaring lights.

Bob ushered them into a small bare room that contained only an examining table and two red plastic chairs. Two neatly folded white hospital smocks and two baskets with nameplates bearing their names were on the table.

From a shelf near the door, Bob produced two little paper cups, each containing a tiny white pill, and two plastic cups of water with fresh ice cubes chilling it nicely.

"If you'll just take these," he said, handing the cups to the ladies, "it will steady your nerves a bit. Dr. Lavalette will be in shortly to see you, and then you'll have your treatment, and then you can have a lovely, relaxing afternoon by the pool. The weather promises to be perfect."

A little less sure of themselves now, they took the pills, drank a bit of the water, and returned the cups to Bob.

"There now," he said. "Don't you worry about a thing."

His smile alone helped set their minds at ease.

"Does the treatment . . . ?" Candace began. "I mean, do we both . . .?"

"Oh yes," said Bob. "Both of you together. We think it's nicer that way."

Left alone, the ladies changed into the hospital smocks, folded their clothing into the baskets, and waited.

Later, when they compared notes on the next hour or so, neither of them had a perfectly clear memory of the doctor coming to see them before the treatment. They agreed that he was tall, that he was wearing a dark blue suit, that he had a wonderful smile and a remarkably calming voice and manner. Afterward, they agreed, they had fuzzy recollections of what must have been an operating room and of the figure of the doctor wearing hospital greens. They remembered nothing else.

*   *   *

Candace awoke in her bed at the cottage.

The first thing she noticed was that she was still wearing the hospital smock. She sat up straight in the bed, quite startled and alarmed for the first time, now that the mysterious deed had actually been done. She certainly felt no different.

Then an attractive young woman whom Candace only vaguely recognized appeared suddenly in the doorway of the room crying, "Candace! Candace! Look! Oh, Candace, you're beautiful! You're as beautiful as I am!"

Candace jumped from the bed. Could this be Beatrice? She looked in the full-length mirror on the wall, one corner of her mind trying to recall if it had been there that morning. Could this be herself she was looking at? Could it? Could it?

The transformation was nothing less than miraculous. The two women admired themselves and each other endlessly, laughing, crying, exclaiming again and again. They were still themselves, but so different: graceful, slender, taut, long-necked and flat-tummied, and, oh the youthful separation!

When they examined themselves more closely, each found that they had the slightest—but very neat and barely noticeable—scars along strategically located parts of their bodies, almost as if tiny incisions had been made and the excess fat—they were even able, in their pleasure at being relieved of the burden, to speak the word out loud—removed neatly from their bodies. And even in the time they spent examining themselves and each other, they could have positively sworn that the scars were already beginning to fade.

A little while later, they were not the least bit surprised when each of them found on top of the dresser in her room a selection of the daintiest, scantiest bathing suits they had ever seen, and all of them in the most flattering colors imaginable.

Time passed. A month's time.

When Candace and Beatrice had reappeared in the shops

and the sitting rooms of East Beaverton, all of their friends had been suitably impressed. Others of the village's ladies had since availed themselves of the services of Dr. Lavalette, and with equally satisfying results. But Candace and Beatrice had been the first, and that knowledge was a great source of contentment to them.

Now, four weeks to the day since their departure from the clinic, they were due to return for "follow-up attention" on Monday next. After sharing such a personal and intimate experience, the two ladies had grown even closer than before, and now shared their most private views and feelings with each other. Only the day before, Beatrice had confided that since leaving the clinic, she had regained four pounds of the weight she had lost there. Candace confessed to regaining three pounds.

On this Friday afternoon, they were stretched out on lounge chairs on Candace's sundeck. Beatrice's bikini was of lime green, Candace's of imported white fishnet. They both had picture-perfect tans. The oriental gardener was puttering around somewhere and, they were both quite certain, stealing furtive glances at them through the azalea bushes.

They were both very, very content. The only difficulty either of them had experienced for weeks and weeks was trouble with the telephone service, but the nice repairman had come by and solved Candace's problem the previous afternoon, and he had done the same for Beatrice only that morning. Nothing could trouble them now.

"I wonder what the follow-up attention consists of," Beatrice said languidly.

"I've been wondering that myself," Candace replied. She slid a hand across the smoothness of her tummy. "I really can't imagine. After all, it's not as if we needed the same treatment all over again. I mean, we've only gained seven pounds between us." The ladies spoke quite frankly to each other these days.

Candace casually slid a hand across the silky skin of her side. There was not a trace of the tiny scar.

"I don't have a single mark, either," Beatrice said meaningfully.

The two women looked at each other.

"You know," Candace said after a thoughtful silence, "I really don't believe either of us needs to go this month. I mean, seven little pounds between the two of us isn't a lot."

"And the price is so very high," stated Beatrice.

"Very," Candace agreed. "And, besides, I should imagine the clinic would be very crowded now."

"I'd imagine so," Beatrice said. "Well, you know, monkey see, monkey do."

"Yes," said Candace.

Neither of the ladies had any great desire to tarnish the aura of their being first at Dr. Lavalette's clinic by demonstrating, before all of East Beaverton, a need to return.

"Yes," Beatrice echoed quietly.

They gave themselves up to the warming rays of the sun, the admiring gaze of the oriental gardener hiding in the azaleas, and the happy knowledge that their telephones were in perfect working order.

More time passed. Exactly one week more.

"Hello?"

"Candace! Hello! This is Bob!"

"Oh. Bob."

"From the clinic! Dr. Lavalette's clinic!"

"Yes."

"We missed you!"

"Yes. Well."

"Is everything all right with you? Are you well?"

"Oh. Just fine. Everything is fine."

"Wonderful! We were so concerned when we didn't see you and Beatrice on Monday. Dr. Lavalette specifically asked me to call and make certain you were both all right."

"We're fine. I mean, I'm fine."

"Yes, I just spoke to Beatrice. She said you'd explain about not coming by on Monday."

"Oh. Well. Yes, well, you see, we've both been tied up. Just very busy. Really, very busy. Charity lunches all week, of course. Fund-raising."

"Of course! I knew there had to be a good reason! And Dr. Lavalette said that himself! He was quite certain you had some good reason for not coming when you were expected!"

"Yes."

"Well, we'll be seeing you on Monday, then, Candace! Both of you! You and Beatrice!"

"Oh."

"Candace, Dr. Lavalette wanted me to mention how very important it is for your health to maintain a steady weight. Our follow-up attention just can't be stressed enough. It's extremely important and, of course, it's part of our total plan. Which makes it part of *your* plan, too, Candace. Yours and Beatrice's."

"Yes. Well."

"So we'll count on seeing you on Monday, then! Both of you! I've already reserved your own cottage for you!"

"Well. I'll have to let you know. I'll have to check with Beatrice. Check my plans. I'll let you know."

And she hung up the phone.

"The nerve!" cried Candace moments later when she called Beatrice. "The gall! Assuming, in the first place, that we *need* more treatments!"

"I know!" cried Beatrice, the outrage clear in her voice. "Oh, Candace, I'm sorry I couldn't reach you to warn you about his call, but he beat me to it. I was so taken aback, I hardly knew what to be saying."

"Well, I knew," Candace told her friend. "I told him we'd let him know when we're ready. When we have the time. *If* we have the time, that is."

"Right!"

"And *if* we need Dr. Lavalette's treatment again."

"Candace, you're so good at this sort of thing. I knew you'd know what to say."

"What I really resent is the bold-faced assumption that we'd *need* follow-up attention."

"That's what I resent too."

"After all," Candace said, "eight or nine pounds between us is hardly anything at all. Especially when you consider how much we lost before!" It was such a relief to be able to speak frankly with a close friend.

"That's right. Eight or nine pounds is hardly anything at all."

"That's right."

"And think of the saving," Beatrice added.

"That's right," Candace said with even greater conviction.

They continued in this vein for a while longer.

One more week passed.

"Candace, this is Bob."

"Oh."

"Candace, we were very disappointed, Dr. Lavalette and I, not to see you and Beatrice this week for your follow-up attention. I can't tell you how distressed we are."

"Oh," said Candace, which was the best she could do on the spur of the moment. Indeed, she and Beatrice had been distressed themselves when they had compared readings, only just that morning, from their bathroom scales. Their combined gain in weight over the past two weeks—and the ladies were rather inclined to blame it on nervousness caused by the hounding they felt they were receiving from Dr. Lavalette and the staff of his clinic—was eight pounds, more than they had jointly gained during the first month after their treatment, for a grand total, between them, of fifteen pounds. The extra odd pound undeniably belonged to Candace and tended to make her a trifle short-tempered.

"Candace?"

"Yes?"

"May Dr. Lavalette and I look forward to seeing you and Beatrice on Monday?"

"Well," said Candace, drawing out the word. She was the kind of person who liked to keep her options open, but she also did not like being pushed.

"Have you spoken to Beatrice yet?" she asked.

"No, not yet."

"Well, then, I'll just have to let you know. That is, *we'll* have to let you know. It just happens that both Beatrice and I have extraordinarily busy schedules just now. We always do at this time of year. For one thing, I know the telephone repairman is coming on Monday. Between nine and six. They're so unreliable, you know, they can never give you an exact time."

"Candace," said Bob, and she could hardly fail to notice the new, vaguely sinister tone in his voice. "I want to stress to you how very essential it is that you continue your treatments, you and Beatrice together. There's no telling what the consequences might be for both of you if you fail to keep them up. I'm certain you'll want to avoid any unfortunate consequences, especially now when you've made such good initial progress. It would be criminal if the weight you've lost were to come creeping back to haunt you after you've made such a good start. That's what would happen, you know. In fact, it may be happening already. That's why Dr. Lavalette wants to impress upon you the need to continue. Without his treatments, you're sure to have to face—"

"We'll be in touch," said Candace and, none too gently, hung up the phone. The fact that the weight Bob referred to was indeed already creeping back on both of them—and more quickly, in fact, on herself—did nothing at all to improve her mood.

On the following Monday afternoon, the ladies were in their accustomed places on Candace's sundeck.

The telephone had rung once that morning and Candace had been a little wary of answering it, fearing it might be Bob reminding them to be on time at the clinic. But it had only been the telephone repairman, inquiring if he could come by to check her line. Candace had put him off till another day.

Their world was gentle and quiet, the warm air cooled by a breeze, their bodies, if somewhat fuller than they'd been six weeks before, beautifully tanned, and the oriental gardener, they both assumed, still lurking in the azalea bushes, which, though bereft now of their dazzling red blossoms, yet provided adequate cover. But they were, both of them, in a foul mood and not much inclined to talk.

"Do you want another drink?" Candace asked.

"No," Beatrice replied. "Thanks. I'm watching my—" She caught herself just in time.

The ladies glanced at each other, then looked quickly away and sank back into moody silence.

A little time passed, the stillness of the afternoon broken only by the rustling of branches in the azalea bushes as the oriental gardener shifted his position for a better view of their still quite attractive bodies.

Candace turned over restlessly to sun her back for a little while.

After a minute, Beatrice did the same.

Candace turned over to lie on her back again.

Beatrice looked across at her friend. "Can't get comfortable?" She turned over too.

"No!"

The rustling in the azalea bushes became quite pronounced, as if the gardener was quite carried away by this ever-changing spectacle of lovely female flesh.

"Oh, for heaven's sake!" cried Candace. She sprang up from the lounge chair.

"What? What?" cried Beatrice. She sprang up too, expecting an intruder.

"That gardener! I'm sick and tired of this!"

"So am I!"

"I'm putting a stop to it this minute!" cried Candace.

Moving as one, they angrily crossed the sundeck in a moment's time. Together, they came to a halt at the end of the row of azalea bushes.

"Come out of there!" Candace exclaimed.

"Yes! Come out!" exclaimed Beatrice.

But it was not the oriental gardener that they saw. It was not the oriental gardener at all.

Instead, they saw a quivering mass of what might have been jelly, its slick, wet surface, all pink and white, rising and falling, expanding and contracting, as if it breathed. The thing had no face or head, and no limbs. It was horribly, horribly *naked,* and looked, except for its shifting, lumpy roundness, the way you'd expect a snake to look if you made a long incision and peeled back its skin. It rolled a little toward them, pulsing with life.

The ladies gasped with one voice and, almost in the same instant, the thing gasped too, in a voice that sounded terribly like their own. It pulsed and pulsed and rolled a little closer still, its wetness glistening in the sun, and then the ladies saw with absolute certainty the thing that their minds had at first denied.

As the horrible fatty ball edged closer and closer to where they stood as if rooted to the deck, its glistening contours shifted ever so subtly and, one moment, it looked a little like Beatrice and, in the next, a little like Candace.

The ladies stood staring at the thing, immobilized by horror, watching its slow expansion and contraction until, from inside the house, came the wonderful, welcome ring of the telephone.

*I believe this was Arizonan Libby Tinker's first profes-
sional sale. It is a brutal piece—not for the weak of
heart or stomach.*

THE HORSE
Libby Tinker

It was a hot day when the colt was born. All around the
corral was flat dusty land. In the distance was a dark
irregular line—misshapen trees straining for the water that
flowed so shallowly on the surface. And sank so deep past
their roots.

The mare knew all this, her dusted muzzle resting on the
hard ground. Her eyes, still glazed with the pain of giving
birth, sought the mark of water. The life she had created
lay by her and she did not care. She closed her eyes; the
blood ran from her, and she died.

The woman stepped from the shack and smiled into the
sun. Her blond hair was unbound and fell to her waist. It
was not clean and did not reflect the light. It lay limply
against her clothing. She smiled at the dirt and pushed at it
with her bare feet as she walked to the one-railed corral
and leaned on it. She stared at the dead mare and the
stained dirt around her. And she stared at the thing that
had been born.

It squirmed, trying to push its feet out of the sac that
still covered part of it. It twisted and bent its scrawny

165

neck. Its head was small and still wet, and it raised its muzzle to breathe the stagnant air.

She stepped into the corral and knelt by its side. It did not know enough to fear or enough to fight. The woman ripped the sac and watched the colt lie panting in the dust, the little body wet and black. She took off her apron and tried to pick the colt up, but she could not hold it. She let it fall into the dirt again and rubbed the side that was up. The hair was matted and dirt-clogged, and the sun was pulling away the wetness.

She rubbed the neck and bony shoulder, the back and hollow side. She rubbed the flank and haunch and one black leg. And screamed.

The colt lay alone in the dirt, his lungs parched with the hot air, his body burning in the hot sun. He could not see, but he could hear, and something had run from him. He moved slowly, gathering his legs to him. He tried to roll onto his knees. His tongue stuck to his mouth. His nostrils were encrusted with bits of mud. His eyes were open, but all they saw was red. He rolled again, and bumped the side of his dam. He sought her belly eagerly but his toothless mouth touched only harsh hair and tasted blood. He sank down in a small huddle and dumbly waited.

In the shack, the woman stood with her back to the closed door and shuddered. Her eyes were closed. Her hands were clenched about the apron. She opened her eyes and stared at it. Its worn-in dirt was covered with spots of mud and blood. She dropped it on the floor and shuddered again. She hugged her elbows as she always did and fingered the rough skin, crooning to herself for comfort. Her eyes slowly closed and opened and she stopped singing. She stooped slowly. She picked up the apron and turned to the door.

The colt flicked an ear as he heard a grating noise. It stopped. The colt lay still, his breathing shallow. His ear flicked forward again as the rustling noise reached him. And now he was aware that something stood by him, knelt by him, and touched his hot body. He tried to move, but there was no strength in him . . . and he listened.

The touch was gone and there were more rustling noises. He breathed a puff of wind that went by his head. Then he felt himself half lifted and tipped over. He struggled a little because he wasn't lying on the ground anymore but on something that clung to his hair. It was placed all around him; a pressure came about his stomach and he struggled again. He moved, but not by his own efforts. His body inched along the ground—he felt the hardness of it, and smelled the dust. He snorted weakly and lay still. He let himself be dragged away from his mother's body and over the hot earth.

She stopped when he was under the corral pole. Her body was wet and her hair hung over her shoulders. She straightened and looked across the yard at the shack. It was not far. Grasping the apron again, she pulled.

At the door, she wiped her forehead and flung her hair back over her shoulders. Opening the door, she propped it with a broken chair leg. She dragged the colt into the shack and kicked away the prop. A bucket sat on a beaten table, a tin cup next to it. She dipped a little water out using the cup. She went to a corner where there were several small sacks. There she hesitated, looking fearfully behind her at the door. Then she kneeled and took a handful of white granules out of one sack. Returning to the table, she placed them in the cup and swished her fingers through the water.

She carried the cup to the colt and knelt. He raised his head a little and she grasped it, sliding herself under him until his head rested on her knees. With coaxing noises she placed two fingers in the water and then forced them past the colt's lips. The colt pushed his tongue against them and tried to shove them away. She dipped her fingers in the water again, and put them back into his mouth. He rolled his gums on them and then licked them. The sweet taste came to his tongue mixed with a bitterness. It was soothing to his throat. She pulled her fingers out and put them into the water. The colt sucked her fingers, and then on a rag soaked in the water. It was the only sound in the shack in the midday sun.

He slept after that, his head pillowed on her lap. She leaned her head against the rough wood wall and slept with him, her hand resting on his neck.

The heat lessened to a faint coolness, but there was no breeze. The sun was throwing shadows from the house, from the corral, and from the dead mare, now bloated and contorted.

She awoke smiling. Her eyes moved to the colt, and she stopped smiling. Her eyes did not look away from the colt as she moved her hand from his neck to her own and rubbed the soreness. She reached out, pulled the cloth away from his body and lifted his front leg gently from the folds. Her eyes held vague fear.

Running her fingers down his leg and along the three toes he had, she touched the tiny clawlike nails. Then soberly she put the leg back against the colt's body and covered him with the apron.

She lifted his head gently and slid herself out. She lowered his head and went to the pail. There was still half a bucket left, and she smiled. She put her cup in the water and scooped up a small bit. Tilting it at her mouth, she drank slowly, carefully. She turned to the corner and pulled out a leather pouch. From this she took a small piece of hard meat. She went back to the colt, chewing on the meat.

The colt awoke several times that night and struggled. She went to him from the cot in a corner of the room, carrying the cup. The colt would suck greedily and then sleep.

The next day she ate the meat and drank the water and fed the colt. She helped him stand on his feet, watching the toes curl and uncurl as he tried to balance. A smile crossed her face when the colt finally stood and then took two steps toward her. He fell again and lay quiet, resting. She ran her hand over his side. His ribs were hard against his coat. She brushed at the mud and laughed to see the dark red he was. Her fingers twined in the little black mane.

She opened the door to the shack and urged him to his

feet again. With an arm around his neck she coaxed him, crooning softly. He followed, hesitating at every wobbly step until he stood in the brightening sun.

His toes moved with more sureness in the dirt, splaying to hold him. He tossed his head up and down.

She let go of him and stood back. The colt swayed, walked forward, and stopped. He whinnied, a high-pitched, squeaky voice, and she laughed. He turned at the sound of her voice. His little ears, beautifully pointed and tipped with black, cocked at her. His straight body moved forward again, the gangly legs almost disjointed. He whinnied again.

He smelled but did not see the mare lying swollen in the corral. The woman saw her but only frowned and turned back to the shack. The colt tried to hurry after her and called to her. She opened the door and let him follow her in. He went to her and sucked on her fingers.

Three days went by. The colt did not thrive nor did he die. The woman fed him, helped him walk until he could run around her. She moved carefully when he slept, feeding herself.

The fourth day she watched the line of trees. She hugged the colt when he came to her, and she fed him, but always she returned to watching the trees. The colt played, aiming kicks at her skirts, but she would not respond. In the afternoon she sat by the wall facing the trees. The colt, just fed, came to her and nuzzled her hair. She smiled and pulled his ear. He collapsed beside her and moved himself comfortably to sleep.

She crooned to him again. She took his foot into her hand and looked at the toes. Her crooning stopped and the fear came into her eyes again. She looked quickly at the trees.

The sun was disappearing behind the trees when he came. She started at the movement and shaded her eyes from the glare of the sun. She watched until she recognized the horse's walk. She watched until she saw the man on his back.

Then she leaped up and prodded the colt into wakefulness.

He bounded to his feet as he caught her fear. She tried to herd him toward the door but he raced around wildly, shying at her flailing arms. She half screamed at him, but he would not heed.

She looked back over her shoulder. He was closer and coming still. She stood with hands clenched, making soft noises in her throat. The colt stopped whirling around her and quivered. His eyes were white-rimmed and his nostrils flared red. His thin body heaved with his quick pants.

She moved to the door, opening it cautiously. The colt watched her. She went in. He nickered anxiously and then ran in after her. She closed the door.

She tried to push the colt to the floor and cover him with the apron he slept on, but he would not lie down. She struggled with him. He panicked and fought against her hands.

The door crashed against the wall. He stood slouched in the doorway, the gloom outlining him. She looked at him with terror in her eyes. The colt was facing him, his lips wrinkled back.

She stepped in front of the colt and tried to speak. Only half-formed sounds came out.

"Whatcha hidin'!" He moved forward, swinging his arm and hitting her. She fell away and the colt cowered back.

"My mare's foal's come! Whatcha hidin' it fer?"

He moved farther into the room, sizing the colt. His eyes narrowed. "What's the matter with it? It ain't right! It's a damned freak!" He whirled on her. "Why'd you let it live? You shoulda killed it quick. Now I got to."

She ran to the colt, trying to gather it to her. Her voice, half croon, half scream came into the stillness. The colt fought against her.

The man shoved her aside. She hit the table with her hip and plopped onto the dirt floor. He drew a knife from his belt and grabbed the colt's mane.

The colt leaped and twisted, lashing out against the painful hold. His breath came fast and his body hit the wall.

The woman flung herself at the man, grasping the hand holding the knife. He lifted her from the floor and shook her off.

"Get away, woman! I don't want no freaks on this place. Get away, I said!"

He lifted the colt and stabbed the knife into its throat. Blood spurted out and sprayed the woman. The colt struggled a moment longer, kicked feebly, and hung its head.

The man dropped it and shoved it with his toe. "I oughta burn it."

The woman crawled to the colt and lifted its head. She gave a cry and gathered what she could onto her lap. She grasped the apron from the floor and covered the colt.

"I oughta burn it," he said.

RETURN OF THE DUST
VAMPIRES

Sharon N. Farber

The man and woman ran across the burning sands, their
faces surprisingly blank and unconcerned considering that
they were being pursued by shambling, dust-colored
monsters.

"I can't go on," the blonde cried.

Dr. Insomnia, leaning on the doorjamb, suggested,
"Leave her." But the tall man paid no attention. He
picked up the woman and stumbled onward, the creatures
coming closer . . .

"Turkey," Dr. Todd remarked. "I'd've left her."

Dr. Insomnia looked in the newspaper. " 'Channel 16:
Desert Vampires, 1955,' " she read. " 'One star'—I'd say
they were being charitable."

"The actor there. Room 418."

She peered at the running man framed in long shot
heading toward electric towers. "My guinea pig?" She
left the call room and went to the nurses' station, skimmed
418's chart, then knocked on his door and entered without
waiting. The patient lay in the patchy light from the neigh-

boring research building. Dr. Insomnia woke him gently and introduced herself.

"Dr. Todd is watching one of your films."

"I'd heard interns suffered," he answered softly.

"Why should the patients be the only ones? We're going to switch your shots tonight—no more morphine. You'll get intravenous enkephalins for the pain."

"Enkeph . . . Do they work?"

"They're the body's own natural painkiller. But as one of my profs used to say, 'If enkephalins were any good, you could buy them on Delmar Street.' If you have any discomfort, make sure you tell me before we begin treatment tomorrow." She twirled her stethoscope. The man sighed and obligingly pulled himself into a seated position and unlaced his gown.

She compared the strong young figure on the TV to the frail dying man on the bed, thinking that neither could be the true him. The man had wasted away until he was sallow skin delineating bones. Despite his height, a single nurse could lift him. His body was consuming itself, cannibalizing the muscles. His cheeks and temples were hollowed, and even the essential fat in the eye sockets was going, making the dark eyes recede into the skull.

"Breathe, Mr. Dutcher."

"Call me Rich."

Dr. Insomnia removed the earpieces and stared into the shadowed eyes. "Rich Dutcher—wait. 'Time Seekers'?"

The man nodded.

"Well, all right! You were Commander Stone. I had a crush on you that was unbelievable." She smiled with one side of her mouth. "It's taken twenty years, but I've finally got Commander Stone naked and in my clutches."

He said weakly, "Cue up diabolical laughter and fade to cut."

I enter my office and Jason is in the comfortable chair, light glinting from his wedding band. Hugging him, I don't let go while he empties a bag of take-out food. Tousling his hair while he steals all the

water chestnuts and I say, "It's nice of you to visit.
It can't be very convenient, since you're dead," and
he says, "Did you return my library books?"

Dr. Insomnia poured a cup of departmental coffee, then
went to her own cubbyhole where she looked about the
stacked journals, offprints, and half-full mugs, expecting
to see Chinese food packets. *The dream's afterglow,* she
thought. Slowly she drifted into full wakefulness, to alter-
nate this state with one of zombielike exhaustion for six-
teen more hours until her daily three or four hours of
sleep.

She ripped yesterday from the desk calendar, half smiling as she remembered the luncheon date with Sean. *Only
lunchtime affairs for the weary.* The phone rang.

"I'll be right there," she told the project technician,
pouring another mug of coffee. A cartoon on the office
wall showed Dr. Insomnia holding an IV bottle and line in
one hand, a Foley catheter and bag in the other, labeled
respectively "Caffeine In" and "Caffeine Out."

She read the morning paper as the patients were brought
in and interfaced, patient and doctor linked by the machine. At eleven Dutcher was wheeled in—a skeleton,
swimming inside an expensive robe.

"You understand what we're doing?"

He nodded. "Grasping at straws."

"You're candid."

"I read the informed-consent information, though I didn't
really understand most of it. 'Somatic self-image'—you
intend to convince me that I'm healthy?" He laughed
weakly. "That'll take some convincing."

"The imager reads off a template—in this case, me—
and sets up resonant signals in your body. It's related to
the placebo effect and to 'faith-healing.'" The technician
began applying the patient's monitoring and invasive electrodes. Dr. Insomnia waved with her unwired hand and
continued. "I haven't eaten in twenty-four hours. We'll
begin by convincing your body that it also is hungry and
can handle food. We can't step up your immune response

and start fighting those metastases until you're in positive
nutritional balance.''

He shrugged. ''It all sounds like the doubletalk in 'Time
Seekers' or those fifties sci-fi flicks—*The Jellyfish from
Hell.*''

''Hey, I saw that,'' the technician said, threading
Dutcher's IV line into the imaging machine. He handed
Dr. Insomnia her headphones, then stepped toward the
patient, holding another pair.

Dr. Insomnia winked. ''Close your eyes, lie still—and
think of the British Empire.''

She watched as Dutcher relaxed under the tranquilizer
injection, the tensed muscles that clothed his skeleton
gradually losing their harsh definition. The electroencepha-
lograph showed increasing low-voltage slow waves. The
pulsing blue light of his heart monitor slowed toward the
steady rhythm of Dr. Insomnia's monitor.

The doctor gazed at an article and found the print slightly
blurred. She closed the journal. Familiarity made dissec-
tion of the sensations difficult. There was the taste of
metal, the itch of electrodes, the tingling of fingers and
toes, the warm skin flush of blood dissipating heat ac-
quired in passage through the analyzer. Dr. Insomnia felt
as if her intellect were fuzzy; her mind seemed poised on
the edge of a flood of memories.

She focused on a brief printout of her own EEG—some
decreased alpha, increased beta, a hint of theta waves. She
was hovering on the border between wakefulness and stage-
one sleep.

''Too much feedback?'' she asked the tech, her voice
deep and isolated under the headphones.

He scanned the gauges, then wrote on a pad, ''Everything checks at this end. You've been working all morning.
Maybe you're just sleepy.''

The blue pulses of the heart monitor synchronized.

Dr. Insomnia tossed the journal onto the floor to join the
pile. She turned off the lights, closed her eyes, and concentrated on the patterns made by the random firing of

retinal neurons. She imagined a tree, a glacier, a bear skiing down the ice. She thought of less and then nothing, suddenly shuddered, and leaped back from the edge of sleep.

"Oh shit," she said, as she had nightly for ten years. "I've *got* to get some sleep." Her bed was striped with moonlight through the blinds. She heard the roar of cars on the busy street below, like surf against the beach, the omnipresent rumble becoming briefly silent as traffic moved on the cross street.

She groped for the TV controls. The picture grew out from the center in an expanding presence of light.

An Aztec priest rants on over a supine, writhing woman in a temple which is a redress of a set from *Flash Gordon,* which is in turn a redress from *Green Hell. You can't fool the doctor.* The entire Aztec nation is a half-dozen extras in loincloths.

"No no no," the woman shrieks preparatory to the sacrifice; suddenly conquistadors enter and rescue her. The dying priest is dragged off by acolytes to be mummified—

"Mummified? An Aztec?"

Jump cut to the 1950s present. A small Mexican archae-ologist is talking to a tall American one. "Hey, 418!" It is Dutcher, a head taller than anyone else in the movie, his face young but with the important lines already set in. His head is bent in a perpetual tilt to see his fellow actors.

Everything is formula and predictable. The mummified priest walks around disposing of bit players. It's really trying to get at Dutcher's love-interest, who is:

(a) the older archaeologist's daughter, and

(b) the reincarnation of the princess who was rescued before the first commercial.

"Millions for defense. Not one penny for script," Dr. Insomnia mutters. The spooky part is seeing Dutcher fro-zen in youth and health. Dr. Insomnia's eyelids drift south-ward as the hero wonders how to electrocute the mummy.

"Throw in a radio while it's bathing," she suggests, and sleeps.

Mother says, "Eat. There are children starving in
Europe." Dinner writhes like a sacrificial victim and
melts. I'm running outside into rain, steaming ground
like a tropical jungle, snakes in the banana, papaya,
pineapple trees. Screeching monkey laughter. Green
hell?

"*Aztec Doom* was on last night," she remarked
around the hovering technician.
  "One of mine?" Rich asked.
  "You weren't very good."
  "For what they paid, why bother?"

Again the body snapped convulsively as sleep neared.
Again the sad grope for the TV controls.
  "It's like nothing I've ever seen before," Rich says
over the sheet-draped, desiccated corpse. People disappear
from the small desert town for another half hour. Then
some teen-agers are trapped and barely escape the monster, an actor in a dust-colored mask and bodysuit. Events
limp forward. Rich carries the young blonde to the electric
towers while the dust vampires pursue, bent on stealing
moisture, flesh, life . . .

Dr. Insomnia sat back, feet on her desk, and contemplated her standard morning exhaustion. Her eyes were red
as Christopher Lee's in *Satanic Rites of Dracula*. She'd
forgotten the last night's dream before she could add it to
her journal, but she had vague memories that it had been
slow-going, like a Russian novel, or introductory chemis-
try for humanities majors. A plodding, sinking feeling.
  "Quagmired in a marshmallow sea," she said aloud,
pleased to have found the proper metaphor. She examined
her breakfast doughnut once more, rotating it a full 360
degrees, staring at the multicolored sprinkles in the icing.
She tossed it in the trash can, a perfect hook shot. Then
she attended a departmental meeting, nodding sagely when
necessary, and adopting an interested expression until her
facial muscles ached. She felt as Rich must have, filming

Desert Vampires, enduring take after take of trying to look concerned while other actors stumbled over their lines and speculated endlessly about the corpse.

Rich's handshake was firmer. "I think it's working," he said. "Look, I'm even drinking juice between meals."

She smiled. Never tell the patient he's fooling himself. What had she accomplished with the other five? Some improved appetite, less nausea—marijuana might do the same. At best, they now had better attitudes.

"I saw *Desert Vampires* last night."

"Not too selective."

"Channel 16 from Las Pulgas will run anything. Sometimes I think aliens have determined that TV waves are bad for us—they'll depopulate the earth or turn us into zombies or something. So the aliens buy up UHF stations all over and beam out vacuous nonsense twenty-four hours a day, even though no one's watching."

He looked thoughtful. "I think I was in that one. Fifty-eight. I played second lead to Gerald Mohr."

She hits the jackpot. A rerun of "Time Seekers."

"It only lasted one season. No one syndicates shows that lasted one season." She lifts one corner of her mouth, her smile self-conscious even when she's alone with the TV. "No one? Channel 16 must take that as a challenge."

Dr. Insomnia loves the show. How can she not? It begins in Time Seekers' top-secret future headquarters. A beehive-hairdoed woman screams. The sun is preparing to go nova. Dr. Meter—she remembers the runt scientist from her youth—whips out his slide rule (slide rule!)—and announces that they only have 14 hours, 58 minutes and 32.5 seconds left to live.

But as it continues, Dr. Insomnia forgets the camp, early sixties futurism. She falls back into her adolescence, when it was only the reassuring presence of "Time Seekers" every Wednesday that gave her purpose, like a tree pointing out a hidden path in an endless plain or a pyramid standing inflexible against erosion.

The hero, blue-eyed and cleft-chinned, fights off various

fiends, eventually arriving at headquarters. Dr. Meter says, "Quick, Rusty. Commander Stone needs you."

Dr. Insomnia holds her breath as the door swings open to the commander's office. The past, especially an adolescent crush, is embarrassing. She always flinches at Herman's Hermits albums or the execrable acting of one of her teen idols. But Stone is a pleasant surprise. Rich is as he should be, face with definite planes and seams in the black and white. Forty-five is kind to him—the lines and shadowed hollows giving character, while the chin is only starting to fall, the stomach to grow, the hair to disappear. His expression is a studied blank, every word and movement minimal but perfectly correct.

"Shit. He can act," she says, quite pleased that she need not be embarrassed.

He sits behind the desk—"Naturally; he's taller than Rusty"—and rattles through the exposition. The hero is almost out the door when Stone's gravelly voice says, offhanded, "Oh, and, Rusty?" Dr. Insomnia says the words along with him. "All time and space depend on you."

The rest of the show is Rusty's heroics through Tudor England and some primitive jungle planet, as he fights thugs and repeatedly rescues a kidnap-prone woman. Insomnia waits for these scattered moments when they cut back to Time Seekers' headquarters. Dr. Meter paces anxiously. Stone sits on the edge of his desk.

"Time is running out."

"I know. We can only hope Rusty succeeds."

And the tag scene: "You did it, Rusty. The Time president wants to thank you."

"He'll have to wait." Sparkle. "I've got a heavy date in Elizabethan England and I don't want to keep the lady waiting." Sprightly music as he winks and leaves. Stone looks furious but, as Dr. Meter shrugs fondly, Stone's expression melts into a rueful grin. Fadeout.

Fog and drums. A row of conga drummers along the lower border of Hippie Hill in Golden Gate Park.

Am I a kid again or—no, I'm me. Hare Krishna chanters. Marijuana smoke overlying eucalyptus scent. Someone playing with soap bubbles; a large one floats over the trees toward Haight Street, unseen behind, the bubble growing and swallowing the park inside it. Standing at the edge of the bubble, translucent, pulsing, rippling with colors like oil on a wet street. A man sits outside the bubble, his back familiar. I must reach him, reach out, reach through the soap wall . . .

"Sorry we're running late. I overslept," she said, marveling at the words.

Rich grinned. "I get to go out in the sun today. I've got some energy to burn." Enthusiasm seemed strange coming from the still cadaverously thin white-haired man.

"Dr. Todd says you're putting away four-course dinners now."

"First course awful, second course dreadful, third . . ."

"In other words, typical hospital food. I'll see if we can have some better meals sent in. Jeeves?" The technician rolled his eyes at the summons and turned on the machinery. White noise welled up in the headphones. Brains grew still in a semblance of sleep . . .

She wheeled Dutcher back to his room. His voice was huskier and slower than Commander Stone's, but it was sounding closer every day. "The best I can say for 'Time Seekers' is that it was work. My first steady acting job after I lost the contract with the studio—I was too tall. Didn't make it as a leading man and they couldn't have a character actor dwarfing the romantic lead. Then I did that awful monster stuff and then TV, villains mostly. I've snuffed more people than Baby Face Nelson.

" 'Time Seekers' was just an excuse to let them use their back lot and old props. Mongol Horde with Enfield rifles—that sort of stuff. My wife would wake me from a dead sleep and I'd say, 'Time and space depend on you, Rusty.' The hardest part of acting is keeping a straight face."

"Well, you kept one very well," she said. He barely needed help getting from the wheelchair to his bed. Stone had always seemed in control, sitting impassively as the universe about him rocked with chaos. She remembered adolescent nights, lying in the dark inventing a background for the character, fantasies explaining his imperturbability. She laughed aloud. "You know, I don't think I recognize you except when you're in the background, half in shadow and slightly out of focus."

"That's because the star's contract specified that he be the one in focus."

She went to the doorway and stopped. "Another cherished mystery bites the dust. Thanks a lot."

Dr. Insomnia's body did not rest. Like every body, it ceaselessly respired, digested, filtered, metabolized, excreted. And it served as mercenary soldier for six other unwell bodies. One night it looked at short strands of nucleic acids and responded with interferon. Another night a hapten inspired B cells to gear up into plasma cells and churn out immunoglobins. Or a tuberculin test awoke the cell-mediated immunity and marshaled the killer T cells.

Dr. Insomnia's body went to war while Dr. Insomnia's brain watched "Time Seekers" and then slept. The roar of traffic subsided on the busy street. Solitary trucks rumbled by, shaking the apartment house. The sun rose over the mountains, illuminating the promise of another smog-filled San Yobebe morning. Light slid in between the slats of the venetian blinds. The traffic built back up to surflike regularity.

Dr. Insomnia still slept.

Desert Vampires as it should be, hopeless and terrifying. We're shot down on some desert planet, Time Seeker uniforms ragged and torn, waiting to die of the cruel heat or alien marauders or indigenous monsters. Commander Stone leads us, torn shirt, scraped cheek, mussed hair. He looks delicious. I'm wearing medic clothes; the others are extras, people from work. "Keep walking," Stone

orders, threatens, cajoles. "Toward the hills." What's
in the hills? More rock and sand and hopelessness.
Someone lags behind and disappears with a scream,
us too tired to react. Only ashes. They pick us off
one by one in the daylight. Jason dies again. Sean
stands there with an astonished wide-eyed look
and crumbles as sand. He's layers collapsing one
by one, while I hide my face in the tatters of
Stone's uniform and his gravelly voice says, "Don't
worry. I won't let them get you." Screaming:
"They've gotten everyone else!" After all my
hopes and expectations, I'm only a screamer
needing to be rescued and feeling disappointed
with myself. But he seems to expect, to like my
helplessness. He says gravely, "They can't get
me. I'm a regular. Rusty will rescue us in the nick of
time." "But I'm not a regular . . ." In a circle
around us, the sand animates, pushing up into the
figures of humans and then shambling forward, so-
lidifying, reaching toward us . . .

She awoke with the blankets on the floor, the sheet's
indentations across her face, and the twenty-four hour flu
in her gut.

The antibody test results came back later that week.
"Just plain old influenza virus, last season's variety,"
Sean, her lunchtime lover, reported in a disappointed voice.
"Any flu capable of downing Dr. Insomnia ought to be a
brave new strain."

"I should be able to fight something so prosaic."

"Maybe you're tired."

She shook her head. "Maybe I'm not tired enough."

Two of the six patients were dead. Three more merely
hung on. Dr. Insomnia fought skirmishes, delayed implacable besiegers who would sooner or later burn, starve, dig
them out. Every day, as dessert, they wheeled in Rich
Dutcher, looking healthier with each session. Dr. Insomnia
looked forward to him as she used to look forward to

"Time Seekers," a joyful cap to a train of miserable events.

"You need more sun," Rich said. "You're pale."

"Thanks, doctor." She coughed and felt a stab of guilt and anxiety. *Mellow out,* she told herself. *It's not like he's immunosuppressed. In fact, right now his reticuloendothelial system is probably a damn sight healthier than yours.* Aloud she said, "Bit of a cold."

They interfaced with the machine. White noise swallowed the remainder of the morning. She blinked, returning to awareness in the warm noon light.

That evening she reviewed Dutcher's chart. Hemoglobin normal. Lymphocyte count high normal. Weight increasing. Radiology noted no new growths, the old ones decreasing to small scars. On the bottom of one page the intern had scribbled, "Query—remission?" The word was sun bursting through clouds.

Rich was awake and cynically watching one of his own movies. "Giant cockroaches," he said. "I had real ones in my apartment while I was making this turkey. They gave me the creeps—my wife had to kill them. But here I am zapping fifty-foot ones with an electric fly swatter."

"Are you implying it's unrealistic?"

He snorted, an old man scowling at himself. "Look at me. That's not acting, it's sleepwalking. I'll never be able to live it down. Fifty years after I'm dead they'll be showing this dreck on the late late show."

"Yeah. Like now, you can watch TV and fall in love with Bogart thirty years after he died."

He looked at her sharply, dark eyes in a pool of light. "Do you always get entranced by flickering images?"

She sighed. "It's so much easier to love people who don't exist. Safer too." She shook her head as if waking to the situation. "Revelations at this early hour? I came in to give you some good news."

He listened gravely as she described his progress. "I'm the only one on whom it's really worked?"

"You know what I think it is? Ego. Only someone with a colossal ego could will himself to health. No offense?"

He laughed. "Don't worry. Von Sternberg said actors are cattle, but we're special cattle. We have charisma. We project. We're immortal. Flies in amber."

She hooked a thumb at the TV. "That's more like a dinosaur in a tar pit. Cattle?" She muttered, "Grade A government-inspected beefcake," glancing obliquely at the screen. Rich, stripped to the waist, was climbing another electric tower. The old actor chuckled and left for his therapeutic walk down the hall and back. Dr. Insomnia watched the tiny man scramble about the tower trying to avoid a huge cockroach.

During the commercial she noticed a spiral-bound notebook on the nightstand. She opened it at random.

I'm outside, running in the rain. Trees—banana, pineapple. (Pineapple on trees?) Screaming noises.

She flipped a page.

The doctor is yelling—she can't make it. I'm shouting "The hills!"

Another.

. . .beside some endless translucent film, and a hand begins to push through . . .

Outside the room, Rich was speaking to a nurse. Inside, in the tube, he questioned a soldier. He was in stereo.

I'm attached by an umbilical IV line to the project machine, swinging the cord like a jump rope. Commander Stone sits in a corner, just staring at me. "Quit it," I say. "Knock it off." His eyes are recessed deep under his brow, like Rich's. The technician sits at the interface control—player piano, ragtime. Then he stands and flakes away as sand. The cord begins pulling me into the machine. Commander Stone reaches out and he's a dust monster, crudely sculpted sand in a Time Seeker's costume. He reaches out, stops, pulls back his hand, and I'm going into the machine, all gaping darkness . . .

The new clock radio read 5:33 in luminescent figures. It was set to go off at seven. She hadn't needed an alarm

clock for over a decade. Her skin felt like burning sand.
She stretched to find a good position to return to sleep and
felt something warm against her back. A body. She was
not alone. A dust monster!

She crawled out slowly, anxious not to awaken the quiet
life-vampire, then went into the kitchen and put up water
for instant coffee. The sky in the eastern window graded
from yellow up to deep blue. She was afraid to return to
bed.

"It's not a dust monster," she said, mouth dry with
fever. "It's Sean, it's got to be Sean. Right?" She was
unable to go and check the hypothesis.

The teapot screamed and it was every black-and-white
thirty-frames-per-second terrified woman screaming for rescue. It was Dr. Insomnia.

They met in the corridor, doctor and patient both wearing robes and slippers. The walls were the same industrial
green as Time Seekers' headquarters. He held up his IV
bottle. "I'm searching for an honest man."

She hoisted her bottle. "I'll see your isotonic saline and
raise you five percent glucose."

Voice suddenly full of concern, he asked, "Do they
know what it is?"

"Not yet. More tests," she replied.

He said, "I'm being discharged soon. Mind if I come
visit?"

"I'll be here." *I'll never leave.* The walk from her
room to the nurses' station and back exhausted her. She
lay down and was asleep.

Running across sand dunes toward the electric
towers. The dune forms into a hand that grabs my
ankle. I fall. Rolling down the dune into more sand
that becomes arms grabbing, holding, smothering
. . . Jason, there is no answer . . . All time and
space depend on you . . . Time. Time is the dust
vampire.

David Morrell is the well-known author of First Blood,
The Totem, *and* Blood Oath. *I recently read his* The
Hundred Year Christmas, *a delightful fantasy that's
unlike those strong titles. I am pleased to report, though,
that "For These and All My Sins" is David Morrell at
his strongest—the kind of yarn that* Whispers *magazine was started to publish.*

FOR THESE AND ALL MY SINS

David Morrell

There was a tree. I remember it. I swear I'd be able to
recognize it. Because it looked so unusual.

It stood on my left, in the distance, by Interstate 80. At
first, it was just a blur in the shimmering heat haze, but as
I drove closer, its skeletal outline became distinct. Skeletal—
that's what struck me first as being strange. After all, in
August, even in the sun-parched Nebraska panhandle, trees
(the few you see) are thick with leaves, but this one was
bare.

So it's dead, I thought. So what? Nothing to frown
about. But then I noticed the second thing about it, and I
guess I'd subconsciously been reacting before I even realized
what its silhouette resembled.

Stronger than resembled.

I felt uneasy. The tree was very menorahlike, a giant

187

counterpart of the candelabrum used in Jewish religious services. Eight candles in a row. Except in this case the candles were barren branches standing straight. I shrugged off an eerie tingle. It's just a freak, an accident of nature, I concluded, though I briefly wondered if someone had pruned the tree to give it that appearance and in the process had unavoidably killed it.

But coincidence or not, the shape struck me as being uncanny—a religious symbol formed by a sterile tree ironically blessing a drought-wracked western plain. I thought of *The Waste Land.*

For the past two weeks, I'd been camping with friends in the Wind River mountains of Wyoming. Fishing, exploring, climbing, mostly sitting around our cook fire, drinking, reminiscing. After our too long postponed reunion, our time together at last had been squandered. Again we'd separated, heading our different ways across the country, back to wives and children, jobs and obligations. For me, that meant Iowa City, home, and the university. As much as I wanted to see my family again, I dreaded the prospect of still another fall semester, preparing classes, grading freshman papers.

Weary from driving (eight hours east since a wrenching emotional farewell breakfast), I glanced from the weird menorah tree and realized I was doing seventy. Slow down, I told myself. You'll end up getting a ticket.

Or killed.

And that's when the engine started shuddering. I drive a second-hand Porsche 912, the kind with four cylinders, from the sixties. I bought it cheap because it needed a lot of body work, but despite its age, it usually worked like a charm. The trouble is, I didn't know the carburetors had to be adjusted for the thinner air of higher altitude, so when I'd reached the mountains in Wyoming, the engine had sputtered, the carburetors had overflowed, and I'd rushed to put out a small but scary, not to mention devastating, fire on the engine. In Lander, a garage had repaired the damage while I went off camping with my friends, but when I'd come back to get it (ransom it really, considering

what the mechanic charged), the accelerator hadn't seemed
as responsive as it used to be. All day, the motor had
sounded a little noisier than usual, and now as it shuddered, it wasn't just noisy, it was thunderous. Oh, Christ,
I thought. The fire must have cracked the engine block.
Whatever was wrong, I didn't dare go much farther. The
steering wheel was jerking in my hands. Scared, I slowed
down to thirty. The roar and shudder persisted. I needed to
find a mechanic fast.

I said this happened in Nebraska's panhandle. Imagine
the state as a low wide rectangle. Cut away the bottom left
corner. The remaining *top* left corner—that's the panhandle, just to the east of Wyoming. It's nothing but broad
flat open range. Scrub grass, sagebrush, tumbleweed. The
land's as desolate as when the pioneers struggled across it
a hundred years ago. A couple more hours into Nebraska,
I wouldn't have worried too much. Towns start showing
up every twenty miles or so. But heading through the
panhandle, I hadn't seen a sign for a town in quite a while.
Despite the false security of the four-lane Interstate, I
might as well have been on the moon.

As a consequence, when I saw the off-ramp, I didn't
think twice. Thanking whatever god had smiled on me, I
struggled with the spastic tremors of the steering wheel
and exited, wincing, as the engine not only roared but
crackled as if bits of metal were breaking off inside and
scraping, gouging. There wasn't a sign for a town at this
exit, but I knew there had to be a reason for the off-ramp.
Reaching a stop sign, I glanced right and left along a
two-lane blacktop but saw no buildings either way. So
which direction? I asked myself. On impulse, I chose the
left and crossed the bridge above the Interstate, only then
realizing I headed toward the menorah tree.

Again I felt that eerie tingle. But the shuddering roar of
the engine distracted me. The accelerator heaved beneath
my foot, sending spasms up my leg. The car could barely
do twenty miles an hour now. I tried to control my
nervous breathing, vaguely sensing the tree as I passed it.

On my left. I'm sure of it. I wasn't so preoccupied that I

wouldn't remember. The tree was on the left of the un-
marked two-lane road.

I'm positive. I know I'm not wrong.

I drove. And drove. The Porsche seemed ready to fall
apart at any moment, jolting, rattling. The road stretched
ahead, leading nowhere, seemingly forever. With the menorah tree behind me, nothing relieved the dismal prairie
landscape. Any time now, I thought. I'll see some buildings. Just another mile or so—if the car can manage that
far.

It did, and another mile after that, but down to fifteen
now. My stomach cramped. I had the terrible sense I
should have gone the other way along this road. For all I
knew, I'd have reached a town in a minute. But now I'd
gone so far in this direction I had to keep going. I wasn't
sure the car could fight its way back to the Interstate.

When I'd first seen the menorah tree, the clock on my
dashboard had shown near five. As I glanced at the clock
again, I winced when I saw near six. Christ, just a few
more hours of light, and even if I found a garage, the
chances were it wouldn't stay open after six. Premonitions
squeezed my chest. I should have stayed on the Interstate,
I thought. There at least, if the car broke down, I could
have flagged down someone going by and asked them to
send a tow truck. Here I hadn't seen any traffic. Visions of
a night spent at the side of the road in my disabled car
were dismally matched by the wearying prospect of the
long hike back to the Interstate. I'd been planning to drive
all night in hopes of reaching home in Iowa City by noon
the next day, but if my luck kept turning sour, I might not
get there for at best another day and likely more, suppos-
ing the engine was as bad as the roar made it seem. I had
to find a phone and tell my wife not to worry when I didn't
reach home at the time I'd said I would. My thoughts
became more urgent. I had to—

That's when I saw the building. In the distance. Hard to
make out, a vague rectangular object, but unmistakably a
building, its metal roof reflecting the glint of the lowering
sun. Then I saw another building, and another. Trees.

Thank God, a town. My heart pounded almost as hard as the engine rattled. I clutched the steering wheel, frantically trying to control it, lurching past a water tower and an empty cattle pen. The buildings became distinct, a lot of them, houses, a car lot, a diner.

And a service station where I lurched to a raw-nerved stop, my hands still shaking from the vibrations of the steering wheel. I shut off the engine, grateful for the sudden quiet, and noticed two men at the pump, their backs to me. Self-conscious about my beard stubble and my sweat-drenched clothes, I got out wearily to ask directions.

Their backs to me. That should have told me right away that something was wrong. I'd made such a racket pulling up it wasn't normal for them not to turn, curious, wondering what the hell was coming.

But they didn't, and I was too exhausted for my instincts to jangle, warning me. Stiff-legged, I approached them. "Excuse me," I said. "I guess you can tell I've got some trouble. Is the mechanic still on duty?"

Neither turned or answered.

They must have heard me, I thought. All the same, I repeated louder. "The mechanic. Is he still on duty?"

No response.

For Christ sake, are they deaf or what? So I walked around to face them.

Even as they pivoted to show me their backs again, I gaped. Because I'd seen a brief glimpse of their faces. Oh, my God. I felt as if an ice-cold needle had pierced my spine. I've never seen a leper. All the same, from what I've read, I imagine a leper might have been less ugly than what I was looking at. Ugly isn't even strong enough to describe what I saw. Not just the swollen goiter bulging from each throat like an obscene Adam's apple. Not just the twisted jaws and cheekbones or the massive lumps on their foreheads. Or the distended lips and misshapen nostrils. Worse, their skin itself seemed rotten, gray, and mushy. Like open festering sores.

I nearly gagged. My throat contracted so I couldn't

breathe. Get control, I told myself. Whatever's wrong with them, it's not their fault. Don't gape like a six-year-old who's never seen someone malformed before. Obviously that's why they didn't want to look at me. Because they hated the disgusted reaction, the awful sickened stare.

They faced the door to the service station now, and I certainly wasn't about to walk in front of them again, so I repeated yet once more. "The mechanic. Where is he?"

As one, they each raised their right arm and pointed horribly twisted fingers toward the right, toward a gravel road that led out of town, parallel to the Interstate miles away.

Well, fuck, I thought. I'm sorry about what's happened to you. I wish there was some way to help you, but right now I need help myself, and you two guys are rude.

I stalked away, my head beginning to ache, my throat feeling raw. A quick glance at my watch showed seven o'clock. The sun, of course, was lower. If I didn't find a mechanic soon . . .

Across the street, on the corner, I saw a restaurant. Perhaps too kind a word. Greasy spoon would have been more accurate. The windows looked grimy. The posters for Pepsi and Schlitz looked ten years old. BAR-B-QUE, a dingy neon sign said. Why not shorten it, I thought, to B.B.Q., which stands for botulism and bad gas?

And why not stop with the jokes? You might be eating there tonight.

That's almost funny now. Eating, I mean. Dear God, I don't know how long I can stand this.

. . . So I walked across the dusty street and opened the fly-covered creaky screen door, peering in at five customers. "Hey, anybody know where—?"

The words caught in my throat. My mind reeled. Because the customers had already shifted, turning, with their backs to me—and *these* had humps and twisted spines and shoulders wrenched in directions nature had never intended. In shock, I hurriedly glanced at the waitress behind the corner, and she'd turned her back as well. The mirror, though. The goddamn mirror. Her face reflecting off it

seemed the result of a hideous genetic experiment. She had
no jaw. And only one eye. I stumbled back, letting the
door swing shut with a creak and a bang, my mind still
retaining the terrible impression of—it couldn't be—two
slits where there should have been a nose.

I'll make this quick. Everywhere I went, growing ever
more apprehensive, I found monsters. The town was like a
hundred horror movies squeezed together. Lon Chaney's
worst makeup inventions almost seemed normal by com-
parison. The island of Dr. Moreau would have been a
resort for beauty-contest winners.

Jesus.

Eight o'clock. The eastern sky was turning gray. The
western horizon was the red of blood. I wondered if I'd
gone insane. A town of monsters, no one speaking to me,
everyone turning away, most pointing toward the gravel
road that headed east out of town.

Appalled, I scrambled to get into the Porsche, turned the
key, and the rest hadn't done the car any good. If anything, the engine roared and shuddered more extremely.
Stomach scalding, I prayed. Though the Porsche shook
and protested, it blessedly managed to move.

A town, I thought. Maybe there's another town a few
miles along that gravel road. Maybe that's why they pointed
down there.

I rattled and heaved and jolted out of town, switching on
my emergency flashers, though I didn't know why since
I'd seen no traffic. All the same, with dusk coming on, it
didn't hurt to be careful.

A quarter mile. Then half a mile. That's as far as I got
before the engine failed completely. It's probable only one
cylinder was working by then. I'd hear a bang, then three
silent beats, then another bang and three more silent beats.
With every bang, the car crept forward a little. Then it finally
wheezed and coasted to a stop. The motor pinged from the
heat. A Porsche doesn't have a radiator, but I swear I heard
a hiss.

And that was that, stuck in the middle of nowhere, a

town of horrors behind me, an empty landscape ahead of me, and an Interstate God knew how far away.

With dark coming on.

On the prairie.

I've said I was frightened. But then I got mad. At my luck and the guy in Lander who'd "fixed" my car, at me and my stupidity for leaving the highway, not to mention my failure to think ahead when I was back in town. I should have bought some soft drinks anyhow, some candy bars and potato chips or something—anything to stop from starving all night out here in the dark. A beer. Hell, considering the way I felt, a six-pack. Might as well get shit-faced.

Angry, I stepped from the car. I leaned against a fender and lit a cigarette and cursed. Eight-thirty now. Dusk thickened. What was I going to do?

I try to convince myself I was being logical. By nine, I'd made my choice. The town was only half a mile away. Ten minutes' walk at most. If that stupid BAR-B-QUE had stayed open, I could still get some beer and chips. At the moment, I didn't care how revolting those people looked. I'd be damned if I was going to spend the night out here with my stomach rumbling. That'd be one discomfort too many.

So I walked, and when I reached the outskirts, night at last had fallen. The lights were on in the BAR-B-QUE; at least my luck hadn't failed entirely. Or so I thought, because they quickly went off as I came closer. Swell, I thought in disgust.

The place stayed dark.

But then the door creaked open. The waitress—a vague white shape—stepped out. She locked the door behind her. I almost asked if she'd mind waiting so I could buy some food. Naturally I assumed she hadn't seen me. That's why she surprised me when she turned.

I blinked, astonished. In contrast with the way the town had treated me, she actually spoke. Her voice was frail and wispy, the words slurred, suggestive of a cleft palate or a harelip. "I saw you," she said. "Through the window. Coming back." Maybe I imagined it, but her whispered cadence sounded musical.

And this is important, too. Though we faced each other, the street had no lights, and the dark had thickened enough I couldn't see her features. For the first time since I'd arrived in town, I felt as if I was having a normal conversation. It wasn't hard to pretend, as long as I forced myself not to remember the horror of what she looked like.

I managed a shrug, a laugh of despair. ''My car broke down. I'm stuck out there.'' Though I knew she couldn't see my gesture, I pointed down the pitch-dark road. ''I hoped you'd still be open so I could get something to eat.''

She didn't answer for a moment. Then abruptly she said, ''I'm sorry. The owner closed a half hour ago. I stayed to clear up and get things ready for tomorrow. The grill's cold.''

''But just some beer? Potato chips or something?''

''Can't. The cash register's empty.''

''But I don't care about change. I'll pay you more than the stuff is worth.''

Again she didn't answer for a moment. ''Beer and potato chips?''

''Please.'' My hopes rose. ''If you wouldn't mind.''

''While you spend the night in your car?''

''Unless there's a hotel.''

''There isn't. You need a decent meal, a proper place to sleep. Considering the trouble you're in.''

She paused. I remember the night was silent. Not even crickets sang.

''I live alone,'' she said, her cadence even more musical. ''You can sleep on the sofa in the living room. I'll broil a steak for you.''

''I couldn't,'' I said. The thought of seeing her face again filled me with panic.

''I won't turn the lights on. I won't disgust you.''

I lied. ''It's just that I don't want to inconvenience you.''

''No trouble.'' She sounded emphatic. ''I want to help. I've always believed in charity.''

She began to walk away. Paralyzed, I thought about it. For sure, the steak sounded good. And the sofa. A hell of a lot better than sleeping hunched in the car.

But Jesus, the way she looked.

And maybe my attitude was painfully familiar to her. How would I feel, I wondered, if I was deformed and people shunned me? Charity. Hadn't she said she believed in charity? Well, maybe it was time I believed in it myself. I followed her, less motivated by the steak and the sofa than by my determination to be kind.

She lived three blocks away, on a street as dark as the one we'd left. The houses were still, no sounds, no sign of anyone. It was the strangest walk of my life.

From what I could tell in the dark, she lived in an old two-story Victorian house. The porch floor squeaked as we crossed it to go inside. And, true to her word, she didn't turn on the lights.

"The living room's through an arch to your left," she said. "The sofa's against the wall straight ahead. I'll fix the steak."

I thanked her and did what she said. The sofa was deep and soft. I hadn't realized how tired I was till I leaned back. In the dark, I heard the sizzle of the steak from somewhere at the back of the house. I assume she turned the kitchen lights on to cook it, but I didn't see even the edge of a glow. Then the fragrance of the beef drifted toward me. Echoing footsteps came near.

"I should have asked how well done you like it. Most customers ask for medium rare." Her wispy voice sounded like wind chimes.

"Great." I no longer cared if she was ugly. By then I was ravenous.

In the dark, she cautiously set up a tray, brought the steak, bread and butter, A-1 sauce (she claimed), and a beer. Though awkward because I couldn't see, I ate amazingly fast. I couldn't get enough of it. Delicious couldn't describe it. Mouth-watering. Taste-bud expanding. Incredible.

I sopped up sauce and steak juice with my final remnant of bread, stuffed it in my mouth, washed it down with my final sip of beer, and sagged back, knowing I'd eaten the best meal of my life.

Throughout, she'd sat in a chair across the room and hadn't spoken once.

"That was wonderful," I said. "I don't know how to thank you."

"You already have."

I wasn't sure what she meant. My belly felt reassuringly packed to the bursting point.

"You haven't asked," she said.

I frowned. "Asked what? I don't understand."

"You do. You're dying to ask. I know you are. They always are."

"They?"

"Why the people here are horribly deformed?"

I felt a chill. In truth, I had been tempted to ask. The town was so unusual, the people so strange, I could barely stifle my curiosity. She'd been so generous, though, I didn't want to draw attention to her infirmity and be rude. At once, her reflection in the mirror at the BAR-B-QUE popped up terribly in my mind. No chin. One eye. Flat slits where there should have been a nose. Oozing sores.

I almost vomited. And not just from the memory. Something was happening in my stomach. It churned and complained, growling, swelling larger, as if it were crammed with a million tiny darting hornets.

"Sins," she said.

I squirmed, afraid.

"Once, long ago," she said, "in the middle ages, certain priests used to travel from village to village. Instead of hearing confessions, they performed a ceremony to cleanse the souls of the villagers. Each member of the group brought something to eat and set it on a table in front of the priest. At last, an enormous meal awaited him. He said the necessary words. All the sins of the village were transferred into the food."

I swallowed bile, unaccountably terrified.

"And then he ate the meal. Their sins," she said. "He stuffed himself with sins."

Her tone was so hateful I wanted to scream and run.

"The villagers knew he'd damned himself to save their

souls. For this, they gave him money. Of course, there were disbelievers who maintained the priest was nothing more than a cheat, a con man tricking the villagers into feeding him and giving him money. They were wrong.''

I heard her stand.

''Because the evidence was clear. The sins had their effect. The evil spread through the sin-eater's body, festering, twisting, bulging to escape.''

I heard her doing something in the corner. I tensed from the sound of scratching.

''And not just priests ate sins,'' she said. ''Sometimes special women did it too. But the problem was, suppose the sin-eater wanted to be redeemed as well? How could a sin-eater get rid of the sins? Get rid of the ugliness. By passing the sins along, of course. By having them eaten by someone else.''

''You're crazy,'' I said. ''I'm getting out of here.''

''No, not just yet.''

I realized the scratching sound was a match being struck. A tiny flame appeared. My stomach soured in pulsing agony.

''A town filled with sin-eaters,'' she said. ''Monsters shunned by the world. Bearable only to each other. Suffering out of charity for the millions of souls who've been redeemed.''

She lit a candle. The light grew larger in the room. I saw her face and gaped again, but this time for a different reason. She was beautiful. Stunning. Gorgeous. Her skin seemed to glow with sensuality.

It also seemed to shimmer, to ripple, to—

''No. My God,'' I said. ''You put something in my food.''

''I told you.''

''Not that foolishness.'' I tried to stand, but my legs felt like plastic. My face seemed to expand, contract and twist. My vision became distorted as if I peered at funhouse mirrors. ''LSD? Was that it? Mescaline? I'm hallucinating.'' Each word echoed more loudly, yet seemed to murmur from far away.

I cringed as she approached, growing more beautiful with every step.

"And it's been so long," she said. "I've been so ugly. So long since anyone wanted me."

Reality cracked. The universe spun. She stripped off her uniform, showing her breasts, her . . . body was . . .

Despite the torture in my stomach, the insanity of my distorted senses, I wanted her. I suddenly needed her as desperately as anything I'd ever coveted.

Passion was endless, powerful, frantic. Rolling, we bumped the tray, sending glass and plate, knife and fork and steak sauce crashing down. A lamp fell, shattering. My naked back slammed against the sharp edge of a table, making me groan. Not from pain. I screamed in ecstasy.

And just before I came with an explosive burst, as if from the core of my soul, as if after foisting her sins upon me she needed something from me in return, I felt her drawing me close to her, down, ever down.

She moaned and pleaded, "Eat me. Eat me."

I lost consciousness. The Nebraska state police claim they found me wandering naked down the middle of Interstate 80 at one o'clock, two days later. They saw I was horribly sunburned. I don't know. I don't remember. All I recall is waking up in the university hospital in Iowa City.

In the psych ward, I found out.

The doctors lie. They claim I'm not ugly. Then why have they locked me up and taken the mirrors away? Why do the nurses flinch when they come in with guards to feed me? They think they're so smart. Despite the thick wire screen across the window, at night I see my reflection. I don't have a chin. There's only one eye. In place of a nose, I've got two flat repulsive slits. I'm being punished. I understand that now. For all the evil in the world.

I used to be a Catholic, but I don't go to church anymore. When I was young, though, learning to go to confession, the nuns made me learn a speech to say to the priest in the booth. *Bless me, Father, for I have sinned. My last confession was* . . . And then I'd tell him how long ago, and then I'd confess, and then I'd finish by saying, *I'm sorry for these and all my sins.* I am, you know. I'm sorry. Except I didn't commit them. The sins aren't mine. I'm innocent.

My wife and children come to visit. I refuse to let them see me. I can't bear to see the sickened reaction in their eyes.

How can a sin-eater get rid of the sins? That's what she said to me. *By passing the sins along, of course. By having them eaten by someone else?*

I've known for several weeks now what I had to do. It was simply a matter of pretending to be calm, of waiting for my chance. I hope the guard wasn't badly hurt. I tried not to hit him too hard. But his head made a terrible sound when I cracked it against the wall.

I've been very clever. I've stolen three cars, and I've never kept one long enough for the state police to catch me. It's taken me two days to return.

That's why the tree's so important. It's my landmark, you see. Remember the off-ramp had no sign. The tree's all I had to give me direction.

But I'm puzzled. Oh, I found the tree all right, its branches in the shape of the menorah candelabrum. And it's so distinctive I can't believe there'd be another like it. But I swear it had eight upright branches then, and it was bare.

But now it's got nine, with the added one slightly taller. And leaves have sprouted.

Dear God, help me. Save me.

I pressed the accelerator to the floor, racing down the two-lane blacktop. As before, the road stretched forever. Doubt made me frantic. I tried not to glance at the rear-view mirror. All the same, I weakened, and my ugliness made me wail.

I saw the building in the distance, the glint of sunlight off the metal roof. I whimpered, rushing closer. And I found the town again. Exactly the same. The water tower. The cattle pen (but it's full now). The service station, the BAR-B-QUE.

I don't understand, though. Everyone's normal. I see no goiters, no hunchbacks, no twisted limbs and festering sores. They stare as I drive past. I can't stand to see their shock and disgust.

. . . I've found her house. I'm in here waiting.

In the hospital, the doctors said I was having delusions. They agreed my initial suspicion might have been correct—that some chemical in my food could have made me hallucinate, and now the effects of the drug persist, making me think I'm ugly, distorting my memory of the trip, even before I ate. I wish I could believe that. I even wish I could believe I've gone crazy. Anything would be better than the truth.

But I know what it is. She *did*. She made me eat her sins. Well, dammit, I'll get even with her. I'll make her take them back.

. . . I've been writing this in her living room while I glance hurriedly out the window. In case something happens to me, so people will understand. It wasn't my fault.

But she'll come home soon. Yes, she will. And then . . .

I hear a car door. On the street, someone's stepping from a station wagon.

Oh, sweet Christ, at last. But no, it's not one person.

Two. A man and a woman.

And the woman isn't . . .

They'll come in. They'll find me.

I don't care. I can't bear this anymore. I have to pass the sins along. I have to . . .

Found a knife in the kitchen. See, I don't know the words. I don't know how to put my sins in the food.

But I remember the last thing she said to me. I know how to do it. I have to use the knife and make them—

Eat me.

Physician number three in Whispers V *is Karl Edward Wagner. He has been with* Whispers *magazine since 1974 and has yet to miss a* Whispers *anthology. He is currently the editor of DAW's* Year's Best Horror *anthologies and his* Whispers IV *tale, "Into Whose Hands," was just chosen for their* Year's Best Fantasy *book. It is my pleasure to present to you this unique modern haunting: 1983's World Fantasy Award winner for Best Novella.*

BEYOND ANY MEASURE
Karl Edward Wagner

I

"In the dream I find myself alone in a room. I hear musical chimes—a sort of music-box tune—and I look around to see where the sound is coming from.

"I'm in a bedroom. Heavy curtains close off the windows and it's quite dark, but I can sense that the furnishings are entirely antique—late Victorian, I think. There's a large four-poster bed, with its curtains drawn. Beside the bed is a small night table upon which a candle is burning. It is from here that the music seems to be coming.

"I walk across the room toward the bed, and as I stand beside it I see a gold watch resting on the night table next to the candlestick. The music-box tune is coming from the watch, I realize. It's one of those old pocket-watch affairs with a case that opens. The case is open now, and I see that the watch's hands are almost at midnight. I sense that on the inside of the watchcase there will be a picture, and I pick up the watch to see whose picture it is.

"The picture is obscured with a red smear. It's fresh blood.

"I look up in sudden fear. From the bed, a hand is pulling aside the curtain.

"That's when I wake up."

"Bravo!" applauded someone.

Lisette frowned momentarily, then realized that the comment was directed toward another of the chattering groups crowded into the gallery. She sipped her champagne; she must be a bit tight, or she'd never have started talking about the dreams.

"What do you think, Dr. Magnus?"

It was the gala reopening of Covent Garden. The venerable fruit, flower, and vegetable market, preserved from the demolition crew, had been renovated into an airy mall of expensive shops and galleries: "London's new shopping experience." Lisette thought it an unhappy hybrid of born-again Victorian exhibition hall and trendy "shoppes." Let the dead past bury its dead. She wondered what they might make of the old Billingsgate fish market, should SAVE win its fight to preserve that landmark, as now seemed unlikely.

"Is this dream, then, a recurrent one, Miss Seyrig?"

She tried to read interest or scepticism in Dr. Magnus's pale blue eyes. They told her nothing.

"Recurrent enough."

To make me mention it to Danielle, she finished in her thoughts. Danielle Borland shared a flat—she'd stopped terming it an apartment even in her mind—with her in a row of terrace houses in Bloomsbury, within an easy walk of London University. The gallery was Maitland Reddin's project; Danielle was another. Whether Maitland really thought to make a business of it or only intended to showcase his many friends' not always evident talents was not open to discussion. His gallery in Knightsbridge was certainly successful, if that meant anything.

"How often is that?" Dr. Magnus touched his glass to his blondbearded lips. He was drinking only Perrier water, and at that was using his glass for little more than to gesture.

"I don't know. Maybe half-a-dozen times since I can remember. And then, that many again since I came to London."

"You're a student at London University, I believe Danielle said?"

"That's right. In art. I'm over here on fellowship."

Danielle had modelled for an occasional session—Lisette now was certain it was solely from a desire to display her body rather than from any financial need—and when a muttered profanity at a dropped brush disclosed a common American heritage, the two *émigrées* had rallied at a pub afterward to exchange news and views. Lisette's bed-sit near the museum was impossible, and Danielle's roommate had just skipped to the Continent with two months' owing. By closing time it was settled.

"How's your glass?"

Danielle, finding them in the crowd, shook her head in mock dismay and refilled Lisette's glass before she could cover it with her hand.

"And you, Dr. Magnus?"

"Quite well, thank you."

"Danielle, let me give you a hand?" Maitland had charmed the two of them into acting as hostesses for his opening.

"Nonsense, darling. When you see me starting to pant with the heat, then call up the reserves. Until then, do keep Dr. Magnus from straying away to the other parties."

Danielle swirled off with her champagne bottle and her smile. The gallery, christened Such Things May Be after Richard Burton (*not* Liz Taylor's ex, Danielle kept explaining and got laughs each time), was ajostle with friends and well-wishers—as were most of the shops tonight: private parties with evening dress and champagne, only a

scattering of displaced tourists gaping and photographing.
She and Danielle were both wearing slit-to-the-thigh crepe
de Chine evening gowns and could have passed for sisters:
Lisette blond, green-eyed, with a dusting of freckles;
Danielle light brunette, hazel-eyed, acclimated to the extensive facial makeup London women favored; both tall without seeming coltish, and close enough of a size to wear
each other's clothes.

"It must be distressing to have the same nightmare over
and again," Dr. Magnus prompted her.

"There have been others as well. Some recurrent, some
not. Similar in that I wake up feeling like I've been
through the sets of some old Hammer film."

"I gather you were not actually troubled with such
nightmares until recently?"

"Not really. Being in London seems to have triggered
them. I suppose it's repressed anxieties over being in a
strange city." It was bad enough that she'd been taking
some of Danielle's pills in order to seek dreamless sleep.

"Is this, then, your first time in London, Miss Seyrig?"

"It is." She added, to seem less the typical American
student: "Although my family was English."

"Your parents?"

"My mother's parents were both from London. They
emigrated to the States just after World War I."

"Then this must have been rather a bit like coming
home for you."

"Not really. I'm the first of our family to go overseas.
And I have no memory of Mother's parents. Grandmother
Keswicke died the morning I was born." Something Mother
never was able to work through emotionally, Lisette added
to herself.

"And have you consulted a physician concerning these
nightmares?"

"I'm afraid your National Health Service is a bit more
than I can cope with." Lisette grimaced at the memory of
the night she had tried to explain to a Pakistani intern why
she wanted sleeping medications.

She suddenly hoped her words hadn't offended Dr.

Magnus; but then, he scarcely looked the type who would approve of socialized medicine. Urbane, perfectly at ease in formal evening attire, he reminded her somewhat of a blond-bearded Peter Cushing. Enter Christopher Lee, in black cape, she mused, glancing toward the door. For that matter, she wasn't at all certain just what sort of doctor Dr. Magnus might be. Danielle had insisted she talk with him, very likely had insisted that Maitland invite him to the private opening: "The man has such *insight!* And he's written a number of books on dreams and the subconscious— and not just rehashes of Freudian silliness!"

"Are you going to be staying in London for some time, Miss Seyrig?"

"At least until the end of the year."

"Too long a time to wait to see whether these bad dreams will go away once you're back home in San Francisco, don't you agree? It can't be very pleasant for you, and you really should look after yourself."

Lisette made no answer. *She* hadn't told Dr. Magnus she was from San Francisco. So then, Danielle had already talked to him about her.

Dr. Magnus smoothly produced his card, discreetly offered it to her. "I should be most happy to explore this further with you on a professional level, should you so wish."

"I don't really think it's worth . . . ."

"Of course it is, my dear. Why otherwise would we be talking? Perhaps next Tuesday afternoon? Is there a convenient time?"

Lisette slipped his card into her handbag. If nothing else, perhaps he could supply her with some barbs or something. "Three?"

"Three it is, then."

II

The passageway was poorly lighted, and Lisette felt a vague sense of dread as she hurried along it, holding the hem of her nightgown away from the gritty filth beneath

her bare feet. Peeling scabs of wallpaper blotched the
leprous plaster, and, when she held the candle close, the
gouges and scratches that patterned the walls with insane
graffiti seemed disquietingly nonrandom. Against the mot-
tled plaster, her figure threw a double shadow: distorted,
one crouching forward, the other following.

A full-length mirror panelled one segment of the passageway, and Lisette paused to study her reflection. Her
face appeared frightened, her blond hair in disorder. She
wondered at her nightgown—pale, silken, billowing, of an
antique mode—not remembering how she came to be wearing it. Nor could she think how it was that she had come to
this place.

Her reflection puzzled her. Her hair seemed longer than
it should be, trailing down across her breasts. Her finely
chiselled features, prominent jawline, straight nose—her
face, except the expression was not hers: lips fuller, more
sensual, redder than her lip gloss glinted; teeth fine and
white. Her green eyes, intense beneath level brows, cat-
cruel, yearning.

Lisette released the hem of her gown, raised her fingers
to her reflection in wonder. Her fingers passed through the
glass, touched the face beyond.

Not a mirror. A doorway. Of a crypt.

The mirror-image fingers that rose to her face twisted in
her hair, pulled her face forward. Glass-cold lips bruised
her own. The dank breath of the tomb flowed into her
mouth.

Dragging herself from the embrace, Lisette felt a scream
rip from her throat . . .

. . . And Danielle was shaking her awake.

III

The business card read DR. INGMAR MAGNUS, followed
simply by CONSULTATIONS and a Kensington address. Not
Harley Street, at any rate. Lisette considered it for the
hundredth time, watching for street names on the corners
of buildings as she walked down Kensington Church Street

from the Notting Hill Gate station. No clue as to what type
of doctor, nor what sort of consultations; wonderfully
vague, and just the thing to circumvent licensing laws, no
doubt.

Danielle had lent her one of his books to read: *The Self
Reborn*, put out by one of those minuscule scholarly pub-
lishers clustered about the British Museum. Lisette found
it a bewildering mélange of occult philosophy and lunatic-
fringe theory—all evidently having something to do with
reincarnation—and gave it up after the first chapter. She
had decided not to keep the appointment until her nightmare Sunday night had given force to Danielle's insistence.

Lisette wore a loose silk blouse above French designer
jeans and ankle-strap sandal-toe high heels. The early
summer heat wave now threatened rain, and she would
have to run for it if the grey skies made good. She turned
into Holland Street and passed the recently closed Equinox bookshop, where Danielle had purchased various works
by Aleister Crowley. A series of back streets—she consulted her map of Central London—brought her to a mod-
estly respectable row of nineteenth-century brick houses,
now done over into offices and flats. She checked the
number on the brass plaque with her card, sucked in her
breath, and entered.

Lisette hadn't known what to expect. She wouldn't have
been surprised, knowing some of Danielle's friends, to
have been greeted with clouds of incense, Eastern music,
robed initiates. Instead she found a disappointingly mundane waiting room, rather small but expensively furnished,
where a pretty Eurasian receptionist took her name and
spoke into an intercom. Lisette noted that there was no one
else—patients? clients?—in the waiting room. She glanced
at her watch and noticed she was several minutes late.

"Please do come in, Miss Seyrig." Dr. Magnus stepped
out of his office and ushered her inside. Lisette had seen a
psychiatrist briefly a few years before at her parents' de-
mand, and Dr. Magnus's office suggested the same—from
the tasteful, relaxed decor, the shelves of scholarly books,
down to the traditional psychoanalyst's couch. She took a

chair beside the modern, rather carefully arranged desk, and Dr. Magnus seated himself comfortably in the leather swivel chair behind it.

"I almost didn't come," Lisette began, somewhat aggressively.

"I'm very pleased that you did decide to come," Dr. Magnus said, with a reassuring smile. "It doesn't require a trained eye to see that something is troubling you. When the unconscious tries to speak to us, it is foolhardy to attempt to ignore its message."

"Meaning that I may be cracking up?"

"I'm sure that must concern you, my dear. However, very often dreams such as yours are evidence of the emergence of a new level of self-awareness—sort of growing pains of the psyche, if you will—and not to be considered a negative experience by any means. They distress you only because you do not understand them—even as a child kept in ignorance through sexual repression is frightened by the changes of puberty. With your cooperation, I hope to help you come to understand the changes of your growing self-awareness, for it is only through a complete realization of one's self that one can achieve personal fulfillment and thereby true inner peace."

"I'm afraid I can't afford to undergo analysis just now."

"Let me begin by emphasizing to you that I am not suggesting psychoanalysis; I do not in the least consider you to be neurotic, Miss Seyrig. What I strongly urge is an *exploration* of your unconsciousness—a discovery of your whole self. My task is only to guide you along the course of your self-discovery, and for this privilege I charge no fee."

"I hadn't realized the National Health Service was this inclusive."

Dr. Magnus laughed easily. "It isn't, of course. My work is supported by a private foundation. There are many others who wish to learn certain truths of our existence, to seek answers where mundane science has not yet so much as realized there are questions. In that regard I am simply another paid researcher, and the results of my investigations are made available to those who share with us this yearning to see beyond the stultifying boundaries of modern science.''

He indicated the book-lined wall behind his desk. Much of one shelf appeared to contain books with his own name prominent upon their spines.

"Do you intend to write a book about me?" Lisette meant to put more of a note of protest in her voice.

"It is possible that I may wish to record some of what we discover together, my dear. But only with scrupulous discretion, and, needless to say, only with your complete permission."

"My dreams." Lisette remembered the book of his that she had tried to read. "Do you consider them to be evidence of some previous incarnation?"

"Perhaps. We can't be certain until we explore them further. Does the idea of reincarnation smack too much of the occult to your liking, Miss Seyrig? Perhaps we should speak in more fashionable terms of Jungian archetypes, genetic memory, or mental telepathy. The fact that the phenomenon has so many designations is ample proof that dreams of a previous existence are a very real part of the unconscious mind. It is undeniable that many people have experienced, in dreams or under hypnosis, memories that can not possibly arise from their personal experience. Whether you believe that the immortal soul leaves the physical body at death to be reborn in the living embryo, or prefer to attribute it to inherited memories engraved upon DNA, or whatever explanation—this is a very real phenomenon and has been observed throughout history.

"As a rule, these memories of past existence are entirely buried within the unconscious. Almost everyone has experienced *déjà vu*. Subjects under hypnosis have spoken in languages and archaic dialects of which their conscious mind has no knowledge, have recounted in detail memories of previous lives. In some cases these submerged memories burst forth as dreams; in these instances the memory is usually one of some emotionally laden experience, something too potent to remain buried. I believe that this is the case with your nightmares—the fact that they are recurrent being evidence of some profound significance in the events they recall.''

Lisette wished for a cigarette; she'd all but stopped buying cigarettes with British prices, and judging by the absence of ashtrays here, Dr. Magnus was a nonsmoker.

''But why have these nightmares only lately become a problem?''

''I think I can explain that easily enough. Your forebears were from London. The dreams became a problem after you arrived in London. While it is usually difficult to define any relationship between the subject and the remembered existence, the timing and the force of your dream regressions would seem to indicate that you may be the reincarnation of someone—an ancestress, perhaps—who lived here in London during this past century.''

''In that case, the nightmares should go away when I return to the States.''

''Not necessarily. Once a doorway to the unconscious is opened, it is not so easily closed again. Moreover, you say that you had experienced these dreams on rare occasions prior to your coming here. I would suggest that what you are experiencing is a natural process—a submerged part of your self is seeking expression, and it would be unwise to deny this shadow stranger within you. I might further argue that your presence here in London is hardly coincidence—that your decision to study here was determined by that part of you who emerges in these dreams.''

Lisette decided she wasn't ready to accept such implications just now. ''What do you propose?''

Dr. Magnus folded his hands as neatly as a bishop at prayer. ''Have you ever undergone hypnosis?''

''No.'' She wished she hadn't made that sound like two syllables.

''It has proved to be extraordinarily efficacious in a great number of cases such as your own, my dear. Please do try to put from your mind the ridiculous trappings and absurd mumbo-jumbo with which the popular imagination connotes hypnotism. Hypnosis is no more than a technique through which we may release the entirety of the unconscious mind to free expression, unrestricted by the countless artificial barriers that make us strangers to ourselves.''

"You want to hypnotize me?" The British inflection came to her, turning her statement into both question and protest.

"With your fullest cooperation, of course. I think it best. Through regressive hypnosis we can explore the significance of these dreams that trouble you, discover the shadow stranger within your self. Remember—this is a part of *you* that cries out for conscious expression. It is only through the full realization of one's identity, of one's total self, that true inner tranquillity may be achieved. Know thyself; and you will find peace.''

"Know myself?"

"Precisely. You must put aside this false sense of guilt, Miss Seyrig. You are not possessed by some alien and hostile force. These dreams, these memories of another existence—this is *you*.''

IV

"Some bloody weirdo made a pass at me this afternoon," Lisette confided.

"On the tube, was it?" Danielle stood on her toes, groping along the top of their bookshelf. Freshly showered, she was wearing only a lace-trimmed teddy—camiknickers, they called them in the shops here—and her straining thigh muscles shaped her buttocks nicely.

"In Kensington, actually. After I had left Dr. Magnus's office." Lisette was lounging in an old satin slip she'd found at a stall in Church Street. They were drinking Bristol Cream out of brandy snifters. It was an intimate sort of evening they loved to share together, when not in the company of Danielle's various friends.

"I was walking down Holland Street, and there was this seedy-looking creep all dressed out in punk regalia, pressing his face against the door where that Equinox bookshop used to be. I made the mistake of glancing at him as I passed, and he must have seen my reflection in the glass, because he spun right around, looked straight at me, and said: 'Darling! What a lovely surprise to see you!' ''

Lisette sipped her sherry. ''Well, I gave him my hardest stare, and would you believe the creep just stood there smiling like he knew me, and so I yelled 'Piss off!' in my loudest American accent, and he just froze there with his mouth hanging open.''

''Here it is,'' Danielle announced. ''I'd shelved it beside Roland Franklyn's *We Pass from View*—that's another you ought to read. I must remember someday to return it to that cute Liverpool writer who lent it to me.''

She settled cozily beside Lisette on the couch, handed her a somewhat smudged paperback, and resumed her glass of sherry. The book was entitled *More Stately Mansions: Evidences of the Infinite* by Dr. Ingmar Magnus and bore an affectionate inscription from the author to Danielle. ''This is the first. The later printings had two of his studies deleted; I can't imagine why. But these are the sort of sessions he was describing to you.''

''He wants to put *me* in one of his books,'' Lisette told her with an extravagant leer. ''Can a woman trust a man who writes such ardent inscriptions to place her under hypnosis?''

''Dr. Magnus is a perfect gentleman,'' Danielle assured her, somewhat huffily. ''He's a distinguished scholar and is thoroughly dedicated to his research. And besides, I've let him hypnotize me on a few occasions.''

''I didn't know that. Whatever for?''

''Dr. Magnus is always seeking suitable subjects. I was fascinated by his work, and when I met him at a party I offered to undergo hypnosis.''

''What happened?''

Danielle seemed envious. ''Nothing worth writing about, I'm afraid. He said I was either too thoroughly integrated, or that my previous lives were too deeply buried. That's often the case, he says, which is why absolute proof of reincarnation is so difficult to demonstrate. After a few sessions I decided I couldn't spare the time to try further.''

"But what was it like?"

"As adventurous as taking a nap. No caped Svengali staring into my eyes. No lambent girasol ring. No swirling lights. Quite dull, actually. Dr. Magnus simply lulls you to sleep."

"Sounds safe enough. So long as I don't get molested walking back from his office."

Playfully Danielle stroked her hair. "You hardly look the punk rock type. You haven't chopped off your hair with garden shears and dyed the stubble green. And not a single safety pin through your cheek."

"Actually I suppose he may not have been a punk rocker. Seemed a bit too old, and he wasn't garish enough. It's just that he was wearing a lot of black leather, and he had gold earrings and some sort of medallion."

"In front of the Equinox, did you say? How curious."

"Well, I think I gave him a good start. I glanced in a window to see whether he was trying to follow me, but he was just standing there looking stunned."

"*Might* have been an honest mistake. Remember the old fellow at Midge and Fiona's party who kept insisting he knew you?"

"And who was pissed out of his skull. Otherwise he might have been able to come up with a more original line."

Lisette paged through *More Stately Mansions* while Danielle selected a Tangerine Dream album from the stack and placed it on her stereo at low volume. The music seemed in keeping with the grey drizzle of the night outside and the coziness within their sitting room. Seeing she was busy reading, Danielle poured sherry for them both and stood studying the bookshelves—a hodgepodge of occult and metaphysical topics stuffed together with art books and recent paperbacks in no particular order. Wedged between Aleister Crowley's *Magick in Theory and Practice* and *How I Discovered My Infinite Self* by "An Initiate" she spotted Dr. Magnus's most recent book, *The Shadow Stranger*. She pulled it down; Dr. Magnus stared thoughtfully from the back of the dust jacket.

"Do you believe in reincarnation?" Lisette asked her.

"I do. Or rather, I do some of the time." Danielle stood behind the couch and bent over Lisette's shoulder to see where she was reading. "Midge Vaughn assures me that in a previous incarnation I was hanged for witchcraft."

"Midge should be grateful she's living in the twentieth century."

"Oh, Midge says we were sisters in the same coven and were hanged together; that's the reason for our close affinity."

"I'll bet Midge says that to all the girls."

"Oh, I like Midge." Danielle sipped her sherry and considered the rows of spines. "Did you say that man was wearing a medallion? Was it a swastika or that sort of thing?"

"No. It was something like a star in a circle. And he wore rings on every finger."

"Wait! Kind of greasy black hair slicked back from a widow's peak to straight over his collar in back? Eyebrows curled up into points like they've been waxed?"

"That's it."

"Ah, Mephisto!"

"Do you know him, then?"

"Not really. I've just seen him a time or two at the Equinox and a few other places. He reminds me of some ham actor playing Mephistopheles. Midge spoke to him once when we were by there, but I gather he's not part of her particular coven. Probably hadn't heard that the Equinox had closed. Never impressed me as a masher; very likely he actually did mistake you for someone."

"Well, they do say that everyone has a double. I wonder if mine is walking somewhere about London, being mistaken for me?"

"And no doubt giving some unsuspecting classmate of yours a resounding slap on the face."

"What if I met her suddenly?"

"Met your double—your *Doppelgänger?* Remember William Wilson? Disaster, darling—*disaster!*"

V

There really wasn't much to it; no production at all. Lisette felt nervous, a bit silly, and perhaps a touch cheated.

"I want you to relax," Dr. Magnus told her. "All you have to do is just relax."

That's what my gynecologist always says too, Lisette thought with a sudden tenseness. She lay on her back on the analyst's couch: her head on a comfortable cushion, legs stretched primly out on the leather upholstery (she'd deliberately worn jeans again), fingers clenched damply over her tummy. A white gown instead of jeans, and I'll be ready for my coffin, she mused uncomfortably.

"Fine. That's it. You're doing fine, Lisette. Very fine. Just relax. Yes, just relax, just like that. Fine, that's it. Relax."

Dr. Magnus's voice was a quiet monotone, monotonously repeating soothing encouragements. He spoke to her tirelessly, patiently, slowly dissolving her anxiety.

"You feel sleepy, Lisette. Relaxed and sleepy. Your breathing is slow and relaxed, slow and relaxed. Think about your breathing now, Lisette. Think how slow and sleepy and deep each breath comes. You're breathing deeper, and you're feeling sleepier. Relax and sleep, Lisette, breathe and sleep. Breathe and sleep . . ."

She *was* thinking about her breathing. She counted the breaths; the slow monotonous syllables of Dr. Magnus's voice seemed to blend into her breathing like a quiet, tuneless lullaby. She *was* sleepy, for that matter. And it was very pleasant to relax here, listening to that dim, droning murmur while he talked on and on. How much longer until the end of the lecture . . .

"You are asleep now, Lisette. You are asleep, yet you can still hear my voice. Now you are falling deeper, deeper, deeper into a pleasant, relaxed sleep, Lisette. Deeper and deeper asleep. Can you still hear my voice?"

"Yes."

"You are asleep, Lisette. In a deep, deep sleep. You will remain in this deep sleep until I shall count to three.

As I count to three, you will slowly arise from your sleep until you are fully awake once again. Do you understand?''

"Yes."

"But when you hear me say the word *amber*, you will again fall into a deep, deep sleep, Lisette, just as you are asleep now. Do you understand?''

"Yes."

"Listen to me as I count, Lisette. One. Two. Three."

Lisette opened her eyes. For a moment her expression was blank, then a sudden confusion. She looked at Dr. Magnus seated beside her, then smiled ruefully. "I was asleep, I'm afraid. Or was I? . . ."

"You did splendidly, Miss Seyrig." Dr. Magnus beamed reassurance. "You passed into a simple hypnotic state, and as you can see now, there was no more cause for concern than in catching an afternoon nap."

"But I'm sure I just dropped off." Lisette glanced at her watch. Her appointment had been for three, and it was now almost four o'clock.

"Why not just settle back and rest some more, Miss Seyrig. That's it, relax again. All you need is to rest a bit, just a pleasant rest."

Her wrist fell back onto the cushions, as her eyes fell shut.

"Amber."

Dr. Magnus studied her calm features for a moment. "You are asleep now, Lisette. Can you hear me?"

"Yes."

"I want you to relax, Lisette. I want you to fall deeper, deeper, deeper into sleep. Deep, deep sleep. Far, far, far into sleep."

He listened to her breathing, then suggested: "You are thinking of your childhood now, Lisette. You are a little girl, not even in school yet. Something is making you very happy. You remember how happy you are. Why are you so happy?"

Lisette made a childish giggle. "It's my birthday party, and Ollie the Clown came to play with us."

"And how old are you today?"

"I'm five." Her right hand twitched, extended fingers and thumb.

"Go deeper now, Lisette. I want you to reach farther back. Far, far back into your memories. Go back to a time before you were a child in San Francisco. Far, farther back, Lisette. I want you to go back to the time of your dreams."

He studied her face. She remained in a deep hypnotic trance, but her expression registered sudden anxiety. It was as if she lay in normal sleep—reacting to some intense nightmare. She moaned.

"Deeper, Lisette. Don't be afraid to remember. Let your mind flow back to another time."

Her features still showed distress, but she seemed less agitated as his voice urged her deeper.

"Where are you?"

"I'm . . . I'm not certain." Her voice came in a well-bred English accent. "It's quite dark. Only a few candles are burning. I'm frightened."

"Go back to a happy moment," Dr. Magnus urged her, as her tone grew sharp with fear. "You are happy now. Something very pleasant and wonderful is happening to you."

Anxiety drained from her features. Her cheeks flushed; she smiled pleasurably.

"Where are you now?"

"I'm dancing. It's a grand ball to celebrate Her Majesty's Diamond Jubilee, and I've never seen such a throng. I'm certain Charles means to propose to me tonight, but he's ever so shy, and now he's simply fuming that Captain Stapledon has the next two dances. He's so dashing in his uniform. Everyone is watching us together."

"What is your name?"

"Elisabeth Beresford."

"Where do you live, Miss Beresford?"

"We have a house in Chelsea . . ."

Her expression abruptly changed. "It's dark again. I'm all alone. I can't see myself, although surely the candles shed sufficient light. There's something there in the candlelight. I'm moving closer.''

"One."

"It's an open coffin." Fear edged her voice.

"Two."

"God in Heaven!"

"Three."

VI

"We," Danielle announced grandly, "are invited to a party."

She produced an engraved card from her bag, presented it to Lisette, then went to hang up her damp raincoat.

"Bloody English summer weather!" Lisette heard her from the kitchen. "Is there any more coffee made? Oh, fantastic!"

She reappeared with a cup of coffee and an opened box of cookies—Lisette couldn't get used to calling them biscuits. "Want some?"

"No, thanks. Bad for my figure."

"And coffee on an empty tummy is bad for the nerves," Danielle said pointedly.

"Who is Beth Garrington?" Lisette studied the invitation.

"Um." Danielle tried to wash down a mouthful of crumbs with too-hot coffee. "Some friend of Midge's. Midge dropped by the gallery this afternoon and gave me the invitation. A costume revel. Rock stars to royalty among the guests. Midge promises that it will be super fun; said the last party Beth threw was unbridled debauchery—there was cocaine being passed around in an antique snuff box for the guests. Can you imagine that much coke!"

"And how did Midge manage the invitation?"

"I gather the discerning Ms. Garrington had admired several of my drawings that Maitland has on display—yea, even unto so far as to purchase one. Midge told her that she knew me and that we two were ornaments for any debauchery."

"The invitation is in both our names."

"Midge *likes* you."

"Midge despises me. She's jealous as a cat."

"Then she must have told our depraved hostess what a lovely couple we make. Besides, Midge is jealous of everyone—even dear Maitland, whose interest in me very obviously is not of the flesh. But don't fret about Midge—Englishwomen are naturally bitchy toward 'foreign' women. They're oh so proper and fashionable, but they never shave their legs. That's why I love mah fellow Americans."

Danielle kissed Lisette chastely on top of her head, powdering her hair with biscuit crumbs. "And I'm cold and wet and dying for a shower. How about you?"

"A masquerade?" Lisette wondered. "What sort of costume? Not something that we'll have to trot off to one of those rental places for, surely?"

"From what Midge suggests, anything goes so long as it's wild. Just create something divinely decadent, and we're sure to knock them dead." Danielle had seen *Cabaret* half-a-dozen times. "It's to be in some back-alley stately old home in Maida Vale, so there's no danger that the tenants downstairs will call the cops."

When Lisette remained silent, Danielle gave her a playful nudge. "Darling, it's a party we're invited to, not a funeral. What is it—didn't your session with Dr. Magnus go well?"

"I suppose it did." Lisette smiled without conviction. "I really can't say; all I did was doze off. Dr. Magnus seemed quite excited about it though. I found it all . . . well, just a little bit scary."

"I thought you said you just dropped off. *What* was scary?"

"It's hard to put into words. It's like when you're starting to have a bad trip on acid: There's nothing wrong that you can explain, but somehow your mind is telling you to be afraid."

Danielle sat down beside her and squeezed her arm about her shoulders. "That sounds to me like Dr. Magnus is getting somewhere. I felt just the same sort of free anxiety the first time I underwent analysis. It's a good sign, darling. It means you're beginning to understand all those troubled secrets the ego keeps locked away."

"Perhaps the ego keeps them locked away for some perfectly good reason."

"Meaning hidden sexual conflicts, I suppose." Danielle's fingers gently massaged Lisette's shoulders and neck. "Oh, Lisette. You mustn't be shy about getting to know yourself. *I* think it's exciting."

Lisette curled up against her, resting her cheek against Danielle's breast while the other girl's fingers soothed the tension from her muscles. She supposed she was over-reacting. After all, the nightmares were what distressed her so; Dr. Magnus seemed completely confident that he could free her from them.

"Which of your drawings did our prospective hostess buy?" Lisette asked, changing the subject.

"Oh, didn't I tell you?" Danielle lifted up her chin. "It was that charcoal study I did of you."

Lisette closed the shower curtains as she stepped into the tub. It was one of those long, narrow, deep tubs beloved of English bathrooms that always made her think of a coffin for two. A Rube Goldberg plumbing arrangement connected the hot and cold faucets, and from the common spout was afixed a rubber hose with a shower head which one might either hang from a hook on the wall or hold in hand. Danielle had replaced the ordinary shower head with a shower massage when she moved in, but she left the previous tenant's shaving mirror, a beveled glass oval in a heavily enameled antique frame, hanging on the wall above the hook.

Lisette glanced at her face in the steamed-up mirror. "I shouldn't have let you display that at the gallery."

"But why not?" Danielle was shampooing, and lather blinded her as she turned about. "Maitland thinks it's one of my best."

Lisette reached around her for the shower attachment.

"It seems a bit personal somehow. All those people looking at me. It's an invasion of privacy."

"But it's thoroughly modest, darling. Not like some topless billboard in Soho."

The drawing was a charcoal-and-pencil study of Lisette, done in what Danielle described as her David Hamilton phase. In sitting for it, Lisette had piled her hair in a high chignon and dressed in an antique cotton camisole and drawers with lace insertions that she'd found at a shop in Westbourne Grove. Danielle called it "Dark Rose." Lisette had thought it made her look fat.

Danielle grasped blindly for the shower massage, and Lisette placed it in her hand. "It just seems a bit too personal to have some total stranger owning my picture." Shampoo coursed like seafoam over Danielle's breasts. Lisette kissed the foam.

"Ah, but soon she won't be a total stranger," Danielle reminded her, her voice muffled by the pulsing shower spray.

Lisette felt Danielle's nipples harden beneath her lips. The brunette still pressed her eyes tightly shut against the force of the shower, but her other hand cupped Lisette's head encouragingly. Lisette gently moved her kisses downward along the other girl's slippery belly, kneeling as she did so. Danielle murmured, and when Lisette's tongue probed her drenched curls, she shifted her legs to let her knees rest beneath the blond girl's shoulders. The shower massage dropped from her fingers.

Lisette made love to her with a passion that surprised her—spontaneous, suddenly fierce, unlike their usual tenderness together. Her lips and tongue pressed into Danielle almost ravenously, her own ecstasy even more intense than that which she was drawing from Danielle. Danielle gasped and clung to the shower rail with one hand, her other fist clenched upon the curtain, sobbing as a long orgasm shuddered through her.

"Please, darling!" Danielle finally managed to beg. "My legs are too wobbly to hold me up any longer!"

She drew away. Lisette raised her face.

"Oh!"

Lisette rose to her feet with drugged movements. Her wide eyes at last registered Danielle's startled expression. She touched her lips and turned to look in the bathroom mirror.

"I'm sorry," Danielle put her arm about her shoulder. "I must have started my period. I didn't realize . . ."

Lisette stared at the blood-smeared face in the fogged shaving mirror.

Danielle caught her as she started to slump.

VII

She was conscious of the cold rain that pelted her face, washing from her nostrils the too-sweet smell of decaying flowers. Slowly she opened her eyes onto darkness and mist. Rain fell steadily, spiritlessly, gluing her white gown to her drenched flesh. She had been walking in her sleep again.

Wakefulness seemed forever in coming to her, so that only by slow degrees did she become aware of herself, of her surroundings. For a moment she felt as if she were a chess piece arrayed upon a board in a darkened room. All about her, stone monuments crowded together, their weathered surfaces streaming with moisture. She felt neither fear nor surprise that she stood in a cemetery.

She pressed her bare arms together across her breasts. Water ran over her pale skin as smoothly as upon the marble tombstones, and though her flesh felt as cold as the drenched marble, she did not feel chilled. She stood barefoot, her hair clinging to her shoulders above the low-necked cotton gown that was all she wore.

Automatically, her steps carried her through the darkness, as if following a familiar path through the maze of glistening stone. She knew where she was: This was Highgate Cemetery. She could not recall how she knew that, since she had no memory of ever having been to this place before. No more could she think how she knew her steps were taking her deeper into the cemetery instead of toward the gate.

A splash of color trickled onto her breast, staining its paleness as the rain dissolved it into a red rose above her heart.

She opened her mouth to scream, and a great bubble of unswallowed blood spewed from her lips.

"Elisabeth! Elisabeth!"

"Lisette! Lisette!"

Whose voice called her?

"Lisette! You can wake up now, Lisette."

Dr. Magnus's face peered into her own. Was there sudden concern behind that urbane mask?

"You're awake now, Miss Seyrig. Everything is all right."

Lisette stared back at him for a moment, uncertain of her reality, as if suddenly awakened from some profound nightmare.

"I . . . I thought I was dead." Her eyes still held her fear.

Dr. Magnus smiled to reassure her. "Somnambulism, my dear. You remembered an episode of sleepwalking from a former life. Tell me, have you yourself ever walked in your sleep?"

Lisette pressed her hands to her face, abruptly examined her fingers. "I don't know. I mean, I don't think so."

She sat up, searched in her bag for her compact. She paused for a moment before opening the mirror.

"Dr. Magnus, I don't think I care to continue these sessions." She stared at her reflection in fascination, not touching her makeup, and when she snapped the case shut, the frightened strain began to relax from her face. She wished she had a cigarette.

Dr. Magnus sighed and pressed his fingertips together, leaning back in his chair; watched her fidget with her clothing as she sat nervously on the edge of the couch.

"Do you really wish to terminate our exploration? We

have, after all, made excellent progress during these last few sessions.''

''Have we?''

''We have, indeed. You have consistently remembered incidents from the life of one Elisabeth Beresford, a young English lady living in London at the close of the last century. To the best of your knowledge of your family history, she is not an ancestress.''

Dr. Magnus leaned forward, seeking to impart his enthusiasm. ''Don't you see how important this is? If Elisabeth Beresford was not your ancestress, then there can be no question of genetic memory being involved. The only explanation must therefore be reincarnation—proof of the immortality of the soul. To establish this I must first confirm the existence of Elisabeth Beresford, and from that demonstrate that no familial bond exists between the two of you. We simply must explore this further.''

''Must we? I meant what progress have we made toward helping me, Dr. Magnus? It's all very good for you to be able to confirm your theories of reincarnation, but that doesn't do anything for me. If anything, the nightmares have grown more disturbing since we began these sessions.''

''Then perhaps we dare not stop.''

''What do you mean?'' Lisette wondered what he might do if she suddenly bolted from the room.

''I mean that the nightmares will grow worse regardless of whether you decide to terminate our sessions. Your unconscious self is struggling to tell you some significant message from a previous existence. It will continue to do so no matter how stubbornly you will yourself not to listen. My task is to help you listen to this voice, to understand the message it must impart to you—and with this understanding and self-awareness, you will experience inner peace. Without my help . . . Well, to be perfectly frank, Miss Seyrig, you are in some danger of a complete emotional breakdown.''

Lisette slumped back against the couch. She felt on the edge of panic and wished Danielle were here to support her.

"Why are my memories always nightmares?" Her voice shook, and she spoke slowly to control it.

"But they aren't always frightening memories, my dear. It's just that the memory of some extremely traumatic experience often seeks to come to the fore. You would expect some tremendously emotion-laden memory to be a potent one."

"Is Elisabeth Beresford . . . dead?"

"Assuming she was approximately twenty years of age at the time of Queen Victoria's Diamond Jubilee, she would have been past one hundred today. Besides, Miss Seyrig, her soul has been born again as your own. It must therefore follow . . ."

"Dr. Magnus. I don't *want* to know how Elisabeth Beresford died."

"Of course," Dr. Magnus told her gently. "Isn't that quite obvious?"

VIII

"For a wonder, it's forgot to rain tonight."

"Thank God for small favors," Lisette commented, thinking July in London had far more to do with monsoons than the romantic city of fogs celebrated in song. "All we need is to get these rained on."

She and Danielle bounced about on the back seat of the black Austin taxi, as their driver democratically seemed as willing to challenge lorries as pedestrians for right of way on the Edgeware Road. Feeling a bit selfconscious, Lisette tugged at the hem of her patent leather trench coat. They had decided to wear brightly embroidered Chinese silk lounging pyjamas that they'd found at one of the vintage clothing shops off the Portobello Road—gauzy enough for stares, but with only a demure trouser leg showing beneath their coats. "We're going to a masquerade party," Lisette had felt obliged to explain to the driver. Her concern was needless, as he hadn't given them a second glance. Either he was used to the current Chinese look in fashion, or else a few seasons of picking up couples at discos and punk rock clubs had inured him to any sort of costume.

The taxi turned into a series of side streets off Maida Vale and eventually made a neat U-turn that seemed almost an automotive pirouette. The frenetic beat of a new wave rock group clattered past the gate of an enclosed courtyard: something Mews—the iron plaque on the brick wall was too rusted to decipher in the dark—but from the lights and noise it must be the right address. A number of expensive-looking cars—Lisette recognized a Rolls or two and at least one Ferrari—were among those crowded against the curb. They squeezed their way past them and made for the source of the revelry, a brick-fronted townhouse of three or more storeys set at the back of the courtyard.

The door was opened by a girl in an abbreviated maid's costume. She checked their invitation while a similarly clad girl took their coats, and a third invited them to select from an assortment of masks and indicated where they might change. Lisette and Danielle chose sequined domino masks that matched the dangling scarves they wore tied low across their brows.

Danielle withdrew an ebony cigarette holder from her bag and considered their reflections with approval. "Divinely decadent," she drawled, gesturing with her black-lacquered nails. "All that time for my eyes, and just to cover them with a mask. Perhaps later—when it's cock's-crow and all unmask . . . Forward, darling."

Lisette kept at her side, feeling a bit lost and out of place. When they passed before a light, it was evident that they wore nothing beneath the silk pyjamas, and Lisette was grateful for the strategic brocade. As they came upon others of the newly arriving guests, she decided there was no danger of outraging anyone's modesty here. Midge had promised, "Anything goes so long as it's wild," and while their costumes might pass for street wear, many of the guests needed to avail themselves of the changing rooms upstairs.

A muscular young man clad only in a leather loincloth and a swordbelt with broadsword descended the stairs leading a buxom girl by a chain affixed to her wrists; aside from her manacles she wore a few scraps of leather. A couple in punk rock gear spat at them in passing; the girl was wearing a set of pasties with dangling razor blades for tassels and a pair of black latex tights that might have been spray paint. Two girls in vintage Christian Dior New Look evening gowns ogled the seminude swordsman from the landing above; Lisette noted their pronounced shoulders and Adam's apples and felt a twinge of envy that hormones and surgery could let them show a better cleavage than she could.

A new wave group called the Needle was performing in a large first-floor room—Lisette supposed it was an actual ballroom, although the house's original tenants would have considered tonight's ball a *danse macabre*. Despite the fact that the decibel level was well past the threshold of pain, most of the guests were congregated here, with smaller, quieter parties gravitating into other rooms. Here, about half were dancing, the rest standing about trying to talk. Marijuana smoke was barely discernible within the harsh haze from British cigarettes.

"There's Midge and Fiona," Danielle shouted in Lisette's ear. She waved energetically and steered a course through the dancers.

Midge was wearing an elaborate medieval gown—a heavily brocaded affair that rose from the floor to midway across her nipples. Her blond hair was piled high in some sort of conical headpiece, complete with flowing scarf. Fiona waited upon her in a page-boy costume.

"Are you just getting here?" Midge asked, running a deprecative glance down Lisette's costume. "There's champagne over on the sideboard. Wait, I'll summon one of the cute little French maids."

Lisette caught two glasses from a passing tray and presented one to Danielle. It was impossible to converse, but then she hadn't anything to talk about with Midge, and Fiona was no more than a shadow.

"Where's our hostess?" Danielle asked.

"Not down yet," Midge managed to shout. "Beth always waits to make a grand entrance at her little dos. You won't miss her.''

"Speaking of entrances . . ." Lisette commented, nodding toward the couple who were just coming onto the dance floor. The woman wore a Nazi SS officer's hat, jackboots, black trousers, and braces across her bare chest. She was astride the back of her male companion, who wore a saddle and bridle in addition to a few other bits of leather harness.

"I can't decide whether that's kinky or just tacky," Lisette said.

"Not like your little sorority teas back home, is it?" Midge smiled.

"Is there any coke about?" Danielle interposed quickly.

"There was a short while ago. Try the library—that's the room just down from where everyone's changing.''

Lisette downed her champagne and grabbed a refill before following Danielle upstairs. A man in fishnet tights, motorcycle boots, and a vest comprised mostly of chain and bits of Nazi medals caught at her arm and seemed to want to dance. Instead of a mask he wore about a pound of eye shadow and black lipstick. She shouted an inaudible excuse, held a finger to her nostril and snifted, and darted after Danielle.

'That was Eddie Teeth, lead singer for the Trepans, whom you just cut," Danielle told her. "Why didn't he grab *me!*''

"You'll get your chance," Lisette told her. "I think he's following us.''

Danielle dragged her to a halt halfway up the stairs.

"Got toot right here, loves.'' Eddie Teeth flipped the silver spoon and phial that dangled amidst the chains on his vest.

"Couldn't take the noise in there any longer," Lisette explained.

"Needle's shit.'' Eddie Teeth wrapped an arm about either waist and propelled them up the stairs. "You gashes sisters? I can dig incest.''

The library was pleasantly crowded—Lisette decided

she didn't want to be cornered with Eddie Teeth. A dozen or more guests stood about, sniffing and conversing energetically. Seated at a table, two of the ubiquitous maids busily cut lines onto mirrors and set them out for the guests, whose number remained more or less constant as people wandered in and left. A cigarette box offered tightly rolled joints.

"That's Thai." Eddie Teeth groped for a handful of the joints, stuck one in each girl's mouth, the rest inside his vest. Danielle giggled and fitted hers to her cigarette holder. Unfastening a silver tube from his vest, Eddie snorted two thick lines from one of the mirrors. "Toot your eyeballs out, loves," he invited them.

One of the maids collected the mirror when they had finished and replaced it with another, a dozen lines of cocaine neatly arranged across its surface. Industriously she began to work a chunk of rock through a sifter to replenish the empty mirror. Lisette watched in fascination. This finally brought home to her the wealth this party represented: All the rest simply seemed to her like something out of a movie, but dealing out coke to more than a hundred guests was an extravagance she could relate to.

"Danielle Borland, isn't it?"

A man dressed as Mephistopheles bowed before them. "Adrian Tregannet. We've met at one of Midge Vaughn's parties, you may recall."

Danielle stared at the face below the domino mask. "Oh, yes. Lisette, it's Mephisto himself."

"Then this is Miss Seyrig, the subject of your charcoal drawing that Beth so admires." Mephisto caught Lisette's hand and bent his lips to it. "Beth is so much looking forward to meeting you both."

Lisette retrieved her hand. "Aren't you the . . ."

"The rude fellow who accosted you in Kensington some days ago," Tregannet finished apologetically. "Yes, I'm afraid so. But you really must forgive me for my forwardness. I actually did mistake you for a very dear friend of mine, you see. Won't you let me make amends over a glass of champagne?"

"Certainly." Lisette decided that she had had quite enough of Eddie Teeth, and Danielle was quite capable of fending for herself if she grew tired of having her breasts squeezed by a famous pop star.

Tregannet quickly returned with two glasses of champagne. Lisette finished another two lines and smiled appreciatively as she accepted a glass. Danielle was trying to shotgun Eddie Teeth through her cigarette holder, and Lisette thought it a good chance to slip away.

"Your roommate is tremendously talented," Tregannet suggested. "Of course, she chose so charming a subject for her drawing."

Slick as snake oil, Lisette thought, letting him take her arm. "How very nice of you to say so. However, I really feel a bit embarrassed to think that some stranger owns a portrait of me in my underwear."

"Utterly chaste, my dear—as chaste as the "Dark Rose" of its title. Beth chose to hang it in her boudoir, so I hardly think it is on public display. I suspect from your garments in the drawing that you must share Beth's appreciation for the dress and manners of this past century."

Which is something I'd never suspect of our hostess, judging from this party, Lisette considered. "I'm quite looking forward to meeting her. I assume then that Ms. is a bit too modern for one of such quiet tastes. Is it Miss or Mrs. Garrington?"

"Ah, I hadn't meant to suggest an impression of a genteel dowager. Beth is entirely of your generation—a few years older than yourself, perhaps. Although I find Ms. too suggestive of American slang, I'm sure Beth would not object. However, there's no occasion for such formality here."

"You seem to know her well, Mr. Tregannet."

"It is an old family. I know her aunt, Julia Weatherford, quite well through our mutual interest in the occult. Perhaps you, too? . . ."

"Not really; Danielle is the one you should chat with about that. My field is art. I'm over here on fellowship at

London University.'' She watched Danielle and Eddie Teeth toddle off to the ballroom and jealously decided that Danielle's taste in her acquaintances left much to be desired. ''Could I have some more champagne?''

''To be sure. I won't be a moment.''

Lisette snorted a few more lines while she waited. A young man dressed as an Edwardian dandy offered her his snuffbox and gravely demonstrated its use. Lisette was struggling with a sneezing fit when Tregannet returned.

''You needn't have gone to all the bother,'' she told him. ''These little French maids are dashing about with trays of champagne.''

''But those glasses have lost the proper chill,'' Tregannet explained. ''To your very good health.''

''Cheers.'' Lisette felt light-headed and promised herself to go easy for a while. ''Does Beth live here with her aunt, then?''

''Her aunt lives on the Continent; I don't believe she's visited London for several years. Beth moved in about ten years ago. Theirs is not a large family, but they are not without wealth, as you can observe. They travel a great deal as well, and it's fortunate that Beth happened to be in London during your stay here. Incidently, just how long will you be staying in London?''

''About a year is all.'' Lisette finished her champagne. ''Then it's back to my dear, dull family in San Francisco.''

''Then there's no one here in London? . . .''

''Decidedly not, Mr. Tregannet. And now if you'll excuse me, I think I'll find the ladies'.''

Cocaine might well be the champagne of drugs, but cocaine and champagne didn't seem to mix well, Lisette mused, turning the bathroom over to the next frantic guest. Her head felt really buzzy, and she thought she might do better if she found a bedroom somewhere and lay down for a moment. But then she'd most likely wake up and find some man on top of her, judging from this lot. She decided she'd lay off the champagne and have just a line or two to shake off the feeling of having been sandbagged.

The crowd in the study had changed during her absence.

Just now it was dominated by a group of guests dressed in costumes from *The Rocky Horror Show,* now closing out its long run at the Comedy Theatre in Piccadilly. Lisette had grown bored with the fad the film version had generated in the States, and pushed her way past the group as they vigorously danced the Time Warp and bellowed out songs from the show.

"Give yourself over to absolute pleasure," someone sang in her ear as she industriously snorted a line from the mirror. "Erotic nightmares beyond any measure," the song continued.

Lisette finished a second line and decided she had had enough. She straightened from the table and broke for the doorway. The tall transvestite dressed as Frankie barred her way with a dramatic gesture, singing ardently: "Don't dream it—be it!"

Lisette blew him a kiss and ducked around him. She wished she could find a quiet place to collect her thoughts. Maybe she should find Danielle first—if she could handle the ballroom that long.

The dance floor was far more crowded than when they'd come in. At least all these jostling bodies seemed to absorb some of the decibels from the blaring banks of amplifiers and speakers. Lisette looked in vain for Danielle amidst the dancers, succeeding only in getting champagne sloshed on her back. She caught sight of Midge, recognizable above the mob by her conical medieval headdress, and pushed her way toward her.

Midge was being fed caviar on bits of toast by Fiona while she talked with an older woman who looked like the pictures Lisette had seen of Marlene Dietrich dressed in men's formal evening wear.

"Have you seen Danielle?" Lisette asked her.

"Why, not recently, darling," Midge smiled, licking caviar from her lips with the tip of her tongue. "I believe she and that rock singer were headed upstairs for a bit more privacy. I'm sure she'll come collect you once they're finished."

"Midge, you're a cunt," Lisette told her through her sweetest smile. She turned away and made for the doorway, trying not to ruin her exit by staggering. Screw Danielle—she needed to have some fresh air.

A crowd had gathered at the foot of the stairway, and she had to push through the doorway to escape the ballroom. Behind her, the Needle mercifully took a break. "She's coming down!" Lisette heard someone whisper breathlessly. The inchoate babel of the party fell to a sudden lull that made Lisette shiver.

At the top of the stairway stood a tall woman, enveloped in a black velvet cloak from her throat to her ankles. Her blond hair was piled high in a complex variation of the once-fashionable French twist. Strings of garnets were entwined in her hair and edged the close-fitting black mask that covered the upper half of her face. For a hushed interval she stood there, gazing imperiously down upon her guests.

Adrian Tregannet leapt to the foot of the stairway. He signed to a pair of maids, who stepped forward to either side of their mistress.

"Milords and miladies!" he announced with a sweeping bow. "Let us pay honor to our betwitching mistress whose feast we celebrate tonight! I give you the lamia who haunted Adam's dreams—Lilith!"

The maids smoothly swept the cloak from their mistress's shoulders. From the multitude at her feet came an audible intake of breath. Beth Garrington was attired in a strapless corselette of gleaming black leather, laced tightly about her waist. The rest of her costume consisted only of knee-length, stiletto-heeled tight boots, above-the-elbow gloves, and a spiked collar around her throat—all of black leather that contrasted starkly against her white skin and blond hair. At first Lisette thought she wore a bullwhip coiled about her body as well, but then the coils moved, and she realized that it was an enormous black snake.

"Lilith!" came the shout, chanted in a tone of awe. "Lilith!"

Acknowledging their worship with a sinuous gesture,

Beth Garrington descended the staircase. The serpent coiled
from gloved arm to gloved arm, entwining her cinched
waist; its eyes considered the revellers imperturbably. Champagne glasses lifted in a toast to Lilith, and the chattering
voice of the party once more began to fill the house.

Tregannet touched Beth's elbow as she greeted her guests
at the foot of the stairway. He whispered into her ear, and
she smiled graciously and moved away with him.

Lisette clung to the staircase newel, watching them
approach. Her head was spinning and she desperately needed
to lie down in some fresh air, but she couldn't trust her
legs to carry her outside. She stared into the eyes of the
serpent, hypnotized by its flickering tongue.

The room seemed to surge in and out of focus. The
masks of the guests seemed to leer and gloat with the
awareness of some secret jest; the dancers in their fantastic
costumes became a grotesque horde of satyrs and wanton
demons, writhing about the ballroom in some witches'
sabbat of obscene mass copulation. As in a nightmare,
Lisette willed her legs to turn and run, realized that her
body was no longer obedient to her will.

"Beth, here's someone you've been dying to meet,"
Lisette heard Tregannet say. "Beth Garrington, allow me
to present Lisette Seyrig."

The lips beneath the black mask curved in a pleasurable
smile. Lisette gazed into the eyes behind the mask, and
discovered that she could no longer feel her body. She
thought she heard Danielle cry out her name.

The eyes remained in her vision long after she slid down
the newel and collapsed upon the floor.

IX

The Catherine Wheel was a pub on Kensington Church
Street. They served good lunches there, and Lisette liked
to stop in before walking down Holland Street for her
sessions with Dr. Magnus. Since today was her final such
session, it seemed appropriate that they should end the
evening here.

"While I dislike repeating myself," Dr. Magnus spoke earnestly, "I really do think we should continue."

Lisette drew on a cigarette and shook her head decisively. "No way, Dr. Magnus. My nerves are shot to hell. I mean, look—when I freak out at a costume party and have to be carted home to bed by my roommate! It was like when I was a kid and got hold of some bad acid: The whole world was some bizarre and sinister freak show for weeks. Once I got my head back on, I said, No more acid."

"That was rather a notorious circle you were travelling in. Further, you were, if I understand you correctly, overindulging a bit that evening."

"A few glasses of champagne and a little toot never did anything before but make me a bit giggly and talkative." Lisette sipped her half of lager; she'd never developed a taste for English bitter, and at least the lager was chilled. They sat across from each other at a table the size of a hubcap; she in the corner of a padded bench against the wall, he at a chair set out into the room, pressed in by a wall of standing bodies. A foot away from her on the padded bench, three young men huddled about a similar table, talking animatedly. For all that, she and Dr. Magnus might have been all alone in the room. Lisette wondered if the psychologist who had coined the faddish concept of "space" had been inspired in a crowded English pub.

"It isn't just that I fainted at the party. It isn't just the nightmares." She paused to find words. "It's just that everything somehow seems to be drifting out of focus, out of control. It's . . . well, it's frightening."

"Precisely why we must continue."

"Precisely why we must not." Lisette sighed. They'd covered this ground already. It had been a moment of weakness when she agreed to allow Dr. Magnus to buy her a drink afterward instead of heading back to the flat. Still, he had been so distressed when she told him she was terminating their sessions.

"I've tried to cooperate with you as best I could, and I'm certain you are entirely sincere in your desire to help me.'' Well, she wasn't all *that* certain, but no point in going into that. ''However, the fact remains that since we began these sessions, my nerves have gone to hell. You say they'd be worse without the sessions, I say the sessions have made them worse, and maybe there's no connection at all—it's just that my nerves have gotten worse, so now I'm going to trust my intuition and try life without these sessions. Fair enough?''

Dr. Magnus gazed uncomfortably at his barely tasted glass of sherry. ''While I fully understand your rationale, I must in all conscience beg you to reconsider, Lisette. You are running risks that . . .''

''Look. If the nightmares go away, then terrific. If they don't, I can always pack up and head back to San Francisco. That way I'll be clear of whatever it is about London that disagrees with me, and if not, I'll see my psychiatrist back home.''

''Very well, then.'' Dr. Magnus squeezed her hand. ''However, please bear in mind that I remain eager to continue our sessions at any time, should you change your mind.''

''That's fair enough, too. And very kind of you.''

Dr. Magnus lifted his glass of sherry to the light. Pensively, he remarked: ''Amber.''

X

''Lisette?''

Danielle locked the front door behind her and hung up her inadequate umbrella in the hallway. She considered her face in the mirror and grimaced at the mess of her hair. ''Lisette? Are you here?''

No answer, and her rain things were not in the hallway. Either she was having a late session with Dr. Magnus, or else she'd wisely decided to duck under cover until this bloody rain let up. After she'd had to carry Lisette home in a taxi when she passed out at the party, Danielle was starting to feel real concern over her state of health.

Danielle kicked off her damp shoes as she entered the

living room. The curtains were drawn against the greyness outside, and she switched on a lamp to brighten the flat a bit. Her dress clung to her like a clammy fishskin; she shivered and thought about a cup of coffee. If Lisette hadn't returned yet, there wouldn't be any brewed. She'd have a warm shower instead, and after that she'd see to the coffee—if Lisette hadn't returned to set a pot going in the meantime.

"Lisette?" Their bedroom was empty. Danielle turned on the overhead light. Christ, it was gloomy! So much for long English summer evenings—with all the rain, she couldn't remember when she'd last seen the sun. She struggled out of her damp dress, spread it flat across her bed with the vague hope that it might not wrinkle too badly, then tossed her bra and tights onto a chair.

Slipping into her bathrobe, Danielle padded back into the living room. Still no sign of Lisette, and it was past nine. Perhaps she'd stopped off at a pub. Crossing to the stereo, Danielle placed the new Blondie album on the turntable and turned up the volume. Let the neighbors complain—at least this would help dispel the evening's gloom.

She cursed the delay needed to adjust the shower temperature to satisfaction, then climbed into the tub. The hot spray felt good, and she stood under it contentedly for several minutes—initially revitalized, then lulled into a delicious sense of relaxation. Through the rush of the spray, she could hear the muffled beat of the stereo. As she reached for the shampoo, she began to move her body with the rhythm.

The shower curtain billowed as the bathroom door opened. Danielle risked a soapy squint around the curtain—she knew the flat was securely locked, but after seeing *Psycho* . . . It was only Lisette, already undressed, her long blond hair falling over her breasts.

"Didn't hear you come in with the stereo going," Danielle greeted her. "Come on in before you catch cold."

Danielle resumed lathering her hair as the shower cur-

tain parted and the other girl stepped into the tub behind
her. Her eyes squeezed shut against the soap, she felt
Lisette's breasts thrust against her back, her flat belly press
against her buttocks. Lisette's hands came around her to
cup her breasts gently.

At least Lisette had gotten over her silly tiff about Eddie
Teeth. She'd explained to Lisette that she'd ditched that
greasy slob when he'd tried to dry hump her on the dance
floor, but how do you reason with a silly thing who faints
at the sight of a snake?

"Jesus, you're chilled to the bone!" Danielle complained with a shiver. "Better stand under the shower and
get warm. Did you get caught in the rain?"

The other girl's fingers continued to caress her breasts,
and instead of answering, her lips teased the nape of
Danielle's neck. Danielle made a delighted sound deep in
her throat, letting the spray rinse the lather from her hair
and over their embraced bodies. Languidly she turned
about to face her lover, closing her arms about Lisette's
shoulders for support.

Lisette's kisses held each taut nipple for a moment,
teasing them almost painfully. Danielle pressed the other
girl's face to her breasts, sighed as her kisses nibbled
upward to her throat. She felt weak with arousal, and only
Lisette's strength held her upright in the tub. Her lover's
lips upon her throat tormented her beyond enduring; Danielle
gasped and lifted Lisette's face to meet her own.

Her mouth was open to receive Lisette's red-lipped kiss,
and it opened wider as Danielle stared into the eyes of her
lover. Her first emotion was one of wonder.

"You're not Lisette!"

It was nearly midnight when Lisette unlocked the door
to their flat and quietly let herself in. Only a few lights
were on, and there was no sign of Danielle—either she had
gone out or more likely had gone to bed.

Lisette hung up her raincoat and wearily pulled off her
shoes. She'd barely caught the last train. She must have

been crazy to let Dr. Magnus talk her into returning to his office for another session that late, but then, he was quite right: As serious as her problems were, she really did need all the help he could give her. She felt a warm sense of gratitude to Dr. Magnus for being there when she so needed his help.

The turntable had stopped, but a light on the amplifier indicated that the power was still on. Lisette cut if off and closed the lid over the turntable. She felt too tired to listen to an album just now.

She became aware that the shower was running. In that case, Danielle hadn't gone to bed. She supposed she really ought to apologize to her for letting Midge's bitchy lies get under her skin. After all, she had ruined the party for Danielle; poor Danielle had had to get her to bed and had left the party without ever getting to meet Beth Garrington, and she was the one Beth had invited in the first place.

"Danielle? I'm back." Lisette called through the bathroom door. "Do you want anything?"

No answer. Lisette looked into their bedroom, just in case Danielle had invited a friend over. No, the beds were still made up; Danielle's clothes were spread out by themselves.

"Danielle?" Lisette raised her voice. Perhaps she couldn't hear over the noise of the shower. "Danielle?" Surely she was all right.

Lisette's feet felt damp. She looked down. A puddle of water was seeping beneath the door. Danielle must not have the shower curtains closed properly.

"Danielle! You're flooding us!"

Lisette opened the door and peered cautiously within. The curtain was closed, right enough. A thin spray still reached through a gap, and the shower had been running long enough for the puddle to spread. It occurred to Lisette that she should see Danielle's silhouette against the translucent shower curtain.

"Danielle!" She began to grow alarmed. "Danielle! Are you all right?"

She pattered across the wet tiles and drew aside the curtain. Danielle lay in the bottom of the tub, the spray falling on her upturned lips, her flesh paler than the porcelain of the tub.

XI

It was early afternoon when they finally allowed her to return to the flat. Had she been able to think of another place to go, she probably would have gone there. Instead, Lisette wearily slumped onto the couch, too spent to pour herself the drink she desperately wanted.

Somehow she had managed to phone the police, through her hysteria make them understand where she was. Once the squad car arrived, she had no further need to act out of her own initiative; she simply was carried along in the rush of police investigation. It wasn't until they were questioning her at New Scotland Yard that she realized she herself was not entirely free from suspicion.

The victim had bled to death, the medical examiner ruled, her blood washed down the tub drain. A safety razor used for shaving legs had been opened, its blade removed. There were razor incisions along both wrists, directed lengthwise, into the radial artery, as opposed to the shallow crosswise cuts utilized by suicides unfamiliar with human anatomy. There was in addition an incision in the left side of the throat. It was either a very determined suicide, or a skillfully concealed murder. In view of the absence of any signs of forced entry or of a struggle, more likely the former. The victim's roommate did admit to a recent quarrel. Laboratory tests would indicate whether the victim might have been drugged or rendered unconscious through a blow. After that, the inquest would decide.

Lisette had explained that she had spent the evening with Dr. Magnus. The fact that she was receiving emotional therapy, as they interpreted it, caused several mental notes to be made. Efforts to reach Dr. Magnus by telephone proved unsuccessful, but his secretary did confirm that Miss Seyrig had shown up for her appointment the previous afternoon. Dr. Magnus would get in touch with them as soon as he returned to his office. No, she did not know why he had cancelled today's appointments, but it was not unusual for Dr. Magnus to dash off suddenly when essential research demanded immediate attention.

After a while they let Lisette make phone calls. She phoned her parents, then wished she hadn't. It was still the night before in California, and it was like turning back the hands of time to no avail. They urged her to take the next flight home, but of course it wasn't all that simple, and it just wasn't feasible for either of them to fly over on a second's notice, since, after all, there really was nothing they could do. She phoned Maitland Reddin, who was stunned at the news and offered to help in any way he could, but Lisette couldn't think of any way. She phoned Midge Vaughn, who hung up on her. She phoned Dr. Magnus, who still couldn't be reached. Mercifully, the police took care of phoning Danielle's next of kin.

A physician at New Scotland Yard had spoken with her briefly and had given her some pills—a sedative to ease her into sleep after her ordeal. They had driven her back to the flat after impressing upon her the need to be present at the inquest. She must not be concerned should any hypothetical assailant yet be lurking about, inasmuch as the flat would be under surveillance.

Lisette stared dully about the flat, still unable to comprehend what had happened. The police had been through—measuring, dusting for fingerprints, leaving things in a mess. Bleakly Lisette tried to convince herself that this was only another nightmare, that in a moment Danielle would pop in and find her asleep on the couch. Christ, what was she going to do with all of Danielle's things? Danielle's mother was remarried and living in Colorado; her father was an executive in a New York investment corporation. Evidently he had made arrangements to have the body shipped back to the States.

"Oh, Danielle." Lisette was too stunned for tears. Perhaps she should check into a hotel for now. No, she couldn't bear being all alone with her thoughts in a strange place. How strange to realize now that she really had no close friends in London other than Danielle—and what friends she did have were mostly people she'd met through Danielle.

She'd left word with Dr. Magnus's secretary for him to call her once he came in. Perhaps she should call there once again, just in case Dr. Magnus had missed her message. Lisette couldn't think what good Dr. Magnus could do, but he was such an understanding person and she felt much better whenever she spoke with him.

She considered the bottle of pills in her bag. Perhaps it would be best to take a couple of them and sleep around the clock. She felt too drained just now to have energy enough to think.

The phone began to ring. Lisette stared at it for a moment without comprehension, then lunged up from the couch to answer it.

"Is this Lisette Seyrig?"

It was a woman's voice—one Lisette didn't recognize. "Yes. Who's calling, please?"

"This is Beth Garrington, Lisette. I hope I'm not disturbing you."

"That's quite all right."

"You poor dear! Maitland Reddin phoned to tell me of the tragedy. I can't tell you how shocked I am. Danielle seemed such a dear from our brief contact, and she had such a great talent."

"Thank you. I'm sorry you weren't able to know her better." Lisette sensed guilt and embarrassment at the memory of that brief contact.

"Darling, you can't be thinking about staying in that flat alone. Is there someone there with you?"

"No, there isn't. That's all right. I'll be fine."

"Don't be silly. Listen, I have enough empty bedrooms in this old barn to open a hotel. Why don't you just pack a few things and come straight over?"

"That's very kind of you, but I really couldn't."

"Nonsense! It's no good for you to be there all by yourself. Strange as this may sound, when I'm not throwing one of these invitational riots, this is a quiet little backwater and things are dull as church. I'd love the company, and it will do you a world of good to get away."

"You're really very kind to invite me, but I . . ."

"Please, Lisette—be reasonable. I have guest rooms here already made up, and I'll send the car around to pick you up. All you need do is say yes and toss a few things into your bag. After a good night's sleep, you'll feel much more like coping with things tomorrow."

When Lisette didn't immediately reply, Beth added carefully: "Besides, Lisette, I understand the police haven't ruled out the possibility of murder. In that event, unless poor Danielle simply forgot to lock up, there is a chance that whoever did this has a key to your flat."

"The police said they'd watch the house."

"He might also be someone you both know and trust, someone Danielle invited in."

Lisette stared wildly at the sinister shadows that lengthened about the flat. Her refuge had been violated. Even familiar objects seemed tainted and alien. She fought back tears. "I don't know what to think." She realized she'd been clutching the receiver for a long silent interval.

"Poor dear! There's nothing you need think about! Now listen. I'm at my solicitor's, tidying up some property matters for Aunt Julia. I'll phone right now to have my car sent around for you. It'll be there by the time you pack your toothbrush and pyjamas, and whisk you straight off to bucolic Maida Vale. The maids will plump up your pillows for you, and you can have a nice nap before I get home for dinner. Poor darling, I'll bet you haven't eaten a thing. Now, say you'll come."

"Thank you. It's awfully good of you. Of course I will."

"Then it's done. Don't worry about a thing, Lisette. I'll see you this evening."

XII

Dr. Magnus hunched forward on the narrow seat of the taxi, wearily massaging his forehead and temples. It might not help his mental fatigue, but maybe the reduced muscle tension would ease his headache. He glanced at his watch. Getting on past ten. He'd had no sleep last night, and it didn't look as if he'd be getting much tonight. If only those girls would answer their phone!

It didn't help matters that his conscience plagued him. He had broken a sacred trust. He should never have made use of post-hypnotic suggestion last night to persuade Lisette to return for a further session. It went against all principles, but there had been no other course: The girl was adamant, and he had to know—he was so close to establishing final proof. If only for one final session of regressive hypnosis . . .

Afterward he had spent a sleepless night, too excited for rest, at work in his study trying to reconcile the conflicting elements of Lisette's released memories with the historical data his research had so far compiled. By morning he had been able to pull together just enough facts to deepen the mystery. He had phoned his secretary at home to cancel all his appointments, and had spent the day at the tedious labor of delving through dusty municipal records and newspaper files, working feverishly as the past reluctantly yielded one bewildering clue after another.

By now Dr. Magnus was exhausted, hungry, and none too clean, but he had managed to establish proof of his theories. He was not elated. In doing so he had uncovered another secret, something undreamed of in his philosophies. He began to hope that his life work was in error.

"Here's the address, sir."

"Thank you, driver." Dr. Magnus awoke from his grim revery and saw that he had reached his destination. Quickly he paid the driver and hurried up the walk to Lisette's flat. Only a few lights were on, and he rang the bell urgently—a helpless sense of foreboding making his movements clumsy.

"Just one moment, sir!"

Dr. Magnus jerked about at the voice. Two men in plain clothes approached him briskly from the pavement.

"Stand easy! We're police."

"Is something the matter, officers?" Obviously something was.

"Might we ask what your business here is, sir?"

"Certainly. I'm a friend of Miss Borland and Miss Seyrig. I haven't been able to reach them by phone, and as I have some rather urgent matters to discuss with Miss Seyrig, I thought perhaps I might try reaching her here at her flat." He realized he was far too nervous.

"Might we see some identification, sir?"

"Is there anything wrong, officers?" Magnus repeated, producing his wallet.

"Dr. Ingmar Magnus." The taller of the pair regarded him quizzically. "I take it you don't keep up with the news, Dr. Magnus."

"Just what is this about!"

"I'm Inspector Bradley, Dr. Magnus, and this is Detective Sergeant Wharton. CID. We've been wanting to ask you a few questions, sir, if you'll just come with us."

It was totally dark when Lisette awoke from troubled sleep. She stared wide-eyed into the darkness for a moment, wondering where she was. Slowly memory supplanted the vague images of her dream. Switching on a lamp beside her bed, Lisette frowned at her watch. It was close to midnight. She had overslept.

Beth's Rolls had come for her almost before she had had time hastily to pack her overnight bag. Once she was at the house in Maida Vale, a maid—wearing a more conventional uniform than those at her last visit—had shown her to a spacious guest room on the top floor. Lisette had taken a sedative pill and gratefully collapsed onto the bed. She'd planned to catch a short nap, then meet her hostess for dinner. Instead she had slept for almost ten solid hours. Beth must be convinced she was a hopeless twit after this.

As so often happens after an overextended nap, Lisette now felt restless. She wished she'd thought to bring a book. The house was completely silent. Surely it was too late to ring for a maid. No doubt Beth had meant to let her sleep through until morning, and by now would have retired herself. Perhaps she should take another pill and go back to sleep herself.

On the other hand, Beth Garrington hardly seemed the type to make it an early night. She might well still be awake, perhaps watching television where the noise wouldn't disturb her guest. In any event, Lisette didn't want to go back to sleep just yet.

She climbed out of bed, realizing that she'd only half undressed before falling asleep. Pulling off bra and panties, Lisette slipped into the antique nightdress of ribbons and lace she'd brought along. She hadn't thought to pack slippers or a robe, but it was a warm night, and the white cotton gown was modest enough for a peek into the hall.

There was a ribbon of light edging the door of the room at the far end of the hall. The rest of the hallway lay in darkness. Lisette stepped quietly from her room. Since Beth hadn't mentioned other guests and the servants' quarters were elsewhere, presumably the light was coming from her hostess's bedroom and indicated she might still be awake. Lisette decided she really should make the effort to meet her hostess while in a conscious state.

She heard a faint sound of music as she tiptoed down the hallway. The door to the room was ajar, and the music came from within. She was in luck; Beth must still be up. At the doorway she knocked softly.

"Beth? Are you awake? It's Lisette."

There was no answer, but the door swung open at her touch.

Lisette started to call out again, but her voice froze in her throat. She recognized the tune she heard, and she knew this room. When she entered the bedroom, she could no more alter her actions than she could control the course of her dreams.

It was a large bedroom, entirely furnished in the mode

of the late Victorian period. The windows were curtained, and the room's only light came from a candle upon a night table beside the huge four-poster bed. An antique gold pocket watch lay upon the night table also, and the watch was chiming an old music-box tune.

Lisette crossed the room, praying that this was no more than another vivid recurrence of her nightmare. She reached the night table and saw that the watch's hands pointed toward midnight. The chimes stopped. She picked up the watch and examined the picture that she knew would be inside the watchcase.

The picture was a photograph of herself.

Lisette let the watch clatter onto the table, stared in terror at the four-poster bed.

From within, a hand drew back the bed curtains.

Lisette wished she could scream, could awaken.

Sweeping aside the curtains, the occupant of the bed sat up and gazed at her.

And Lisette stared back at herself.

"Can't you drive a bit faster than this!"

Inspector Bradley resisted the urge to wink at Detective Sergeant Wharton. "Sit back, Dr. Magnus. We'll be there in good time. I trust you'll have rehearsed some apologies for when we disrupt a peaceful household in the middle of the night."

"I only pray such apologies will be necessary," Dr. Magnus said, continuing to sit forward as if that would inspire the driver to go faster.

It hadn't been easy, Dr. Magnus reflected. He dared not tell them the truth. He suspected that Bradley had agreed to make a late night call on Beth Garrington more to check out his alibi than from any credence he gave to Magnus's improvised tale.

Buried all day in frenzied research, Dr. Magnus hadn't listened to the news, had ignored the tawdry London tabloids with their lurid headlines: "Naked Beauty Slashed in Tub" "Nude Model Slain in Bath" "Party Girl Suicide or

Ripper's Victim?'' His shock of learning of Danielle's death was seconded by the shock of discovering that he was one of the "important leads" police were following.

It had taken all his powers of persuasion to convince them to release him—or at least, to accompany him to the house in Maida Vale. Ironically, he and Lisette were the only ones who could account for each other's presence elsewhere at the time of Danielle's death. While the CID might have been sceptical as to the nature of their late-night session at Dr. Magnus's office, there were a few corroborating details. A barman at the Catherine Wheel had remembered the distinguished gent with the beard leaving after his lady friend had dropped off of a sudden. The cleaning lady had heard voices and left his office undisturbed. This much they'd already checked in verifying Lisette's whereabouts that night. Half a dozen harassed records clerks could testify as to Dr. Magnus's presence for today.

Dr. Magnus grimly reviewed the results of his research. There was an Elisabeth Beresford, born in London in 1879 of a well-to-do family who lived in Cheyne Row on the Chelsea Embankment. Elisabeth Beresford married a Captain Donald Stapledon in 1899 and moved to India with her husband. She returned to London, evidently suffering from consumption contracted while abroad, and died in 1900. She was buried in Highgate Cemetery. That much Dr. Magnus had initially learned with some difficulty. From that basis he had pressed on for additional corroborating details, both from Lisette's released memories and from research into records of the period.

It had been particularly difficult to trace the subsequent branches of the family—something he must do in order to establish that Elisabeth Beresford could not have been an ancestress of Lisette Seyrig. And it disturbed him that he had been unable to locate the tomb of Elisabeth Stapledon, née Beresford, in Highgate Cemetery.

Last night he had pushed Lisette as relentlessly as he dared. Out of her resurfacing visions of horror he finally found a clue. These were not images from nightmare, not symbolic representations of buried fears. They were literal memories.

Because of the sensation involved and the considerable station of the families concerned, public records had discreetly avoided reference to the tragedy, as had the better newspapers. The yellow journals were less reticent, and here Dr. Magnus began to know fear.

Elisabeth Stapledon had been buried alive.

At her final wishes, the body had not been embalmed. The papers suggested that this was a clear premonition of her fate, and quoted passages from Edgar Allan Poe. Captain Stapledon paid an evening visit to his wife's tomb and discovered her wandering in a dazed condition about the graves. This was more than a month after her entombment.

The newspapers were full of pseudoscientific theories, spiritualist explanations, and long accounts of Indian mystics who had remained in a state of suspended animation for weeks on end. No one seems to have explained exactly how Elisabeth Stapledon escaped from both coffin and crypt, but it was supposed that desperate strength had wrenched loose the screws, while, providentially, the crypt had not been properly locked after a previous visit.

Husband and wife understandably went abroad immediately afterward in order to escape publicity and for Elisabeth Stapledon to recover from her ordeal. This she very quickly did, but evidently the shock was more than Captain Stapledon could endure. He died in 1902, and his wife returned to London soon after, inheriting his extensive fortune and properties, including their house in Maida Vale. When she later inherited her own family's estate— her sole brother fell in the Boer War—she was a lady of great wealth.

Elisabeth Stapledon became one of the most notorious hostesses of the Edwardian era and on until the close of the First World War. Her beauty was considered remarkable, and men marvelled, while her rivals bemoaned, that she scarcely seemed to age with the passing years. After the war, she left London to travel about the exotic East. In 1924 news came of her death in India.

Her estate passed to her daughter, Jane Stapledon, born abroad in 1901. While Elisabeth Stapledon made occasional references to her daughter, Jane was raised and educated in Europe and never seemed to have come to London until her arrival in 1925. Some had suggested that the mother had wished to keep her daughter pure from her own Bohemian life-style, but when Jane Stapledon appeared it seemed more likely that her mother's motives for her seclusion had been born of jealousy. Jane Stapledon had all her mother's beauty—indeed, her older admirers vowed she was the very image of Elisabeth in her youth. She also had inherited her mother's taste for wild living; with a new circle of friends from her own age group, she took up where her mother had left off. The newspapers were particularly scandalized by her association with Aleister Crowley and others of his circle. Although her dissipations bridged the years of Flaming Youth to the Lost Generation, even her enemies had to admit she carried her years extremely well. In 1943 Jane Stapledon was missing and presumed dead after an air raid levelled and burned a section of London where she had gone to dine with friends.

Papers in the hands of her solicitor left her estate to a daughter living in America, Julia Weatherford, born in Miami in 1934. Evidently her mother had enjoyed a typical whirlwind resort romance with an American millionaire while wintering in Florida. Their marriage was a secret one, annulled following Julia's birth, and her daughter had been left with her former husband. Julia Weatherford arrived from the States early in 1946. Any doubts as to the authenticity of her claim were instantly banished, for she was the very picture of her mother in her younger days. Julia again seemed to have the family's wild streak, and she carried on the tradition of wild parties and bizarre acquaintances through the Beat Generation to the Flower Children. Her older friends thought it amazing that Julia in a minidress might easily be mistaken as being of the same age group as her young pot-smoking hippie friends. But it might have been that at last her youth began to fade, because since 1967 Julia Weatherford had been living more or less in seclusion in Europe, occasionally visited by her niece.

Her niece, Beth Garrington, born in 1950, was the orphaned daughter of Julia's American half-sister and a wealthy young Englishman from Julia's collection. After her parents' death in a plane crash in 1970, Beth had become her aunt's protégée and carried on the mad life in London. It was apparent that Beth Garrington would inherit her aunt's property as well. It was also apparent that she was the spitting image of her Aunt Julia when the latter was her age. It would be most interesting to see the two of them together. And that, of course, no one had ever done.

At first Dr. Magnus had been unwilling to accept the truth of the dread secret he had uncovered. And yet, with the knowledge of Lisette's released memories, he knew there could be no other conclusion.

It was astonishing how thoroughly a woman who thrived on notoriety could avoid having her photograph published. After all, changing fashions and new hair styles, careful adjustments with cosmetics, could only do so much, and while the mind's eye had an inaccurate memory, a camera lens did not. Dr. Magnus did succeed in finding a few photographs through persistent research. Given a good theatrical costume and makeup crew, they all might have been taken of the same woman on the same day.

They might also all have been taken of Lisette Seyrig.

However, Dr. Magnus knew that it *would* be possible to see Beth Garrington and Lisette Seyrig together.

And he prayed he would be in time to prevent it.

With this knowledge tormenting his thoughts, it was a miracle that Dr. Magnus had held onto sanity well enough to persuade New Scotland Yard to make this late-night drive to Maida Vale—desperate, in view of what he knew to be true. He had suffered a shock as severe as any that night when they told him at last where Lisette had gone.

"She's quite all right. She's staying with a friend."

"Might I ask where?"

"A chauffered Rolls picked her up. We checked registration, and it belongs to a Miss Elisabeth Garrington in Maida Vale."

Dr. Magnus had been frantic then, had demanded that they take him there instantly. A telephone call informed them that Miss Seyrig was sleeping under sedation and could not be disturbed; she would return his call in the morning.

Controlling his panic, Dr. Magnus had managed to contrive a disjointed tangle of half-truths and plausible lies—anything to convince them to get over to the Garrington house as quickly as possible. They already knew he was one of those occult kooks. Very well, he assured them that Beth Garrington was involved in a secret society of drug fiends and satanists (all true enough), that Danielle and Lisette had been lured to their most recent orgy for unspeakable purposes. Lisette had been secretly drugged, but Danielle had escaped to carry her roommate home before they could be used for whatever depraved rites awaited them—perhaps ritual sacrifice. Danielle had been murdered —either to shut her up or as part of the ritual—and now they had Lisette in their clutches as well.

All very melodramatic, but enough of it was true. Inspector Bradley knew of the sex-and-drug orgies that took place there, but there was firm pressure from higher up to look the other way. Further, he knew enough about some of the more bizarre cult groups in London to consider that ritual murder was quite feasible given the proper combination of sick minds and illegal drugs. And while it hadn't been made public, the medical examiner was of the opinion that the slashes to the Borland girl's throat and wrists had been an attempt to disguise the fact that she had already bled to death from two deep punctures through the jugular vein.

A demented killer, obviously. A ritual murder? You couldn't discount it just yet. Inspector Bradley had ordered a car.

* * *

"Who are you, Lisette Seyrig, that you wear my face?"

Beth Garrington rose sinuously from her bed. She was dressed in an off-the-shoulder nightgown of antique lace, much the same as that which Lisette wore. Her green eyes—the eyes behind the mask that had so shaken Lisette when last they'd met—held her in their spell.

"When first faithful Adrian swore he'd seen my double, I thought his brain had begun to reel with final madness. But after he followed you to your little gallery and brought me there to see your portrait, I knew I had encountered something beyond even my experience."

Lisette stood frozen with dread fascination as her nightmare came to life. Her twin paced about her, appraising her coolly as a serpent considers its hypnotized victim.

"Who are you, Lisette Seyrig, that yours is the face I have seen in my dreams, the face that haunted my nightmares as I lay dying, the face that I thought was my own?"

Lisette forced her lips to speak. *"Who* are you?"

"My name? I change that whenever it becomes prudent for me to do so. Tonight I am Beth Garrington. Long ago I was Elisabeth Beresford."

"How can this be possible?" Lisette hoped she was dealing with a madwoman but knew her hope was false.

"A spirit came to me in my dreams and slowly stole away my mortal life, in return giving me eternal life. You understand what I say, even though your reason insists that such things cannot be."

She unfastened Lisette's gown and let it fall to the floor, then did the same with her own. Standing face to face, their nude bodies seemed one a reflection of the other.

Elisabeth took Lisette's face in her hands and kissed her full on the lips. The kiss was a long one; her breath was cold in Lisette's mouth. When Elisabeth released her lips and gazed longingly into her eyes, Lisette saw the pointed fangs that now curved downward from her upper jaw.

"Will you cry out, I wonder? If so, let it be in ecstasy

and not in fear. I shan't drain you and discard you as I did your silly friend. No, Lisette, my newfound sister. I shall take your life in tiny kisses from night to night—kisses that you will long for with your entire being. And in the end you shall pass over to serve me as my willing chattel—as have the few others I have chosen over the years.''

Lisette trembled beneath her touch, powerless to break away. From the buried depths of her unconscious mind, understanding slowly emerged. She did not resist when Elisabeth led her to the bed and lay down beside her on the silken sheets. Lisette was past knowing fear.

Elisabeth stretched her naked body upon Lisette's warmer flesh, lying between her thighs as would a lover. Her cool fingers caressed Lisette; her kisses teased a path from her belly across her breasts and to the hollow of her throat.

Elisabeth paused and gazed into Lisette's eyes. Her fangs gleamed with a reflection of the inhuman lust in her expression.

''And now I give you a kiss sweeter than any passion your mortal brain dare imagine, Lisette Seyrig—even as once I first received such a kiss from a dream-spirit whose eyes stared into mine from my own face. Why have you haunted my dreams, Lisette Seyrig?''

Lisette returned her gaze silently, without emotion. Nor did she flinch when Elisabeth's lips closed tightly against her throat, and the only sound was a barely perceptible tearing, like the bursting of a maidenhead, and the soft movement of suctioning lips.

Elisabeth suddenly broke away with an inarticulate cry of pain. Her lips smeared with scarlet, she stared down at Lisette in bewildered fear. Lisette, blood streaming from the wound on her throat, stared back at her with a smile of unholy hatred.

''*What* are you, Lisette Seyrig?''

''I am Elisabeth Beresford.'' Lisette's tone was implacable. ''In another lifetime you drove my soul from my body and stole my flesh for your own. Now I have come back to reclaim that which once was mine.''

Elisabeth sought to leap away, but Lisette's arms embraced her with sudden, terrible strength—pulling their naked bodies together in a horrid imitation of two lovers at the moment of ecstasy.

The scream that echoed into the night was not one of ecstasy.

At the sound of the scream—afterward they never agreed whether it was two voices together or only one—Inspector Bradley ceased listening to the maid's outraged protests and burst past her into the house.

"Upstairs! On the double!" He ordered needlessly. Already Dr. Magnus had lunged past him and was sprinting up the stairway.

"I think it came from the next floor up! Check inside all the rooms!" Later he cursed himself for not posting a man at the door, for by the time he was again able to think rationally, there was no trace of the servants.

In the master bedroom at the end of the third floor hallway, they found two bodies behind the curtains of the big four-poster bed. One had only just been murdered; her nude body was drenched in the blood from her torn throat—seemingly far too much blood for one body. The other body was a desiccated corpse, obviously dead for a great many years. The dead girl's limbs obscenely embraced the mouldering cadaver that lay atop her, and her teeth, in final spasm, were locked in the lich's throat. As they gaped in horror, clumps of hair and bits of dried skin could be seen to drop away.

Detective Sergeant Wharton looked away and vomited on the floor.

"I owe you a sincere apology, Dr. Magnus." Inspector Bradley's face was grim. "You were right. Ritual murder by a gang of sick degenerates. Detective Sergeant! Leave off that and put out an all-points bulletin for Beth Garrington. And round up anyone else you find here! Move, man!"

"If only I'd understood in time," Dr. Magnus muttered. He was obviously at the point of collapse.

"No, *I* should have listened to you sooner," Bradley growled. "We might have been in time to prevent this.

The devils must have fled down some servants' stairway when they heard us burst in. I confess I've bungled this badly.''

''She was a vampire, you see,'' Dr. Magnus told him dully, groping to explain. ''A vampire loses its soul when it becomes one of the undead. But the soul is deathless; it lives on even when its previous incarnation has become a soulless demon. Elisabeth Beresford's soul lived on, until Elisabeth Beresford found reincarnation in Lisette Seyrig. Don't you see? Elisabeth Beresford met her own reincarnation, and that meant destruction for them both.''

Inspector Bradley had been only half listening. ''Dr. Magnus, you've done all you can. I think you should go down to the car with Detective Sergeant Wharton now and rest until the ambulance arrives.''

''But you must see that I was right!'' Dr. Magnus pleaded. Madness danced in his eyes. ''If the soul is immortal and infinite, then time has no meaning for the soul. Elisabeth Beresford was haunting herself.''